THE ART OF ESCAPE
On Melville's Bachelor Machines

Taras Alexander Sak

Shumpusha Publishing

© Copyright by Taras A. Sak 2025

All Rights Reserved

For Kai, Anna, and Naoko

And in loving memory of
Robert S. Sak
(1945–2001)

Acknowledgments

First of all, I must thank my teachers. The late William Spanos' writing on *Moby-Dick*, particularly his reading of Father Mapple's sermon in the context of the war in Vietnam and the larger sweep of American expansionism and empire, initially inspired me to gather the courage necessary to leave an unhappy situation in California and return to Binghamton in order to study the work of Herman Melville. Professor Spanos' reading of the American "canon" greatly influenced my own, and it was in and through his teaching and scholarship that I revisited our greatest of literary authors. William Haver, regardless of the subject matter, taught me nothing less than how to think—by which I mean how to think *critically*, how to engage a text and reconsider my own assumptions or premises—and thereby inspired me to become the teacher (and person) that I am today. I suppose that I can never repay them, except by providing similar inspiration, generosity, and care for my own students.

I must also acknowledge the many people who have helped me on a more personal level. In Binghamton, Vern Walker, Ally Hwang, Markus Zisselsberger, Amy Smith, the late Ben Van Wyke, Matt Laferty, and Matt and Julia Friday were great colleagues and friends. The Fridays, in particular, provided invaluable moral support at critical junctures, and without such friendship I would surely have given up. In Mie, Dimitar Antonov, Thierry Guthmann, Akira Noda, Mitsuaki Hayase and Nobuhiro Miyachi provided me with much encouragement and support. In Kyushu, David Farnell, Greg Bevan, Elmar Lenhart, Stephen Laker, Nobumitsu Ukai, Nobuaki Nishioka, the late Kazuhiko Murai and Yasushi Takano each helped me in his own way and contributed to the completion of this project. In Hiroshima, Katsuya Shima, Toshiki Tatara, Keisuke Koguchi, Hironobu Matsuoka, Ken Nakagawa, Hidefumi Miyake, Kenichi Yamakawa, and John McLean provided encouragement and support. I must also acknowledge the friendship and generosity of Mike Gorman.

This book is based on my doctoral dissertation and has been funded in large part through the Publication Support Fund for FY 2024, granted by Yasuda Women's University. I am grateful to my university for generous research and financial support, as well as to Shumpusha Publishing in Yokohama, especially to editor Koichi Okada for his thorough assistance and professionalism. Most of all, the support of my family—in Japan, my in-laws; in the US, my aunts, uncles, cousins, and mother and sister in particular—must be acknowledged. They never gave up on me, even when it seemed hopeless. My mother, sister, and wife—the three long-suffering women in my life—listened patiently for innumerable hours not only about Melville but also about the lengthy struggle involved in the writing of a dissertation. For their understanding and love, I am truly grateful. Naoko never lost faith in me, even when things looked grim, and we learned how to work together and become better partners. For that alone I am grateful. Finally, though he died over twenty years ago, my father was very much a living presence during the writing of this book. When doubts crept in, and things looked their worst, I recalled his good humor, tenacity, and love of life—because of this I was able to carry on. To him, and to my teachers, colleagues, friends and loved ones—and also to Herman Melville, whose art made all of this possible in the first place—I humbly dedicate this work. All errors or shortcomings are, of course, my own.

Table of Contents

Acknowledgments   5

Introduction   11

Chapter 1: Mad Fathers; or, Escaping the Nation   21

The Berkshires   24

Storming Heaven: Moby-Dick; or, the Whale   38

"*The Hemispheres are Counterparts*": the Transatlantic Fiction   56

Chapter 2: Lost Sons (and Daughters); or, Escaping the Family   77

The Isle of Shoals   80

The Avenging Dream: Pierre; or, the Ambiguities   87

The Vanquished: Melville's Female Characters   132

Chapter 3: An (Un)Holy Ghost; or, Escaping the Subject   143

The Sand Dunes   144

"*Quite an Original*": The Confidence-Man: His Masquerade   146

The Inhuman Sea: Melville's Poetry   190

Conclusion   199

Bibliography   207

Index   215

[L]iterature... exists only when it discovers beneath apparent persons the power of an impersonal... [it] begins only when a third person is born in us that strips us of the power to say "I"

(Gilles Deleuze, "Literature and Life," *Essays Critical and Clinical*, 3)

Introduction

To leave, to escape, is to trace a line. The highest aim of literature, according to [D.H.] Lawrence, is "To leave, to leave, to escape... to cross the horizon, enter into another life... It is thus that Melville finds himself in the middle of the Pacific. He has really crossed the line of the horizon."

Gilles Deleuze[1]

In *The Scarlet Letter* (1850), there is a curious digression concerning a group of sailors, what author Nathaniel Hawthorne (1804–1864) calls "specimens of the nautical brotherhood" (203), who intrude upon both the narrative and the New England Holiday that is the setting of the novel's climax, the scene centering upon the Reverend Arthur Dimmesdale's Election Sermon. It is tempting to see this passage as a reflection of the details of Hawthorne's biography—more specifically, nostalgia or longing for his father, who was captain of a vessel that plied the Spanish Main, as do these mariners in *The Scarlet Letter*, but who died of fever in Suriname when Hawthorne was four years old—or perhaps in terms of the mariners' function in providing an analogy to the outsider or pariah status of Dimmesdale and his lover, Hester Prynne, who find comfort not only in the wilderness, beyond the limits of the Puritan community, but also in their dream of flight upon the open seas, among these sailors who likewise stand outside the bounds of civilization. In

---

[1] "On the Superiority of Anglo-American Literature" in *Dialogues II*, trans. Hugh Tomlinson and Barbara Habberjam (New York: Columbia University Press, 1987): 36, ellipsis in original.

other words, the sailors are outsiders, much like Hester and Dimmesdale, and they will convey the star-crossed lovers to the Old World, where they, accompanied by their daughter Pearl, will disappear. Hawthorne describes it thus:

> The picture of human life in the market-place, though its general tint was the sad gray, brown, or black of the English emigrants, was yet enlivened by some diversity of hue. A party of Indians [...] stood apart [...] Nor, wild as were these painted barbarians, were they the wildest feature of the scene. This distinction could more justly be claimed by some mariners, — a part of the crew of the vessel from the Spanish Main,—who had come ashore to see the humors of Election Day. They were rough-looking desperadoes, with sun-blackened faces, and an immensity of beard [...] From beneath their broad-brimmed hats of palm-leaf, gleamed eyes which, even in good nature and merriment, had a kind of animal ferocity. They transgressed, without fear or scruple, the rules of behaviour that were binding on all others [...] It remarkably characterized the incomplete morality of the age, rigid as we call it, that a license was allowed for the seafaring class, not merely for their freaks on shore, but for far more desperate deeds on their proper element [...] [T]he sea, in those old times, heaved, swelled, and foamed very much at its own will, or subject only to the tempestuous wind, with hardly any attempts at regulation by human law. (202–203)

The mariners—"rough-looking desperadoes," a term favored by Melville—stand outside the law of the community and therefore provide the doomed lovers with hope for a chance to escape—a chance that, as every reader of *The Scarlet Letter* knows, is quickly closed to them, since Roger Chillingworth, Hester's husband in disguise, disfigured and hell-bent on revenge, has also managed to secure passage to Europe on the same vessel. But for the moment, at least, that opportunity arises, a chance to escape into a space outside the bounds of reputable society, a space that challenges or throws that society into question, one remarkably similar to what Michel Foucault called a "heterotopia."[2] However, and crucially, Hawthorne closes this escape route, almost as quickly as it had opened, and the lovers are trapped once more. Here, for Hawthorne, lies the true "moral" of the story—one cannot escape one's sin or one's duty, as D.H. Lawrence long ago pointed out[3] —and the temptation of escape is simply that: temptation, and nothing more. Hester still hopes to flee, while the saintly Dimmesdale realizes the futility of escape and goes to his reward after having poured his soul into the Election Sermon, confessing and exposing his sin, and foiling Chillingworth's plans for revenge.

I cite this passage and revisit this well-known scene in order to illustrate the difference between Hawthorne and his contemporary, Herman Melville (1819–1891), the subject of the following study. For Melville, escape was indeed possible, and such "heterotopic" spaces—the whaling ship *Pequod* in *Moby-Dick*, the metropolis of New York City in *Pierre*, and the steamboat *Fidèle* in *The Confidence-Man*—were the settings of his most powerful work, each novel a drama of escape. Lawrence described Hawthorne as a "sugary, blue-eyed little darling" (12), and it appears that it was precisely in this respect that his comments were intended: that Hawthorne would not leave the bounds of his society, his community, its mores or laws. On the other hand, Melville

---

[2]   See his lecture, "Of Other Spaces," trans. Jay Miskowiec, *Diacritics*, 16 (Spring 1986): 22–27. I will discuss this notion of "heterotopic space" later in this study. For another reading of this concept as it appears in Melville and Joseph Conrad, see Cesare Casarino, *Modernity at Sea: Melville, Marx, Conrad in Crisis* (Minneapolis: University of Minnesota Press, 2002).

[3]   See chapter 7 of his *Studies in Classic American Literature* (New York: Thomas Seltzer).

did—not only in literature but in his own life. Melville escaped.[4]

It is this aspect of Melville's work and life that interests me most, this moment when his Ishmael-like outcasts or orphans turn their backs on society and law and plunge into uncharted waters, so to speak. In other words, when they turn away from their societies and cross the line of the horizon, as Lawrence phrased it. And it is this moment—more precisely this movement of escape or taking flight—that will be the focus of this monograph, in which I examine the "major" texts mentioned above (*Moby-Dick*, *Pierre* and *The Confidence-Man*), alongside selected "minor" works to which they are variously related, in order to chart this movement, speculate as to what Melville is escaping from, and consider the contemporary relevance of Melville's "art of escape."

The period under scrutiny in this study, 1850–1857, covers what biographer Leon Howard has called a period of "second growth," or what we may alternately think of as Melville's "major period," following the immature work that precedes *Moby-Dick* (composed in 1850–51) and the period of "silence" and withdrawal from the public eye that followed his voyage to the Levant in late-1856 and the appearance of the final novel published in his lifetime, *The Confidence-Man* (1857), while he was abroad. What he discovered during this period of crisis—marked by increasingly poor health, growing family obligations, declining sales, and unsympathetic, if not bitterly

---

[4] Denis Donoghue makes a very similar point in "Melville Beyond Culture," *The Sewanee Review*, Vol. 118, No. 3 (Summer 2010): 351–366. In this provocative essay, Donoghue asserts that Melville "harbored a desire to live not only in a general sense beyond culture [in Lionel Trilling's sense], but beyond law, family, and every force in life that imposed itself as a condition" (364). In this study, I argue much the same thing, but attempt to understand why and how he does this.

hostile reviews—was a power of vision engendered by his passionate encounter with Nathaniel Hawthorne, and their brief, yet intense and far-reaching friendship frames my study.

My first chapter, "Storming Heaven," explores the manner in which this passionate friendship manifested itself in Melville's writing by utilizing Gilles Deleuze and Félix Guattari's concept of the "bachelor-machine." They borrow the term from Michel Carrouges's *Les Machines célibataires*, a study of various fantastic machines that appear in nineteenth-century literature. When Deleuze and Guattari adopt the term "bachelor machines" (a translation of *machine célibataire*), they stress the anti-conjugal and anti-familial nature of desire, which completely ignores distinctions between "legitimate" or "illegitimate" sexual relations, and they employ it in a highly provocative reading of the work and life of Franz Kafka.[5] The series of sisters, maids and prostitutes we meet in Kafka's fiction are all agents of anti-conjugal, anti-familial desire, as are the various homoerotic doubles, brothers and bureaucrats.

When speaking of Kafka's (or Melville's) "bachelor-machine," however, it is important to note that it is comprised of all of these anti-conjugal figures and that its desire reaches far beyond the connections opened up or produced by them. "The bachelor is a state of desire much larger and more intense than incestuous desire and homosexual desire" (70), Deleuze and Guattari tell us, for such desire is ultimately impersonal, indifferently human or non-human. "With no family," they write, "no conjugality, the bachelor is all the more social, social-dangerous, social-traitor, a collective in himself" (71). This is precisely what is at stake in the bachelor-machines of Ahab, of

---

[5]   *Kafka: Toward a Minor Literature*, trans. Dana Polan (Minneapolis: University of Minnesota Press, 1986).

Pierre and of the mysterious, shape-shifting figure known as "the confidence man," which will be explored, respectively, in the chapters that follow this introduction.

Chapter one begins with some biographical contextualization before moving on to a discussion of the essay "Hawthorne and His Mosses" (*Literary World*, August 17 and 24, 1850), ostensibly a review of Hawthorne's *Mosses from an Old Manse* (1846), which in fact proved to be more of a literary manifesto—the closest Melville ever came to articulating a theory of literature—that registered the depth of Hawthorne's impact upon Melville. The chapter then moves on to letters and other documents relating to the Melville-Hawthorne friendship, which attest to Melville's desire to construct a "society of brothers," centered upon Hawthorne and a dream of collaboration that, on the surface, takes the form of writing but, in fact, lies much deeper, eventually intensifying and (possibly) driving the two friends apart. Chapter one ends by looking ahead, to the end of the timeframe of my study, at a text that in many ways is a revisiting, rewriting or repetition—namely, "The Piazza," written for the publication of a collection of short stories entitled *The Piazza Tales* (1856). This story is in dialogue not only with Melville's "Mosses" essay, but also with Hawthorne's "The Old Manse" (from *Mosses from an Old Manse*).

Between these two texts, which span the period under scrutiny in my study, I discuss in the bulk of the first chapter *Moby-Dick* (1851), Melville's masterwork, by focusing upon the figure of Ahab and his construction of a transnational (bachelor) machine that is comprised of his own broken body, with its various prostheses, the *Pequod*, the ship's crew, and the parts of dead whales and wrecked ships that have crossed its path, all of which become extensions of Ahab's own body, his will and desire. In his defiance, Ahab constructs an interracial, interspecies, and—most crucially for my purposes—transnational machine that turns away and attempts to escape from the nation-state and its mythology. This critique of the nation-state, particularly the myth of "exceptionalism" that subtends the American imaginary, is echoed in several of the "minor," transatlantic fictions, also discussed in chapter one, in the section entitled "The Hemispheres are Counterparts." Starting with an analysis of *Redburn* (1849), a text that to some extent predates Melville's period of "second growth"—but, in fact, plays a crucial role in precipitating that dynamic period of creativity—I attempt to build upon the work of William Spanos, who has interrogated Melville's untimely critique of several aspects of the hegemonic culture of his day, including the crucial concept of American exceptionalism, which is grounded upon an absolute break with the so-called "Old World," a break which Melville sought to deny and discredit.

I begin this section by looking at *Redburn*, before continuing with a reading of the three transatlantic "diptyches," Jay Leyda's term for three stories written in late-1853 at *Arrowhead*, Melville's home in the Berkshire Mountains, and submitted for publication sometime in the spring of 1854. I revisit these texts—"Poor Man's Pudding and Rich Man's Crumbs," "The Paradise of Bachelors and the Tartarus of Maids," and "The Two Temples"—followed by *Israel Potter* (serialized from July 1854, published as a novel in 1855) in order to demonstrate how Melville is deliberately using the techniques of repetition, juxtaposition, and a shifting, transatlantic setting—what he himself calls "inverted similitude"—in order to specifically critique the idea that the "New World" has definitively broken with or somehow improved upon the "Old," with Europe. In this context, the novel *Pierre* is briefly discussed; however, in the following chapter, it is the main focus.

Chapter two, "The Avenging Dream," explores the novel *Pierre* (1852) and what I am calling, once again employing a concept from Deleuze and Guattari, the character Pierre's "schizo-incest" for his (possible) half-sister, Isabel. Most commentators have focused upon the "Oedipal-incest" between Pierre and his mother, Mrs. Glendinning—understandably so, since Melville holds out the bait for us, as it were, by having them refer to one another as "brother" and "sister" and otherwise act in an overtly, even theatrically incestuous manner—but this has drawn attention away from Pierre's relation to Isabel, upon which Deleuze has notably focused. I attempt to elaborate upon Deleuze's insights concerning this schizo-incestuous coupling, and then draw some conclusions concerning the connective function of such female figures in Melville's writing from this point (1852) onwards, showing how they help enable Melville's escape from the Oedipal configuration, the so-called "family romance" and conjugality. The women—Isabel, Pierre's betrothed, Lucy Tartan, and the servant-girl Delly—form a series of such "sisters" that we will encounter again, later in this period of Melville's major phase.

This is discussed in the section entitled "The Vanquished," which addresses the point at which Melville had been abandoned by both his reading public and, perhaps more painfully, by Hawthorne. It is not by coincidence that he concerns himself at this stage with figures of abandonment—most strikingly, with female figures, quite unlike any of those who preceded them in his work. At this critical juncture in Melville's life and career, the story of the abandoned wife of a sailor, Agatha, which is the basis for his dream of literary collaboration with Hawthorne, takes center stage. The so-called "Agatha story" (perhaps a completed but lost novel entitled *The Isle of the Cross*) is itself repeated in several of the stories in *The Piazza Tales*, most poignantly and powerfully in "The Encantadas," with the figure of Agatha herself repeated, first, in the character of Hunilla, "the Chola [mestiza] widow," who is the main character of the eighth and longest "sketch" of that short story, and second in the character Marianna, in "The Piazza," a story that brings us back, full-circle, to Hawthorne and the "Mosses" essay, and back to the beginning of Melville's major phase. Melville's greatest achievement at this penultimate stage in his transformation is his creation of a series of anti-familial, anti-conjugal bachelors and "sisters," who have assisted him in declaring war on domesticity, the very foundation—as more than one contemporary reviewer of *Pierre* noted in horror—of society. In the process, Melville found himself abandoned by Hawthorne, to whom he will soon bid farewell.

This final stage of Melville's major or mature phase is explored at length in chapter three, "Quite an Original." Repetition, doubling, masks or what Tony Tanner calls "reversibility" is taken to its absolute limit in the first half of the final text under consideration in this study (and the last published during the period under scrutiny), *The Confidence-Man* (1857), where the avatars, masks, doubles or simulacra—as they have been variously called by critics—of the confidence man are repeated in a vertiginous succession. This process is transformed, however, in the second half of the novel, where reversibility gives way to a new phenomenon, which Tanner calls "interchangeability," revealing the groundlessness of identity or subjectivity. The parade of disguises or masks of the confidence man gives way to the lone figure of "the cosmopolitan," an enigmatic figure whom Melville alternately (and mysteriously) calls "an original," and which may be best understood by reading it through the concept of the simulacrum as envisioned by Deleuze.

In this final chapter, I attempt to illustrate how, after taking reversibility to its limit, and staging the confidence man's dizzying "masquerade," Melville reaches a point where he has finally left Hawthorne— and all that Hawthorne had come to mean to him—behind. For Melville, at this point, writing—indeed, as William C. Spengemann has argued, words, language, art—had been completely transformed, much as he, himself, had been transformed in and through the process of writing. Now, in Spengemann's words, "writing points ahead in time, deriving its meaning not once and for all, from unchanging and eternal truths, but endlessly, from its own unforeseeable, inescapable consequences, taking on new meanings with each successive unfolding of events" (Introduction of *Pierre*, xiv)—much as Melville had described to Hawthorne his own "unfolding," or growth and development—that it, itself, has set in motion. Indeed, as Spengemann points out, instead of standing for the fixed meanings from which they arose, words now create and continually recreate their meanings, "accumulating semantic complexity as long as they continue" and reverberate, as long as they are read.

At the time of their parting, Melville made a comment to Hawthorne concerning how he had "made up his mind to be annihilated." This comment has, in turn, been widely discussed, but in the main interpreted as marking Melville's depression and despair, in keeping with the popular image of him being a "morbid" writer at this late stage of his career. However, in my final chapter, I revisit and re-examine the "annihilation" comment, placing it in its proper Miltonian context, which brings us back, full-circle, to Ahab and Pierre, Melville's defiant sufferers, at once mournful and unrepentant, bidding farewell to their lost Paradises. This is where Hawthorne left Melville, and where we shall as well, amidst the sand dunes in 1856–57—sorrowful yet unrepentant, defiant to the end, and still standing ahead of us, on the farther shore. What Melville found as he played the confidence man's "masquerade" to its bitter end and crossed over to the other shore was what he would later, in his poetry, call "the Inhuman Sea," something that he could only capture in verse, and to which I will briefly turn in my conclusion. Before doing so, however, we must first explore Melville's art of escape.

Chapter 1
Mad Fathers; or, Escaping the Nation

[The] motive [of] mutiny was the root, the radical of Melville. There are [those] who see this need of his to rebel against authority... as theological... I take it to be more vital, and speaking to our time, of the order of revolution, a reflection of the social and economic violence of America in his time, and a projection of what we now are experiencing. We know nothing if we do not see this chaos as of long shaping... Mutiny, translated from the sea, is known on land as revolution.

—Charles Olson, *Collected Prose*[6]

Gilles Deleuze, whose work continually refers back to the fiction of Herman Melville, once wrote that "[i]t is never the beginning or the end which are interesting; the beginning and end are points. What is interesting is the middle."[7] This seems especially appropriate when discussing Melville, a writer who found himself occupying an uneasy place between the Boston and New York literary/cultural establishments, between rural and urban America, and to some extent between the country's Atlantic-dominated past and Pacific-oriented future. In terms of his aesthetic concerns and practice, Melville seems even more the hybrid, straddling his era, the (mid-) nineteenth century, and our own, with one foot firmly planted in each. However, I begin at this point,

---

[6] Ed. Donald Allen and Benjamin Friedlander (Berkeley: University of California Press, 1997): 389, n. 67; qtd. with ellipsis added in James Zeigler, "Charles Olson's American Studies: *Call Me Ishmael* and the Cold War," *Arizona Quarterly*, Vol. 63, No. 2 (Summer 2007): 62.

[7] "On the Superiority of Anglo-American Literature," 39.

as it were the middle of Melville's career—that is, if, following Robert Milder, Hershel Parker and others,[8] we consider the poetry that sustained Melville beyond the frame of my study, which ends with the year 1857 while only glimpsing at Melville's verse, as a kind of "second act"—quite deliberately and with a clear sense of purpose. For this period of Melville's career, whether we envision it as the middle or the conclusion, saw the publication of his greatest work and yet is perhaps the least understood. My attention will be focused upon the work Melville produced during this "middle period," as I am calling it, one which is often neglected since most scholars and critics rightly consider *Moby-Dick; or, The Whale* (1851) Melville's masterpiece. The work after *Moby-Dick*, leading up to Melville's farewell to prose (with the publication in 1857 of *The Confidence-Man: His Masquerade*) and a long period of experimentation in poetry, is normally seen as demonstrating a marked decline in his abilities, reflecting his physical and spiritual exhaustion. This is unfortunate because the fiction of Melville's "middle period" is in fact vigorous and profound, particularly in its engagement with and revelation of his shifting artistic vision and what I have termed his "art of escape."

One way to begin is by engaging with what I call Melville's "sea-change," a shift in his poetics that can be traced to the highly experimental *Mardi: and a Voyage Thither* (1849), noted by Jean-Jacques Mayoux in his literary

---

[8]   Recent studies that reconsider Melville's post-1857 work, a period that had been largely neglected, include: Robert Milder, *Exiled Royalties: Melville and the Life We Imagine* (NY: Oxford University Press, 2006); Hershel Parker, *Melville: The Making of the Poet* (Evanston: Northwestern University Press, 2008); and Edgar A. Dryden, *Monumental Melville: The Formation of a Literary Career* (Stanford: Stanford University Press, 2004). Milder uses and discusses the phrase "second act" in Chapter 7 of his study.

biography of Melville.[9] Mayoux's observation, which greatly informs Deleuze's reading of Melville, runs as follows:

> For those who wish to understand Melville, *Mardi* is a key [...] Instead of narrating, he composes; instead of following the data furnished by his memories, he creates symbols [...] Moved by a kind of inner necessity, his imagination goes off in a direction it has taken before, obeying an instinctive reflex of his body and soul: that of escape, of flight. To desert, to flee the ship. This time it happens in mid-ocean, and we should note here a more or less conscious desire to lose himself far more completely than in *Typee*, among the cannibals. (51)

To be sure, the novel that followed *Mardi*, the highly autobiographical and poignant *Redburn: His First Voyage* (1849), is an uneven, perhaps immature book, as Melville would often claim (dismissing it alongside *White Jacket*, written and published shortly after, in 1850), but the scenes of what Mayoux describes as "humiliating poverty" are a real achievement, demonstrating a new level of technical skill as well as a new depth of sympathy and compassion. This "sea-change" was no doubt in part the result of Melville's voyages abroad, the first of which is poignantly recounted in *Redburn*, in which the déclassé protagonist finds himself face to face with misery and pauperism as he sails to England and back again to the US on a merchant vessel.

Melville's journeys, I suggest, helped the provincial, largely self-educated young man develop a sense of sympathy for what he will later call "the vanquished"—a notable accomplishment in his time, when immigrants

---

[9] Jean-Jacques Mayoux, *Melville*, trans. John Ashberry (New York: Grove Press, 1960): see, esp., 50–55.

and the poor were often demonized—but before we can understand the Melville of this "middle period," we need to recognize a further shift, from his early, rather detached or distanced observation of suffering to an experience of participation (or even and immersion) in suffering. My second point, related to the one above regarding Melville's "sea-change" is that something happened to Melville which somehow enabled the shift in tone and perspective that is palpable in all of the work that follows *Moby-Dick*. This, I argue, was his brief, passionate, but ultimately disappointing friendship with Nathaniel Hawthorne.

The Berkshires

This relationship or encounter, at the heart of which lies an intense, fourteen-month period during which the two were neighbors in the Berkshire mountains of western Massachusetts, has been the source of endless speculation, comprising an ongoing debate within Melville scholarship that stretches back to the very beginnings of the "Melville revival" of the 1920s (in Weaver and Mumford's groundbreaking work),[10] through such classic mid-century studies as Matthiessen's *American Renaissance* (1941),[11] Harrison Hayford's dissertation (on Hawthorne and Melville, 1945),[12] and Newton

---

[10] Raymond Weaver, *Herman Melville: Mariner and Mystic* (New York: George H. Doran, 1921); Lewis Mumford, *Herman Melville* (New York: Literary Guild of America, 1929).

[11] F.O. Matthiessen, *American Renaissance: Art and Expression in the Age of Emerson and Whitman* (New York: Oxford Univ. Press, 1941).

[12] Harrison Hayford, "Melville and Hawthorne: A Biographical and Critical Study." Ph.D. diss., Yale University (1945).

Arvin's 1950 Melville biography,[13] before reaching a new level of intensity in the 1970s with the work of Charles N. Watson (the so-called "estrangement theory")[14] and, especially, the provocative and highly speculative psychosexual biography by Edwin Haviland Miller, who asserted that Hawthorne fled in "homosexual panic" from Melville's advances.[15] There is a very useful summary of the scholarship in the Introduction to *Hawthorne and Melville: Writing a Relationship* (2008), a collection of essays edited by Argersinger and Person,[16] and most recently Jay Parini's creative re-imagining of this friendship has appeared in his novel, *The Passages of H.M.* (2010).[17]

Charles Olson's *Call Me Ishmael* (1947),[18] an iconoclastic and profoundly influential mid-century study, long ago drew attention to the importance of this friendship on Melville's writing, yet it has been neglected in the current debate (it goes unmentioned by Aregersinger and Person, for example). Olson was one of the first critics to note the importance of Melville's journeys, a topic he introduces precisely as he begins exploring Shakespeare's influence on Melville (particularly *King Lear* on *Moby-Dick*), and then continues in the

---

[13]   Newton Arvin, *Melville* (New York: William Sloane Associates, 1950).
[14]   Charles N. Watson, "The Estrangement of Hawthorne and Melville," *The New England Quarterly*, Vol. 46, No. 3 (Sept., 1973): 380–402.
[15]   Edwin Haviland Miller, *Melville* (New York: Persea Books, 1975); see, especially, 234–250. Miller does not use the exact phrase, "homosexual panic," which is discussed in Eve Kosofsky Sedgwick's *Epistemology of the Closet* (Berkeley: University of California Press, 1990), especially in chapter 4.
[16]   Jana L. Argersinger and Leland S. Person, "Hawthorne and Melville: Writing, Relationship, and Missing Letters," in *Hawthorne and Melville: Writing a Relationship*, edited by Argersinger and Person, (Athens: Univ. of Georgia Press, 2008): 1–24.
[17]   Jay Parini, *The Passages of H.M.* (New York: Doubleday, 2010).
[18]   Charles Olson, *Call Me Ishmael* (San Francisco: City Lights Books, 1947).

chapters that immediately follow ("American Shiloh" and "Man, to man"). Here, he examines Shakespeare's effect on Melville by turning to the figure of Hawthorne in Melville's essay, "Hawthorne and His Mosses," begun just before the two met for the first time (in early August, 1850), and then substantially expanded or revised before publication. In it, Melville prophesied the birth of an "American Shakespeare," a figure to which he likened Hawthorne. Olson then considers the theme of "Timonism," as Melville phrased it—in other words, a person betrayed or "undone by his friends." "Like Timon," Olson writes, "Melville found only disappointment. He lost Jack Chase, and Hawthorne, shyest grape, hid from him" (46). Here, Olson invokes the symbol of vines and grapes in Melville's later poetry, which undoubtedly allude to Hawthorne (a point I will take up later in this study). From Olson, then, we begin to see the significance of Melville's literal dislocation, his turn to the sea, his turn away from land, from home, from family and all that this entailed, and also his displacement or estrangement, most crucially from Hawthorne, but also, as we shall see, from the nation-state.

Robert Martin and Leland Person, in an important essay entitled "Missing Letters: Hawthorne, Melville and Scholarly Desire" (2000),[19] take this a step further, by calling on scholars to shift the focus of their attention, and with it the terms of this important debate in Melville studies, "from gossip to politics" (113): in other words, to raise the level of discourse concerning this friendship from psychosexual speculation to a higher level of engagement in order to produce a more serious study of the encounter's effects on the two

---

[19] Robert K. Martin and Leland S. Person, "Missing Letters: Hawthorne, Melville, and Scholarly Desire," *ESQ: A Journal of the American Renaissance*, Vol. 46, Nos. 1&2 (2000): 99–122.

authors' literary careers, particularly Melville's. To do so, we must examine the friendship in more detail. First, we must return to the site of the Hawthorne-Melville encounter, to their face-to-face meeting in the Berkshires. This is the point when Hawthorne became, in Hennig Cohen's words, a "catalytic force" in Melville's creative life.[20] In subsequent pages, I will pursue this thesis farther than have past or present Melville scholars, attempting to illustrate how Hawthorne initially (in 1850) proved to be a catalyst that drove Melville beyond the text he had then been working on, what was undoubtedly a much simpler, more orthodox "romance of adventure"[21]—the first draft of what would eventually become *Moby-Dick*—and then drove Melville to venture even farther.

Hawthorne was indeed a kind of catalyst that drove Melville in a direction that has not been well understood, much less explored or charted. This is one of my principal aims: in other words, to address the question of what Hawthorne—or, more precisely, what Melville's encounter with Hawthorne and all that the latter had come to mean to him—precipitated in Melville's writing, what it allowed or inspired him to do. For, in many ways, Melville still stands ahead of his readers; he still outdistances us, still eludes or escapes our grasp. As a result, and despite several decades of truly remarkable scholarship, we still have a great deal of catching up to do. It is hoped that the present study will, at least in some small way, contribute to that ongoing effort.

---

[20]   Hennig Cohen, "Herman Melville (1819–1891)" in *Dictionary of Literary Biography, Volume 3: Antebellum Writers in New York and the South*, ed. Joel Myerson (Detroit: Gale Research, 1979): 232.

[21]   "[F]ounded upon certain wild legends in the Southern Sperm Whale Fisheries," as Melville described the manuscript of the then in-progress *Moby-Dick* to publisher Richard Bentley (WHM 14: 163).

In order to approach that moment when Melville first encountered Hawthorne in the flesh, so to speak, it is necessary to briefly look at events immediately prior to that meeting, which I will briefly summarize. Melville completed the final proof sheets of *Omoo: A Narrative of Adventure in the South Seas* (1847) at the start (January) of 1847 and most likely began thinking of his next project. He got married later that year, in August. Laden with new responsibilities, the popular young author of travel books embarked upon his most daring and ambitious undertaking to date, an allegorical novel, *Mardi: and a Voyage Thither*, which took him eighteen months to complete. It was clearly indebted to Rabelais and Swift, as Newton Arvin long ago pointed out,[22] and offered glimpses of what was soon to come (in *Moby-Dick*, for example). Though Melville had been spurred to write something completely fictional, even fantastical, by those who would pigeonhole him as a mere "travel writer"—all the while charging him with aggrandizing or even fabricating his "non-fictional," real-life experiences—*Mardi* was, eventually, misunderstood by readers and dismissed by critics. In any case, Melville had finished the final proofs of *Mardi* and then submitted the book to his publishers in January 1849, just before the birth of his first child, Malcolm, in February. In the interim, in the space of those two years (January 1847 to January 1849), a great deal happens, but for lack of space I will draw upon Leon Howard's apt summary:

> The United States was still in the process of bringing home its troops from war with Mexico [...] The problem of Anglo-American relations was still an uneasy one, with the Oregon controversy fresh in people's minds and with the prospect of further imperialistic conflicts growing out of the

---

[22] Newton Arvin, *Herman Melville* (New York: William Sloan Associates, 1950): 91.

current war. Internally, the country was being torn by factional strife [punctuated by political conventions and a Presidential election]: the slavery question was causing the Democratic party to split [...] and a highly vocal group of "Conscience" Whigs were threatening to add their strength to a growing new party of "Free Soilers." In Europe, the French Revolution of 1848 had broken out, and all New York had been set agog by the reports of it.[23]

It was in this context that Melville revised and expanded *Mardi*, adding more overtly political content before sending it off to the publishers. In May 1849, as Robert Milder has pointed out, Melville signs his name for the first and only time to a "political" petition, appearing in the *New York Herald*, which urges the English Shakespearean actor, William Macready, to continue his performances at the Astor Place Opera House in the face of politically motivated protests fueled by xenophobia, jingoism and class antagonism, which subsequently erupted in disastrous violence known as the Astor Place Riots. This may have contributed to Melville's desire to leave New York City and move to the countryside; in any event, he did so, taking his family in the summer of 1850 to Arrowhead, a farm he purchased near Pittsfield, Massachusetts, where he would soon come into contact with Nathaniel Hawthorne, surely his most important literary friendship, and then compose what would be his literary declaration of independence, the justly famous "Hawthorne and His Mosses." Biographers agree with Robert Milder when he writes that the "poor sales of *Mardi* sent Melville back to his sailor experiences to keep afloat his growing family," which now included his infant son, Malcolm. Remarkably, in a span of only a few months during the spring

---

[23] Leon Howard, *Herman Melville: A Biography* (Berkeley: University of California Press, 1951): 122–123.

and summer of 1849, Melville wrote *Redburn* and *White-Jacket*—"two *jobs*, which I have done for money," he told his father-in-law, Judge Shaw; however, working within those constraints, he added, "I have not repressed myself much—so far as *they* are concerned; but have spoken pretty much as I feel" (WHM 14: 138–139; qtd. in Milder 28).

Redburn: His First Voyage (1849), based on Melville's voyage to Liverpool ten years earlier, and *White-Jacket; or, The World in a Man-of-War* (1850), inspired by his journey home from the Pacific aboard the warship *United States*, renamed the *Neversink*, were indeed straightforward, even frank and revealing, accounts drawn from his life, from his first and final youthful voyages. *Redburn*, as Milder succinctly puts it, "draws upon [Melville's] youthful hardships after his father's bankruptcy and death to depict what F. O. Matthiessen called 'the latent economic factor in tragedy [that] remained part of Melville's vision at every subsequent stage of his writing,'"[24] whereas *White-Jacket* "focuses polemically upon flogging in the U.S. Navy" (28). The latter novel's "wider subject," Milder emphasizes, "announced by its metaphoric subtitle, is [in fact] the nature of power relations within a martially oriented, if not militaristic and increasingly bellicose, class-based society" (Ibid.). Although *Redburn* and *White-Jacket* are not "overtly metaphysical novels," neither are they lacking in what Milder calls Melville's "interrogations of the universe and his emerging sense of tragedy" (29)—important themes that will be fully explored in *Moby-Dick* (and beyond). Milder describes it thus: "As chapters on sickness, death, and the 'armed neutrality' of Fate darken the close of *White-Jacket*, *Redburn*'s plea

---

[24]   *American Renaissance: Art and Expression in the Age of Emerson and Whitman* (New York: Oxford University Press, 1941): 400; qtd. in Milder, "Brief Biography," 28.

for a brotherhood of man under the fatherhood of God gives way to the mature Melvillean vision of a brotherhood of man asserted in the absence of God."[25] This is, of course, the great theme of Melville's "mature" writing.

Sadly, *Redburn* and *White-Jacket,* though well-received by critics, did little to bolster Melville's financial situation, complicated as their publication was by copyright issues (involving pirated or illegal copies) in Britain. After travelling to the UK in order to arrange for the publication of *White-Jacket,* in early 1850, Melville returned to America and "seems to have set to work almost immediately on the book that would eventually become *Moby-Dick; or, The Whale* (1851)" (Milder 31). The writing apparently went very well, at least initially: by May 1, he reported that he was "half way in the work" (WHM 14:162), and later than month he told English publisher Richard Bentley (in the letter cited above) that he would have "a new work" finished "in the latter part of the coming autumn" (WHM 14:163), a timetable confirmed by Evert Duyckinck in a letter dated August 7 that describes Melville's whaling book as "mostly done."[26] As it turned out, however, "*Moby-Dick* would not be completed until the following summer, a delay which has prompted speculation among scholars that sometime during the later months of 1850, *Moby-Dick* underwent not only a significant enlargement, as Melville consulted additional sourcebooks on whaling, for example, but also a profound revision or reconception: what might have begun as a loose and episodic whaling narrative patterned after *White-Jacket*" (Milder 31) had

---

[25] Robert Milder, "Brief Biography" in *A Historical Guide to Herman Melville*, ed. Giles Gunn (Oxford: Oxford University Press, 2005): 29.

[26] Originally in Luther S. Mansfeld, "Glimpses of Herman Melville's Life in Pittsfield, 1850–1851; Some Unpublished Letters of Evert A. Duyckinck," *American Literature* 9 (1937): 32; qtd. in Milder, "Brief Biography," 31.

instead become a grand symbolic, metaphysical, or allegorical quest. In the process, Melville had produced the masterwork we now know.

Milder asserts that "the catalysts that seem to have transformed *Moby-Dick* and helped to transform its author were Melville's (re)immersion in Shakespeare," as Olson pointed out long ago,[27] Melville's "reading of Carlyle,"[28] and—most crucially, for my purposes—"his discovery of Hawthorne's *Mosses from an Old Manse* (1846) followed by his meeting with Hawthorne himself," two events or encounters that combined to produce what Melville called a "shock of recognition" (WHM 9: 249), recorded in his enthusiastic review essay, the aforementioned "Hawthorne and His Mosses," published in Evert Duyckinck's *Literary World* on August 17 and 24, 1850 (Milder 31). Melville met Hawthorne on August 5th, at what is (perhaps) the most famous literary gathering in 19th century American letters, in the Berkshires of Western Massachusetts, where Melville and his family were staying. "The two writers took to each other immediately," according to Milder, "with Hawthorne making the thoroughly uncharacteristic gesture of inviting Melville to visit at the small red cottage in nearby Lenox to which he had moved his own family after leaving Salem" (Ibid.). In September, with a loan from his father-in-law, Judge Lemuel Shaw, Melville bought a farm, which he named "Arrowhead," in Pittsfield, only a few miles from Lenox; in Milder's apt summary, "for the next fourteen months, until Hawthorne left the Berkshires in November 1851, the two men periodically exchanged letters and visits in what would become one of the most extraordinary friendships in

---

[27] See his *Call Me Ishmael*, esp. 47–73.
[28] Especially *Sartor Resartus* and *On Heroes, Hero-Worship, and the Heroic in History*, according to Milder in "Brief Biography," 31 and in *Exiled Royalties*, 65–66 and passim.

American letters" (Ibid.).

According to Milder, "Melville had interested Hawthorne from the time of *Typee: A Peep at Polynesian Life* (1846), his first novel, when Hawthorne had recognized in its author a freshness and breadth of experience, including erotic experience, that he himself admired and perhaps had even envied" (32). On the other hand, for Melville, Hawthorne was "nothing short of a revelation" (Ibid.)—that "shock of recognition," mentioned earlier, "seemed to signify for Melville an American artist of the highest order so sympathetically attuned to his own inner life as to combine, in one person, the roles of friend, brother, father, soulmate, teacher, ideal reader, and perhaps fantasized lover."[29] *Moby-Dick* certainly owes much of its boundless ambition to this "shock of recognition," this encounter with Hawthorne, which Melville described in the "Mosses" review in terms of fertilization or impregnation[30] —after all, it is notably dedicated to Hawthorne, to point to the most obvious fact—but "this only begins to suggest the investment of emotion and self-esteem that Melville poured into the relationship even after time and circumstances had distanced him from Hawthorne, indeed even years after Hawthorne's death in 1864" (Milder 32), as we shall see.

Reviews of *Moby-Dick* were mixed—the Epilogue ("The drama's done. Why then here does any one step forth? —Because one did survive the wreck.") was not even printed in the UK, which left readers bewildered (if no one survived, then who was telling the tale?). Across the Atlantic, as Milder informs us, "Melville must have been particularly stung by Evert Duyckinck's

---

[29] Milder 32, and see Miller, Cohen, Parker, Martin, Person and Argersinger, for examples of these readings.
[30] Melville had written that Hawthorne had "dropped germinous seeds into my Southern soul" (WHM 9: 250).

criticisms in the *Literary World*" (32), but he found consolation, apparently, in Hawthorne's reception of the novel (though Hawthorne's letter, responding to *Moby-Dick*, has never been located: most likely it was burned by Melville). "A sense of unspeakable security is in me this moment," he wrote in a famous letter of November 1851, "on account of your having understood the book," referring to *Moby-Dick*. "I have written a wicked book," he continued, "and feel spotless as the lamb. Ineffable socialities are in me" (WHM 14: 212). That same month, however, "Hawthorne left the Berkshires, and Melville, embittered by the reception and disappointing sales of his book, was forced to deal simultaneously with the loss of" what Milder succinctly calls "the most enlivening intellectual and spiritual intimacy in his life" ("A Brief Biography," 35).

It may be useful, before moving on to my readings of Melville's texts, to look more closely at a remarkable postscript (actually one of two) appended to the well-known, oft-cited letter of November 1851 to Hawthorne, quoted above. It is as follows:

> "P.S. I can't stop yet. If the world was entirely made up of Magians, I'll let you know what I should do. I should have a paper-mill established at one end of the house, and so have an endless riband of foolscap rolling in upon my desk; and upon that endless riband I should write a thousand—a million—billion thoughts, all under the form of a letter to you. The divine magnet is on you, and my magnet responds. Which is the biggest? A foolish question—they are *One*." (WHM 14: 213)

Everything is contained in this postscript: Melville's garrulousness, his bombast—bordering on grandiloquence—and boundless energy, his enthusiasm, recklessness and utter sincerity. And nowhere is Melville clearer in his feelings toward Hawthorne. "I can't stop yet," he writes, bringing to mind his well-known request to Duyckinck to send him "fifty fast-writing youths" to keep up with the breakneck speed with which he was, just a few months prior to this letter to Hawthone, composing *Moby-Dick*. "Give me a condor's quill! Give me Vesuvius' crater for an inkstand!" he had boasted at the time, in chapter 104 ("The Fossil Whale") of *Moby-Dick*—flush with the excitement of having just met Hawthorne in the flesh. This desire "to say it all in one sentence, between one Cap [capital letter] and one period," as Faulkner once famously put it in a letter to Malcolm Cowley, is not only evident in the letter (and numerous postscripts) to Hawthorne, but in all of Melville's writing. He truly "can't stop yet."

The image of the paper-mill will certainly remind readers familiar with Melville of the infernal setting of "The Tartarus of Maids," a short story set in a hellish paper factory, but for my purposes the idea of an "endless riband of foolscap"—similar, perhaps, to Freud's "mystic writing-pad" or even to actual, single ribbon of paper upon which Kerouac typed the manuscript of *On the Road*—is more pertinent. On this endless sheet of paper, Melville will pour out his heart and soul, his innermost thoughts and desires, "all," as he emphasizes, "under the form of a letter" to Hawthorne. This last point is crucial. Melville will communicate these thoughts and desires to Hawthorne, hoping for but not expecting a reply, as he makes clear in this second postscript. In this way, it is perhaps as close to prayer as the famously skeptical Melville allowed himself to indulge. He will also dream of collaborating with the older and better-established writer—a dream that sustains him for a while, but ultimately disappoints. We can also detect hints of the rivalry—"Which is the biggest?"—and sacredness, desire, even love—the "divine magnet"—which Melville attached to Hawthorne. These elements, in addition to the notion of "escape," are the points of departure for this study. We must ask ourselves why Melville feels that, as he phrases it in the same letter, he has written a "wicked book" in *Moby-Dick*, and why it is that Hawthorne alone, according to Melville, has grasped its "true meaning." This leads us to the question of the impact of Hawthorne upon the composition of Melville's masterwork.

Once again returning to Olson, who was among the first commentators to advance the thesis that Melville had substantially revised the novel—perhaps even adding the character Ahab only *after* his initial encounter with Hawthorne[31] —we can discern a notable Hawthornean element in the work. Besides the "Puritanic gloom" that Melville so admired in his "Mosses" review, the two writers also shared, among many other things, a penchant for Miltonian, "Satanic" (anti-)heroes, a point that may be illustrated by pointing to Roger Chillingworth in Hawthorne's *The Scarlet Letter* (1850) and Captain Ahab in Melville's *Moby-Dick*. In this brief section, then, before moving on to a closer engagement with Ahab, I would like to investigate one possible source—Milton's Satan, via Hawthorne—for the tragic grandeur of Melville's most famous character. This will also serve as an introduction to the recurring motif of the defiant sufferer, the unyielding "heaven assaulter" who will appear in Melville's major fiction during the period under consideration in this study: the characters Pierre (discussed in chapter two) and the "confidence-man" (discussed in chapter three). Ahab's defiance, in other words, establishes a pattern that will be repeated in the works produced during this major phase of Melville's career.

As Milder points out, Olson wrote that "[t]he germinous seeds Hawthorne has dropped in Melville's July soil begin to grow: Bulkington, the secret member of the crew in *Moby-Dick*, is here [in "Hawthorne and His Mosses"] hidden in what Melville quotes as Hawthorne's self-portrait—the 'seeker,' rough-hewn and brawny, of large, warm heart and powerful intellect" (39). Olson's phrase "Melville's July soil" in fact alludes to the persona of "a Virginian Spending July in Vermont," a fictional Southerner from whose point

---

[31]   See *Call Me Ishmael*, especially 35.

of view Melville wrote the review essay on Hawthorne in 1850. In this light, according to Milder, Bulkington becomes a crucial presence, who could be associated with Melville's Virginian narrator celebrating his literary hero, Nathaniel Hawthorne, to whom *Moby-Dick* is, of course, dedicated.

Suddenly, however, Bulkington disappears from the novel in the chapter entitled "The Lee Shore" in such a way that he may emerge—or rather, "be submerged," in Milder's apt phrase—as a mythically elevated presence (Melville uses the very term "apotheosis," for example, in this chapter). The literal and figurative or symbolic disappearance of this quester-hero, who resists the "slavish shore" while maintaining his faith in "landlessness" as "the highest truth," clearly anticipates Ahab, whose first appearance (in chapter 29, "Enter Ahab"), in turn, seems to be structured in a way that suggests, at least on one level, that he has replaced Bulkington, whose disappearance is described in chapter 26 (the aforementioned "Lee Shore"). Thus, the role of Bulkington as a kind of "seeker" in the story's early chapters is passed on to the character of Ahab, whose dominating presence accelerates the narrative to its tragic end. Whether or not Bulkington "became" Ahab in the process of Melville's composition, it may safely be said that "[w]ith all the purity of symbolic form, Bulkington prefigures the proud and angry Ahab who hurls humanity's ultimate challenge against the powers of earth, sea, and air."[32] Not surprisingly, Bulkington described as a "demigod" (MD 107) recalls Ahab referred to as an "ungodly, God-like man" (79)—and, most importantly, his transformation reveals the influence of Hawthorne.

Hawthorne, I suggest, allows Melville to transform Ahab—perhaps even, as Olson has claimed, to have created him in the first place—and, in the

---

[32] Richard Blau, *The Body Impolitic: A Reading of Four Novels by Herman Melville* (Amsterdam: Rodopi, 1979): 74.

process, transform both his masterwork and himself as an artist. For Ahab is the first truly "original" character in Melville's work, I would argue—though Ahab is, as mentioned above, modeled to some extent after Milton's Satan (and is foreshadowed by the villainous yet piteous Claggart in *Redburn*, a mixture of "wickedness" and "woe"). This "defiant sufferer" sets the stage for the fiction that will follow, until Melville's farewell to prose in 1857 with *The Confidence-Man*. All of Melville's work during this period is, in essence, preoccupied with the misapprehended sign (as noted in the Introduction to this study), "dead letters"—especially ones addressed to Hawthorne, as we saw with the postscript examined earlier. However, despite being in dialogue with Hawthorne (or attempting to correspond in some way with Hawthorne or his fiction), these works begin to take on greater significance, as Melville develops his critique—first, of the nation-state, to be discussed in this chapter; second, of the family, the focus of chapter two; and third, of the subject, examined in chapter three. This is where Melville parts ways with Hawthorne, where he essentially leaves him (alongside Bulkington) on "the lee shore." Here, we must recall Melville's words from *Mardi*: "better to sink in boundless deeps, than float on vulgar shoals; and give me, ye gods, an utter wreck, if wreck I do" (M 557). Melville did not shy away from risking failure or "shipwreck," but instead ventured out—escaping land, and voyaging the horizon, over "boundless deeps." At this point, we must turn to Ahab, the first of the defiant sufferers to be examined in this study, and ask why he is heading away from land: in other words, we must ask from what, exactly, is Ahab attempting to escape?

Storming Heaven: Moby-Dick; or, the Whale

Of what is Captain Ahab in Melville guilty? Of having chosen Moby Dick, the white whale, instead of obeying the law of the group of fishermen, according to which all whales are fit to hunt. In that lies Ahab's demonic element, his treason, his relationship with Leviathan—this choice of object which engages him in a whale-becoming himself. (Deleuze, "On the Superiority of Anglo-American Literature," 42)

We must now focus upon the moments in *Moby-Dick* when its "monomaniacal" captain turns away—from land, or to put it alternately, from his duties and responsibilities—and in the section that follows, I will isolate these moments and comment upon them. The first is made clear during a conversation, really more a heated argument, with his first mate, Starbuck. "But what's this long face about, Mr. Starbuck; wilt thou not chase the white whale? art not game for Moby Dick?" asks Ahab, to which Starbuck replies: "I am game for his crooked jaw, and for jaws of Death too, Captain Ahab, if it fairly comes in the way of the business we follow; but I came here to hunt whales, not my commander's vengeance. How many barrels will thy vengeance yield thee even if thou gettest it, Captain Ahab? it will not fetch three much in our Nantucket market." Ahab is incensed, and shouts: "Nantucket market! Hoot! But come closer, Starbuck; thou requirest a little lower layer. If money's to be the measurer, man, and the accountants have computed their great counting-house the globe, by girding it with guineas, one to every three parts of an inch; then, let me tell thee, that my vengeance will fetch a great premium *here*!" We then hear from an onlooker, Mister Stubb, who reports: "He smites his chest," whispered Stubb, "what's that for? methinks it rings most vast, but hollow." "Vengeance on a dumb brute!" cries Starbuck, "that simply smote thee from blindest instinct! Madness! To be enraged with a dumb thing, Captain Ahab, seems blasphemous." Ahab then delivers one of his best-known lines: "Hark ye yet again,—the little lower layer. All visible objects are but pasteboard masks [...] Talk not to me of blasphemy, man; I'd strike the sun if it insulted me" (MD 164).[33] Here, we can see Ahab not only turning away from the Nantucket market—much like Hawthorne's mariners, mentioned at the beginning of the Introduction, who are unbound by the moral strictures of Puritan society, centering as it does upon the marketplace—but also from the sun, which is a clear allusion to Milton's Satan and his defiance.

As if to emphasize this point, Melville has Ahab deliver a soliloquy worthy of Shakespeare (who undoubtedly inspired it, as Olson has decisively shown):[34] "Oh! time was, when as the sunrise nobly spurred me, so the sunset soothed. No more. This lovely light, it lights not me; all loveliness is anguish to me, since I can ne'er enjoy. Gifted with the high perception, I lack the low, enjoying power; damned, most subtly and most malignantly! damned in the midst of Paradise!" (MD 167). The Miltonian echoes are very strong in this passage, as should be clear; also, we must note how this speech is placed right before Ahab's famous words, "Swerve me? ye cannot swerve me [...] The path to my fixed purpose is laid with iron rails [...] unerringly I rush!" (168), which have been analyzed by Leo Marx and William Spanos, to name but two of the most persuasive readings. Marx sees Ahab as embodying the new technology of the railroad, while Spanos sees him as the epitome of the imperial, metaphysical perspective that has characterized so-called "Western Civilization" from the Romans through the European colonial powers down

---

[33] We must note not only the sun metaphor, which is profoundly Miltonian, but also the placement of this memorable exchange, just before the Satanic "communion" scene in which Ahab has all hands drink to the death of Moby Dick. This is repeated, later in the novel, in the equally well-known harpoon baptism scene.

[34] In *Call Me Ishmael*, especially 59–63 and 68–69.

to the present-day American Empire.[35] And as both Marx and Spanos have noted, it is as if Ahab, the *Pequod* and its crew have now somehow become a machine. When Ahab nails a gold doubloon to the mast, as a prize to whoever is first to sight the white whale, Starbuck notices that a sound, "so strangely muffled and inarticulate," seems to be coming from Ahab: "the mechanical humming of the wheels of his vitality in him" (162). In the very next chapter (37, "Sunset"), Ahab meditates upon the crew and reflects that "my one cogged circle fits into all their various wheels, and they revolve" (167). As it turns out, immediately after this scene, Ahab's machine and the fixed, iron, and "unswerving" path that it will be forced to follow is in fact soon revealed.

Indeed, in Chapter 44, "The Chart," we are told by the narrator that Ahab has planned the entire voyage of the *Pequod*, secretly mapping its course, with the purpose of intersecting the trajectory of the white whale known as "Moby Dick," somewhere in his Equatorial feeding-grounds, called the "Season-on-the-Line" (200) by whalemen. Ahab arranges to leave at precisely the start of this so-called "season" so that he could sail for a full calendar year, rather than wait ashore, all the while hunting miscellaneous whales as cover for his real purpose—to search for the whale known as "Moby Dick," which Deleuze noted (cited in the epigraph to this section, above)— then rush "unswervingly," as if on "iron rails," to meet the white whale "on the line," in his "cruising ground" during this feeding-season, one year hence. In this way, he might camouflage his true purpose and keep crewmembers like

---

[35] Leo Marx, *The Machine in the Garden: Technology and the Pastoral Ideal in America* (Oxford: Oxford University Press, 1964): 294–310; William V. Spanos, *The Errant Art of Moby-Dick: The Canon, the Cold War, and the Struggle for American Studies* (Durham: Duke University Press, 1995): especially 131–135.

Starbuck distracted, satisfied, and none the wiser. But Ahab's purpose is clear, as is the fact that he has planned the entire voyage around the projected movements of this one whale, now likened (significantly) to the sun. Allow me to quote this remarkable passage, where Ahab's plan is revealed, in full:

> That particular set time and place were conjoined in the one technical phrase—the Season-on-the-Line. For there and then, for several consecutive years, Moby Dick had been periodically descried, lingering in those waters for awhile, as the sun, in its annual round, loiters for a predicted interval in any one sign of the Zodiac [...] Now, the Pequod had sailed from Nantucket at the very beginning of the Season-on-the-Line. No possible endeavor then could enable her commander to make the great passage southwards, double Cape Horn, and then running down sixty degrees of latitude arrive in the equatorial Pacific in time to cruise there. Therefore, he must wait for the next ensuing season. Yet the premature hour of the Pequod's sailing had [...] been covertly selected by Ahab, with a view to this very complexion of things. Because, an interval of three hundred and sixty-five days and nights was before him; an interval which, instead of impatiently enduring ashore, he would spend in a miscellaneous hunt; if by chance the White Whale [...] should turn up [...] any wind [...] might blow Moby Dick into the devious zig-zag world-circle of the Pequod's circumnavigating wake. (200–201)

Here, we see that for Ahab all other considerations are set aside in deference to his main purpose: in this manner, the ship itself, the *Pequod*, along with its crew, has truly become as one with Ahab and his mad quest. This becomes all the more obvious in the famous "Try-Works" chapter (96), which Olson first pointed to as being an allegory of American industry,[36] albeit with a (diabolical) twist: this floating factory is in fact "remorselessly commissioned

---

[36] In *Call Me Ishmael*, especially 16–25.

to some vengeful deed" (462–3), and though it burns whale blubber into oil for the aforementioned Nantucket market, it is in fact burning with the single-minded purpose of Ahab's plan, which runs counter to all financial considerations: "as the wind howled on, and the sea leaped, and the ship groaned and dived, and yet steadfastly shot her red hell further and further into the blackness of the sea and the night, and scornfully champed the white bone [the whale's skeleton] in her mouth, and viciously spat round her on all sides; then the rushing Pequod, freighted with savages, and laden with fire, and burning a corpse, and plunging into that blackness of darkness, seemed the material counterpart of her monomaniac commander's soul" (463). The ship itself has been turned away from its initial purpose and, as such, has become a veritable extension of Ahab: in other words, it has now been completely transformed into a type of "machine."

Melville makes this even clearer in Chapter 100, "Leg and Arm," when Ahab and the "rushing" *Pequod* meet the *Samuel Enderby*, a whaler out of London, and have a "gam," or meeting, with her captain. This is one of several such scenes in the novel—increasing in frequency and intensity as the *Pequod* approaches Moby Dick—in which Ahab repeatedly and single-mindedly asks the question, "Hast seen the White Whale?" Captain Boomer, of the *Enderby*, has lost an arm to Moby Dick, but seeks him no more; unlike Ahab, he has learned his lesson. Ahab asks him, "Did'st thou cross his wake again?" (meaning after the initial encounter, during which his arm was torn off), to which Boomer replies, "Twice." Ahab then asks, "But could not fasten?" but Boomer turns the tables, so to speak, and questions Ahab: "Didn't want to try to; ain't one limb enough?" (481) Boomer assumes that Ahab, who likewise lost a limb to the White Whale, will steer clear of the monster: "'[H]e's best let alone; don't you think so, Captain?'—glancing at the ivory leg. [To which Ahab responds,] 'He is. But he will still be hunted, for all that. What is best let alone, that accursed thing is not always what least allures.

He's all a magnet!'" Boomer and his ship's surgeon, Bunger, stare incredulously at Ahab, and ask Fedallah, Ahab's "Parsee" stowaway who has for all intents and purposes supplanted Starbuck as Ahab's first mate, "Is your Captain crazy?" to which Fedallah merely presses his finger to his lip before "slid[ing]" away (482). Here, we can see that not only do these whale-ships (and their captains and crew) take on a mechanical or machine-like aspect—with the body parts of their prey used as decoration, weaponry, fuel, food, or even artificial limbs, prostheses—but also that Ahab has voyaged beyond "common sense" or reason; however, it is in later "gams," which I will subsequently discuss, that Ahab's "mad" quest, his purpose in escape, in turning away from home, land, the market and sun, is truly revealed.

Before proceeding, it may be useful to pause on this "machine"-like aspect of the *Pequod* and the possible purposes to which it was designed. As Joseph Fruscione has shown in a recent essay,[37] Melville's fiction often interrogates the various discourses that underpin race and colonialism: from his earliest, often scathing (and consequently censored) critique of Christianity and Christian missionaries in Polynesia in *Typee* and *Omoo*, to his questioning of the underlying assumptions and latent racism of Francis Parkman's *The Oregon Trail* in a review essay written two years before the publication of *Moby-Dick* (entitled "Mr. Parkman's Trail"), Melville "did not shy away from examining the systems of power that buttress racial hierarchies and imperialism, particularly their ways of focusing colonial and racial oppression on the bodies of nonwhites" (Fruscione 3). "The savage is born a savage; and the civilized being but inherits his civilization, nothing more," Melville wrote

---

[37] "'What is Called Savagery': Race, Visual Perception, and Bodily Contact in *Moby-Dick*," *Leviathan*, Vol. 10, No. 1 (March 2008): 3–24; I draw heavily upon this excellent essay in the section that follows.

in the Parkman review (PT 231; qtd. in Fruscione, 3), anticipating the manner in which he would depict the multinational and multi-racial or -cultural crew of the *Pequod* in *Moby-Dick*. In this novel, "civilized" and "savage" intersect and bleed into one another, not only in the racially diverse bodies of the crew but most of all in the person—the very body—of Captain Ahab. As Carolyn Karcher and Samuel Otter have shown,[38] cultural constructions of different racial bodies subtended the concept of "race" in nineteenth-century America, as well as in *Moby-Dick*. Whether the would-be narrator Ishmael is describing the harpooners or the white whale, itself, the text "teems with descriptions of bodies and their colors" (Ibid.). As Fruscione points out, Ishmael and Queequeg sharing a bed in "The Spouter-Inn," Queequeg "birthing" Tashtego in "Cistern and Buckets," and Fedallah's mutilated body tied to Moby Dick in "The Chase, Third Day" (soon to be joined by Ahab's broken body, as well)—"these are but a few examples of interracial bodily contact, sometimes embodying harmony, at other times violence and power, but always joining notions of the 'civilized' and the 'savage' in interracial encounters in which different-colored bodies are hybridized, quite to the contrary of the hierarchies of the nineteenth-century nation-state" (Ibid.). Melville forces different identities—racial and national—to intersect with each other on the *Pequod*, a polyglot ship or "cannibal craft" that "was appareled like any barbaric Ethiopian emperor," and whose diverse international crew comprises different types of people and bodies, reflecting the cross-cultural or trans-national aspect of the whaling industry, taken more generally. To this

---

[38] Carolyn Karcher, *Shadow Over the Promised Land* (Baton Rouge: Louisiana State University Press, 1980) and Samuel Otter, *Melville's Anatomies* (Berkeley: University of California Press, 1999) examine 19th century racial pseudoscience (qtd. in Fruscione, 4).

end, at a crucial point in the narrative, Melville describes the crew as an "Anacharsis Clootz deputation from all the isles of the sea, and all the ends of the earth."[39] This is, in fact, a favorite metaphor of Melville's and one which we shall see repeated later.

However, diverse though the crew may be, Melville reminds us that they are, in many respects, united—a point that Fruscione emphasizes. They are on the same ship, of course, and as mentioned above they all participate in Ahab's quest for Moby Dick, bloodthirstily vowing "A sharp eye for the White Whale; a sharp lance for Moby Dick!" in unison. In this way, the *Pequod* is the site for Melville's mixing of races and nationalities, all unified under Ahab, welded or forged not only into a machine but also into a kind of family or brotherhood. This is not to say that the ship is without strife, contradiction or complexity—for it undeniably is, as we can see in several scenes in which the crew fights among itself, each sailor choosing sides based upon nationality or race ("Midnight, Forecastle" being perhaps the best-known, by turns comical and frightening), and at times the *Pequod* seems to be "staging interracial or international physical contact in the service of mirroring or embodying nineteenth-century racial hierarchies and colonialism;"[40] but it is to say that Ahab (and Melville, through him), through this very ship, the *Pequod*, somehow forges a multicultural and transnational "machine" that strives to escape the bounds of race and, especially, the nation-state.

Melville personifies the *Pequod* as a machine, a symbolic hybrid of

---

[39] In fact, Melville invokes Anacharsis Clootz on two other occasions: first, in *The Confidence-Man* (9) and, later, in *Billy Budd* (43).

[40] See Geoffrey Sanborn, *The Sign of the Cannibal: Melville and the Making of a Postcolonial Reader* (Durham: Duke University Press, 1998) for the fullest account of precisely this aspect of *Moby-Dick*.

Ahab, the polyglot crew, parts of whales and of various ships, even wood from Japan (the masts, it should be remembered, had to be replaced in a typhoon). The "old hull's complexion was darkened," while the ship "trick[ed] herself forth in the chased bones of her enemies." The body imagery, as Fruscione stresses, underscores the *Pequod*'s figurative physicality: it has a "claw-footed look," and its "venerable bow looked bearded," its "masts stood stiffly up like [...] spines," its "open bulwarks were garnished like one continuous jaw, with the long sharp teeth of the sperm whale [...] to fasten her old hempen thews and tendons to," and its tiller was "carved from the long narrow lower jaw of her hereditary foe" (MD 70; qtd. in Fruscione, 8). As a "body" containing virtually all of the text's other bodies, the *Pequod* is defined by its hybridity, as well as its unity of purpose; later in the narrative, Melville emphasizes how the hunt for the white whale fuses the crew's bodies to both Ahab and the ship as follows:

> They were one man, not thirty. For as the one ship that held them all; though it was put together of all contrasting things—oak, and maple, and pine wood; iron, and pitch, and hemp—yet all these ran into each other in the one concrete hull [...] both balanced and directed by the long central keel; [...] all the individualities of the crew, this man's valor, that man's fear; guilt and guiltlessness, all varieties were welded into oneness, and were all directed to that fatal goal which Ahab their one lord and keel did point to. The rigging lived. The mast-heads, like the tops of tall palms, were outspreadingly tufted with arms and legs. (557; qtd. in Ibid.)

Melville's "humanization" of the *Pequod*—with Ahab as the "keel," as Fruscione makes abundantly clear—creates a single body (or machine) composed of thirty smaller bodies (of various "races" and nationalities) and of various materials. The *Pequod* is indeed a "heterotopic" space, a venue where the diverse crew can explore the boundaries of their bodies and class- or race-determined positions in the various hierarchies that exist back on shore (despite the violence of the aforementioned "Midnight, Forecastle" chapter and the ship's preexisting racial hierarchy). Identities take on new meaning through physical contact, as Melville recasts them, and the power relations that subtend them, in favor of that "oneness" so clearly described above, as the crew prepares for its next encounter with Moby Dick. Nowhere is this clearer, perhaps, than in the chapter entitled "The Candles," which I will describe in more detail later in this chapter. The storm and the St. Elmo's fire aboard the ship bring about a remarkable scene of interracial bodily contact: Ahab holds the lightning-rod's chain in his hand, rests his foot on Fedallah's back, and boldly challenges the storm, eventually grasping the glowing harpoon and addressing the mesmerized crew (505–508). Here and elsewhere, as Fruscione has argued, Melville is restaging and challenging, unsettling and resetting the rigid hierarchy of the nineteenth-century racial body, by bringing numerous bodies—white and nonwhite, "civilized" and "savage"—into frequent contact with one another, thus creating various interracial (even interspecies, as in the case of Ahab and his whalebone-leg) hybrids that subvert and recast dominant power relations. The *Pequod* is, in this and other ways, a type of community in which bodies intersect and new identities are (per)formed, fusing figuratively if not physically into hybrid races and species that challenge the very foundations of the nation-state.

Indeed, Ahab and Pip, the black cabin-boy from Alabama, form an "important bodily engagement" (Fruscione, 17) or machine, one that challenges the America of the 1850s, particularly the "peculiar institution" of chattel slavery in the South, as their pairing circumvents the ship's otherwise rigid hierarchy (in terms of officers and crew, in addition to race or nationality). Ahab sees his crew and ship as physical and figurative extensions of his own body, as can be seen when he exhorts the men to return to the *Pequod* after Moby Dick staves their boats—"Ye are not other men, but my arms and legs; and so obey me" (568; qtd. in Ibid.)—or when, just before this, he had addressed the ship directly, as follows: "But aye, old mast, we both grow old together; sound in our hulls, though, are we not, my ship? Aye, minus a leg, that's all. By heaven this dead wood has the better of my live flesh every way" (565; qtd. in Fruscione, 18). Beyond this fusing of captain and ship, according to Fruscione's highly suggestive reading, Ahab's connection with Pip, who is (after "The Castaway" chapter, in which he falls overboard and nearly drowns) bordering on madness, raises another challenge to the order of things, fusing the ship's highest and lowest roles. Melville twice gives us a richly suggestive hybrid: Pip and Ahab's joining hands, and Pip's offering to replace Ahab's leg (severed by Moby Dick) with his own body. In the chapter entitled "The Log and Line," their union crystallizes when Ahab essentially adopts the abandoned and abject Pip: "Ahab's cabin shall be Pip's home henceforth, while Ahab lives. Thou touchest my inmost center, boy; thou are tied to me by cords woven of my heart-strings"; to which Pip replies,

> "What's this? here's velvet shark-skin," intently gazing at Ahab's hand, and feeling it. "Ah, now, had poor Pip but felt so kind a thing as this, perhaps he had ne'er been lost! This seems to me, sir, as a manrope; something that weak souls may hold by. Oh, sir, let old Perth [the blacksmith] now come and rivet these hands together; the black one with the white, for I will not let this go." (522; qtd. in Ibid.)

"Holding and looking at Ahab's hand," Fruscione concludes, "Pip experiences a feeling of belonging; Ahab, too, breaks free of his isolation and welcomes Pip into his privacy: thus, these two outcasts form their own community" (Ibid.). This Ahab-Pip hybrid is revisited in "The Cabin," again juxtaposing the top and bottom bodies of the *Pequod*'s hierarchy. Here, Pip wants to become part of Ahab, in effect an extension of his fragmented body. After

Ahab asks Pip to retire below and "sit here in my own screwed chair," Pip offers to complete his incomplete captain: "No, no, no! ye have not a whole body, sir; do ye but use poor me for your one lost leg; only tread upon me, sir; I ask no more, so I remain a part of ye" (534; qtd. in Fruscione, 19). Later, in the same scene, Pip tells Ahab that "[t]hey tell me, sir, that Stubb did once desert poor little Pip, whose drowned bones now show white, for all the blackness of his living skin. But I will never desert ye, sir, as Stubb did him. Sir, I must go with ye" (Ibid). "These symbolic color contrasts," according to Fruscione, "work on multiple levels"—Pip and Ahab, Pip and Ahab's leg, Pip's very bones and flesh—all of which transgress social and racial boundaries and "reinforce the Ahab-Pip hybrid created when they joined hands" (Ibid.). As John Bryant has noted in this scene, "In replacing ebony for ivory, Pip proposes to heal Ahab's physical wound [...] through a symbolic integration of selves that is [...] both metaphysical and political."[41] Like Ishmael and Queequeg, this Ahab-Pip hybrid or coupling challenges the racial hierarchies of Melville's day, though this is not to say that it is without its complexities. After all, Ahab and Pip reflect a marked hierarchy that is undeniably topped (quite literally) by Ahab, with Pip continually calling Ahab "master" (far more than he addresses him "captain," another point underscored by Fruscione), thus showing how Melville's resonant interracial hybrids rely upon or reflect nineteenth-century American racial hierarchies while, at the same time, threatening to undercut them. This can also be seen in the aforementioned chapter, "Midnight, Forecastle," in which the crew's revelry, attended and punctuated by their racial consciousness, spills over into violence—though, it must be added, their symbolic unity (in diversity) is once more reasserted as

---

[41] John Bryant, *Melville and Repose: The Rhetoric of Humor in the American Renaissance* (New York: Oxford University Press, 1993); qtd. in Fruscione, 19.

Ahab immediately fuses them together into one body in order to hunt down the white whale.

Returning to our earlier focus upon moments when Ahab turns away from his duties and responsibilities as commander of a whaling vessel—moments when he steers, so to speak, this transnational machine towards his own ends—we see another dynamic at work: this time increasing tension between Ahab as captain and his strait-laced first mate, Starbuck. In Chapter 109, a pivotal scene in the narrative in which Starbuck confronts Ahab over the leaking sperm whale oil, the first mate begs to "up Burtons [hoist the tackle] and break out [lift all the barrels of whale oil out of the hold, to find the leak or leaks and make repairs]" (516). Ahab is enraged, and refuses: "Let it leak!" he screams. Starbuck once again reminds him of his responsibility, asking "What will the owners say, sir?" to which Ahab roars, "Let the owners stand on Nantucket beach and outyell the Typhoons. What cares Ahab? Owners, owners? Thou are always parting to me, Starbuck, about those miserly owners, as if the owners were my conscience. But look ye, the only real owner of anything is its commander; and hark ye, my conscience is in this ship's keel.—On deck!" Starbuck hesitates and Ahab seizes a loaded musket, which he then points at Starbuck while screaming, "There is one God that is Lord over the earth, and one Captain that is lord over the Pequod.—On deck!" (517). After this, however, Ahab thinks matters over by himself. Crazed in his desire to chase and kill Moby Dick, yet he is still sane enough at this point to realize that his purposes will be best served—and this "important chief officer of his ship," Starbuck, will remain loyal to him—if he maintains the appearance of trying to bring a full cargo of oil back to Nantucket. Swallowing his pride, Ahab returns to the deck and orders the barrels lifted and repaired, thus delaying his vengeance. However, this is only a temporary measure, and though Starbuck is appeased for the moment, Ahab's defiance and his true purposes will soon be made clear enough.

In Chapter 118, "The Quadrant," Melville takes a further step in this direction and we see yet another reference to the sun at a moment of Ahab's defiance. Melville's meaning here is plain: Ahab's feud is akin to Satan's feud with God in Milton. In this scene, we may recall Satan's defiance in *Paradise Lost*: "Then falling into a moment's revery, [Ahab] again looked up towards the sun and murmured to himself: 'Thou sea-mark! thou high and mighty Pilot! thou tellest me where I *am*—but canst thou cast the least hint where I *shall* be? Or canst thou tell where some other thing besides me is this moment living? Where is Moby Dick?'" he demands. "Then," the narrator tells us, "gazing at his quadrant [...] he muttered: 'Foolish toy! babies' plaything of haughty Admirals, and Commodores, and Captains [...] Thou canst not tell where one drop of water or one grain of sand will be to-morrow noon; and yet with thy impotence thou insultest the sun! Science! Curse thee, thou vain toy; and cursed be all the things that cast man's eyes aloft to heaven, whose live vividness but scorches him, as these old eyes are even now scorched with thy light, O Sun!'" (544). Ahab then dashes the quadrant to the deck, smashing it, before trampling the broken pieces. This occurs right before the crucial scene, in Chapter 119, "The Candles," in which St. Elmo's Fire, or ball lightning, sets the three (Japanese) masts aflame, "like three gigantic wax tapers before an altar" (549), while the three "pagan" harpooners'—Daggoo, Tashtego and Queequeg's—eyes, teeth and tattoos literally glow in the dark. Ahab quickly masters the scene, making one of his most memorable speeches ("I own thy speechless, placeless power!" he exclaims; 550, repeated on 551), while brandishing a burning harpoon. He reminds the terrified crew that "All your oaths to hunt the White Whale are as binding as mine; and heart, soul, and body, lungs and life, old Ahab is bound," before extinguishing the flaming harpoon and, with it, "the last fear" (552). He has thus consecrated their bond, baptizing them with fire much as he had done earlier baptizing the same harpoon with these same three "pagan" harpooners' blood (and the famous line, "Ego non baptizo te in nomine patris, sed in nomine diaboli!" 489, in Chapter 113, "The Forge"). Now, the chase is ready to begin, without any subterfuge; however, Ahab's resolve will be repeatedly tested.

In the famous "gam" in Chapter 128, for example, involving the *Pequod* and the *Rachel*—which winds up rescuing Ishmael later in the narrative, after the *Pequod* sinks—Ahab is asked by Captain Gardiner of the *Rachel* (a man he knows, out of Nantucket) to help join the search for a lost whaleboat, adrift since their encounter with Moby Dick the day before. Gardiner's son is one of the missing, so he is desperate; besides this, it is customary for whalers to assist one another in such emergencies; but Ahab ignores Gardiner's pleas, and continues on with his hunt for the White Whale. Here, Ahab turns his back on all human contact, "normal" sociality and friendship. In the next "gam," the *Pequod* meets the *Delight* (Chapter 131) and, yet again, Ahab ignores all convention and rules of behavior: this "most miserably misnamed" (587) ship, in mourning for one of its whaleboats, is conducting a funeral, from which Ahab turns and flees. Not only does he neglect to pay his respects to the corpses being lowered into the sea by the grieving crew of the *Delight*, he goes so far as to boast of possessing the one harpoon in the world that can kill Moby Dick—the same harpoon, encountered earlier in Chapters 113 and 119, that was "[t]empered in blood, and tempered by lightning" (587). Here, Ahab is beyond all human relations or sympathies, and Melville makes it clear that his fate is sealed.

However, there is a moment in the following chapter in which Ahab comes closest to turning away from his "mad" quest and turning back to Nantucket. In "The Symphony" (Chapter 132), Ahab meets Starbuck yet again, on a "clear steel-blue day" in which "[a]loft, like a royal czar and king, the sun seemed giving this gentle air to this bold and rolling sea; even as bride to groom," while Ahab, for the first time, gazes upward:

Tied up and twisted; gnarled and knotted with wrinkles; haggardly firm and unyielding; his eyes glowing like coals, that still glow in the ashes of ruin; untottering Ahab stood forth in the clearness of the morn; lifting his splintered helmet of a brow to the fair girl's forehead of heaven. (589)

It is a strange moment in the text, when Ahab seems to grow younger, or at least gentler with nostalgia—and when he comes closest to what Giles Deleuze and Félix Guattari would call "reoedipalization:" that is, returning to "conjugality," to hearth and home, to wife and child and his role as father and husband.[42] Ahab then continues in this vein:

> "Oh, Starbuck! it is a mild, mild wind, and a mild looking sky [...] I feel deadly faint, bowed, and humped, as though I were Adam, staggering beneath the piled centuries since Paradise [...] stand close to me, Starbuck; let me look into a human eye; it is better than to gaze into the sea or sky; better than to gaze upon God. By the green land; by the bright hearth-stone! this is a magic glass, man; I see my wife and my child in thine eye [...] [I see] the far away home [...] in that eye!" (590–591)

In this manner, Ahab exchanges pleasant memories of home with Starbuck; but at last, just as Starbuck thinks that Ahab will turn back, Ahab in fact turns away, once more, and this time for good: "But Ahab's glance was averted; like a blighted fruit tree he shook, and cast his last, cindered apple to the soil. 'What is it, what nameless, inscrutable, unearthly thing is it; what cozening, hidden lord and master, and cruel, remorseless emperor commands me; that

---

[42] The term occurs throughout their work, but is perhaps discussed most clearly in *Kafka: Toward a Minor Literature*, trans. Dana Polan (Minneapolis: University of Minnesota Press, 1986), especially 14–15.

against all natural lovings and longings, I so keep pushing, and crowding, and jamming myself on all the time[?]'" (592) In a Miltonian flourish, he then compares the sun to "an errand-boy in heaven" and concludes that "some invisible power," "God" or "Fate" has been driving him, and will drive him further still, to doom.

Once more will Starbuck and Ahab's eyes meet: in the final chapter (135), "The Chase—Third Day," just before Ahab lowers for the third and final time to pursue the White Whale (which, in fact, is now pursuing Ahab). Once again, however, Ahab will turn from Starbuck—as well as from all human contact:

> "'Starbuck!' 'Sir?' 'For the third time my soul's ship starts upon this voyage, Starbuck.' 'Aye, sir, thou wilt have it so.' 'Some ships sail from their ports, and ever afterwards are missing, Starbuck!' 'Truth, sir: saddest truth.' 'Some men die at ebb tide; some at low water; some at the full of the flood;—and I feel now like a billow that's all one crested comb, Starbuck. I am old;—shake hands with me, man.' Their hands met; their eyes fastened; Starbuck's tears the glue. 'Oh, my captain, my captain!—noble heart—go not—go not!—see, it's a brave man that weeps; how great the agony of the persuasion then!' 'Lower away!'—cried Ahab, tossing the mate's arm from him. 'Stand by the crew!' In an instant the boat was pulling round close under the stern." (616)

Here, Ahab turns from all human contact, for the final time, and is followed by vulture-like sharks to his doom. However, there is one final moment in which Ahab again turns away, just before his death.

Later in the same chapter, which recounts Ahab's third lowering for the White Whale, the third day of the doomed chase, there is one final turning-away. After delivering a deathblow to the *Pequod*, and maliciously allowing Ahab to watch it sink before his own eyes, the whale seems to offer his body to Ahab's diabolically baptized and consecrated harpoon, laying "quiescent" "but within a few yards of Ahab's [whale]boat" (622). Ahab echoes Milton's Satan in crying, "I turn my body from the sun" (Ibid.), just before casting his harpoon at Moby Dick: "Towards three I roll, thou all-destroying but unconquering whale; to the last I grapple with thee; from hell's heart I stab at thee; for hate's sake I spit my last breath at thee" (623). We should note the phrase, "from hell's heart I stab at thee," which is another clear echo of Milton. Ahab's defiance, then, must be viewed from the perspective of these Miltonian elements or echoes, yet without reducing Melville's art to some form of "Romantic Satanism" of the order of Byron (though we cannot deny Melville's interest in and familiarity with Byron).[43] There is something more at stake in Ahab's turning-away—something that will be repeated, and transformed, in both Pierre's and the Confidence-Man's defiance, which will be discussed in later chapters.

"The Hemispheres are Counterparts": the Transatlantic Fiction

From what is Ahab turning, what is he fleeing? What, in other words, is embodied by Starbuck or represented by the land? It should be clear from the above examples that Ahab has not only turned his back on the sun, on land, on profit and on home, but also, and perhaps most crucially, on the nation-state—as we shall see echoed in what I am calling Melville's "minor" work of this period: *Moby-Dick's* precursor, *Redburn*, the three transatlantic "diptyches" written for magazine publication, and also *Israel Potter*, which likewise was written for serial publication but later released as a novel. In this final section of chapter one, then, I will focus upon one text written before

---

[43] See Spanos' *The Errant Art of Moby-Dick*, 232–239, for a critique of this reductive reading.

Melville's "major" or "mature" period, and then two composed in *Moby-Dick*'s turbulent wake: first, *Redburn: His First Voyage* (1849), followed by *Pierre; or, The Ambiguities* (1852; here, only very briefly, as this novel is the focus of much of chapter two) and *Israel Potter: His Fifty Years of Exile* (serialized from July 1854, published as a novel in 1855), which I consider related in important ways. Here, I draw upon the work of William Spanos, whose project has consistently been one of retrieving the *political* Melville, an artist relevant to our contemporary occasion, by focusing our attention on the post-*Moby-Dick* writing and charting the ways in which it subverts or critiques what Spanos calls "the hegemonic discourse" of American national identity, in particular the central myth of "American exceptionalism," inherited from the Puritan founders. We can think of "American exceptionalism" as a pervasive belief that the US has, since its conception, maintained a special status, unique among nations and empires, as the "redeemer nation" on a divinely ordained "errand in the wilderness," something that the Puritan fathers never tired of reminding their people—the "saving remnant" escaped from a decaying, corrupt "Old World"—in a ritualistic sermon that Sacvan Bercovitch has charted and called "the American Jeremiad,"[44] which chastises the New Israelites for their backsliding, warns of the wrath to come should they shirk their responsibilities, but also assures victory, restoring confidence in the mission. Father Mapple's sermon in *Moby-Dick* is surely Melville's most obvious appropriation (and parody, as Spanos has demonstrated)[45] of this rhetoric, and my understanding of it owes much to Bercovitch's indispensable study, upon which Spanos builds his own argument for the

---

[44] Sacvan Bercovitch, *The American Jeremiad* (Madison: University of Wisconsin Press, 1978).

[45] See *The Errant Art of Moby-Dick*, 93–114.

contemporary political relevance of Melville's subversive employment of the Jeremiad tradition and Puritan Typology, more generally (particularly in this "middle period", where it is at its most intense).

Melville, himself, provides us with a means to engage the Puritan foundations of American culture, through an intriguing phrase that I will use to organize my readings of these transatlantic, "minor" texts. It comes from *Israel Potter*, which is the most direct treatment of the Puritan past, as the very name of the protagonist itself testifies. In a crucial scene, describing a British and an American ship engaged in a spectacular, "fratricidal" battle that serves as the very fulcrum of the narrative, Melville uses the phrase, "a type, a parallel, and a prophecy"[46] through which he hints at a deeper level of meaning for both the "engagement" at sea and the American nation-state itself, explicitly referring to the Typology of the Puritan fathers. "Typology" is a "method of interpretation of the Bible in which persons, events, and things in the Old Testament are regarded as 'types' or 'shadows' of persons, events, and things in the Christian dispensation, the latter being referred to as 'antitypes' or 'fulfilments' of the types" (Dwens xxv). As such, it is an attempt by the Church fathers to legitimate the Christian Bible much as, later, the Puritan fathers attempted to read their own struggles in terms of the ancient

---

[46] The quote, in full, is as follows: "There would seem to be something singularly indicatory in this engagement. It may involve at once a type, a parallel, and a prophecy[...] intrepid, unprincipled, reckless, predatory, with boundless ambition, civilized in externals but a savage at heart, America is, or may yet be, the Paul Jones of nations" (*Israel Potter* 136).

Israelites—a tradition Spanos has decisively shown is alive and well today.[47]

In this section, I want to very briefly turn to two aspects of the three texts under scrutiny: first, the motif of fathers and sons; second, the setting, which in all three novels involves a hellish descent into the city, with the additional dimension of a transatlantic journey in *Redburn* and *Israel Potter*. By looking at these two particular elements, I believe we can avoid the shortcomings of both New Critical and New Historicist approaches to Melville, the first of which tends to isolate the text at the expense of social or political contextualization, while the second often over-invests the biographical. Let us begin by examining the father/son motif running through these texts. In *Redburn*, which I read as "a type" (using Melville's phrase), Melville constructs his novel around the search by a lost son or orphan for his vanished father. Wellingborough Redburn, the protagonist, a "son-of-a-gentleman" now sweeping out pigpens on board a merchant ship bound for Liverpool, clutches in his hands a travel guide handed down from his now-deceased father, who died raving mad and under crippling debt (as did Melville's own father). Everything in the story seems to build toward the central event, in which Redburn wanders the streets of Liverpool looking for traces of his father, who had made an earlier, similar journey, but finds to his chagrin that his father's guidebook and map are sorely out-of-date and the Liverpool in his book bears no resemblance to the one before his eyes. Once he tosses away the useless book, he begins to see the reality of Liverpool, which I will discuss shortly. For now, I want to simply draw attention to the father that has failed

---

[47] See his *America's Shadow: An Anatomy of Empire* (Minneapolis: University of Minnesota Press, 2000) or *American Exceptionalism in the Age of Globalization: The Specter of Vietnam* (Albany: SUNY Press, 2008) for an elaboration of this argument.

Redburn, the lost son who, as Melville phrases it, "has learned to think much and bitterly before [his] time" and has had his "warm soul" "flogged out by adversity" (11). As in the tradition of Typology, Redburn is attempting to fulfill or become the "anti-type" of his father. This journey has been read in terms of psychoanalysis,[48] but it may be more useful instead to view it in terms of the consistent typological strain running through Melville's work of the mid- to late-1850s. If we turn to *Pierre*, which I read as "a parallel" (drawing again upon Melville's phrase) to *Redburn* in this respect, I believe a pattern will emerge.

In *Pierre*, we meet another lost son of an absent father, but in this case a true "son-of-a-gentleman," the last in a long and distinguished line of rural gentry. Pierre Glendinning comes to find, however, that the unblemished image of his dead father is in fact a mask, hiding a much darker side, which is embodied by an illegitimate daughter (Pierre's half-sister), Isabel, who appears one day and drastically alters Pierre's destiny. This double-image of Pierre's father is symbolized by his portraits, one prominently on display while another is hidden and a third is revealed at the very end of the novel, all of which function much as the guidebook does in *Redburn*, comprising the very heart of the story. Everything builds toward Pierre's encounters with these three paintings, as we saw with Redburn's climactic discovery in Liverpool, but with much darker, more disastrous consequences. In any case, both novels feature ruined fathers and disillusioned sons, but it would not be until *Israel Potter* that Melville "politicized" this motif.

This is what I am calling "a prophecy," again using Melville's phrase.

---

[48] By Régis Durand, for example, in his persuasive "'The Captive King': The Absent Father in Melville's Text," in *The Fictional Father: Lacanian Readings of the Text*, edited by Robert Con Davis (Amherst: Univ. of Massachusetts Press, 1981): 48–72.

Now, the lost son, after defying his biological father, seeks new father figures and finds nothing but misery. He meets none other than Benjamin Franklin, John Paul Jones and Ethan Allen, Revolutionary or "Founding" Fathers, who variously use and abuse him, landing him in prison, in battle, and ultimately in poverty and exile. The message here seems clear: in Deleuze's words, "There are only monstrous, devouring fathers, and petrified, fatherless sons."[49] Israel Potter, after forty-five years of wandering in the "English deserts", finally comes "home" to the United States to retrieve his pension, accompanied by his only surviving child (a son), only to find himself forgotten and his own childhood home vanished. Melville's own words, concerning America being the "Paul Jones of nations," suggest that the wildest and most "barbaric" of the monstrous fathers encountered by Israel Potter may indeed be the nation's destiny, if it ignores this "prophecy."

Before moving on, we should look at the typological setting of the three texts, beginning with *Redburn* and Liverpool. After realizing that his father's guidebook and map to the city have failed him, Redburn casts them aside, much as he earlier did with Adam Smith's *Wealth of Nations*, admitting to himself that "I am not the traveler my father was" (185). He is now ready to see the city for what it really is and what he finds along the docks and in the slums horrifies him. The most powerful chapters begin at this point: the most affecting scene occurs when Redburn tries, in vain, to help a dying mother and her starving children. This deeply moving realism is repeated on the homeward voyage as Melville describes "the emigrants" fleeing famine in Ireland, heading to New York. In both sections, Melville seems to be

---

[49]   Gilles Deleuze, "Bartleby; or, the Formula," in *Essays Critical and Clinical*, trans. Daniel W. Smith and Michael A. Greco (Minneapolis: University of Minnesota Press, 1997): 84.

fictionalizing something he has Redburn say—that "to be a born American citizen seems a guarantee against pauperism" (234), though, as we shall see, he will later mock and subvert this statement in both *Pierre* and *Israel Potter*, among other work of the 1850s. *Pierre* parallels Redburn's descent into an urban hell, but is in this case a journey from a bucolic rural setting to a nightmarish cityscape. "Old World" social ills (pauperism, crime, and vice) are all on display in New York City, which extends an extremely rude welcome to Pierre and Isabel. The optimism of *Redburn* and "Hawthorne and His Mosses" now gone, Melville turns his attention toward the realities of life for the "other half" in the "New World," which mirror the "Old," as *Israel Potter* and the work that follows will make clear.

Turning to the setting of *Israel Potter*, we see Melville repeating both Redburn and Pierre's journeys, across the Atlantic and from the countryside to the city. In this case, we have in Israel an unmistakable "American pauper," who finds himself in a desperate situation whether it is in the London slums, the streets of Boston, or his native Berkshire hills. Through him, we meet forgotten veterans and ruined farmers in both Old and New worlds, people orphaned by war and industrialization, in effect "pauperized" and driven to the cities or "out West." Is it a "prophecy?" The short fiction that follows *Israel Potter* and the bitter satire of *The Confidence-Man*, examined in the following chapters of this study, seem to strongly support this thesis. At any rate, Melville's larger point in these texts seems clear: America is not "exceptional," the "Old" and "New Worlds" are in fact very much the same—or, as he will say in his three transatlantic "diptyches" composed at about the same time as *Israel Potter*, "the hemispheres are counterparts." In the final section of chapter one, I want to examine these "diptyches" that seem to repeat the same critique of the novels discussed above, before concluding.

After the disappointing reception of his most experimental novel to date, *Mardi,* in 1849, Herman Melville told his British publisher, Bentley that he would refrain from writing anything similar, famously promising "no metaphysics, no conic sections, nothing but cakes & ale" (WHM 14: 132; qtd. in Winter, 17). The novels that immediately followed, *Redburn* and *White Jacket*, were certainly a return to form: tales set at sea that were geared for transatlantic popularity; however, *Moby-Dick* and *Pierre*, which came next, proved to be alarming, even disastrous relapses into metaphysics, particularly when we consider Melville's dire personal situation, with more mouths to feed and increasing debts. Once again restraining his more ambitious metaphysical aspirations, Melville entered the next phase of his career writing short fiction for two magazines, *Harper's New Monthly* and *Putnam's Monthly*, publishing his work anonymously (though the identity of the author was more or less an "open secret") and being paid relatively well.

The magazine sketches were intended for a popular audience expecting "cakes & ale," to be sure, yet they were themselves highly experimental, featuring a form flexible enough to accommodate Melville's increasingly subversive critique of American social and political values, as Marvin Fisher and many others have shown. One example of this formal experimentation is on display in three stories written in late-1853 at Arrowhead and submitted for publication sometime in the spring of 1854. These texts—"Poor Man's Pudding and Rich Man's Crumbs," "The Paradise of Bachelors and the Tartarus of Maids," and "The Two Temples," which are usually grouped together—share several thematic and structural similarities: each is a satire of contemporary British and American socioeconomic conditions, and each is a set of paired narratives.

Referring to the form of the two-paneled medieval religious painting, Jay Leyda first classified these three works as "diptychs" in his *Complete Short*

Stories of Herman Melville,[50] describing them as follows:

> The striking pictorial quality of all Melville's writings found a precise reflection within the medium of the short story in the form of the diptych. At least three times he displayed pairs of contrasting images [...] to make the light one brighter, and the dark one blacker.

For Leyda, Melville was continuing his "policy of concealment" (xxi) in this way, attempting through anonymity and a strategy of what Fisher called "going under" to subvert or critique many of the social conditions of his day, if only obliquely or indirectly. More recent critics have followed Leyda in categorizing these stories as "diptychs," viewing them for example as "morally constrastive pictorial pairs."[51] I also read the three stories as "paired narratives" characterized by a "striking pictorial quality," and in what follows I show how they provide readers with an important bridge between, on the one hand, the earlier social criticism of *Redburn*, *Pierre* and *Israel Potter*, and, on the other, the later work, including the cryptic sketches of "The Encantadas" (published in *The Piazza Tales*, 1856) and the biting satire of *The Confidence-Man* (1857)—the first of which is filled with doubles, while the second is, itself, structured in two, "panel"-like parts. The continuity of the three sketches with the serialized novel, *Israel Potter*, which was in fact written after their composition but published before them, has been noted by several scholars,

---

[50] Jay Leyda (ed.), *The Complete Short Stories of Herman Melville*, (New York: Random House, 1949), xx; qtd. in Winter, 18.

[51] Aaron Winter, "Seeds of Discontent: The Expanding Satiric Range of Melville's Transatlantic Diptychs," *Leviathan*, Vol. 8, No. 2 (June 2006): 17–35.

most notably Judith Hiltner,[52] and the social critique they offer, particularly through the transatlantic settings that they share not only with *Israel Potter* but also with the earlier *Redburn*, has been the focus of numerous studies (such as Rowland, Cook, Duban, and Lee).[53] In this final section of chapter one, I will bring together some of these studies in order to take a fresh look at the stories, revisiting the three diptychs in order to demonstrate how Melville is deliberately using the techniques of repetition, juxtaposition, and a shifting, transatlantic setting—what he himself calls "inverted similitude"—in order to specifically critique at least three crucial aspects of American identity, American Exceptionalism, Laissez-Faire Economics, and Messianic Nationalism, from which Ahab had attempted to escape.

Melville's phrase, "inverted similitude" (PT 327), refers to what Paul Giles has described as "elaborate parallels" that work "through contrast;" a contrast that "depends upon prior analogies."[54] In Melville's own words,

---

[52] Judith R. Hiltner, "From Pisgah to Egypt: Narrative Continuities in Melville's *Israel Potter* and 'The Two Temples,'" *Journal of Narrative Technique* Vol. 19, No. 3 (1989): 300–311.

[53] Beryl Rowland, "Sitting Up with a Corpse: Malthus according to Melville in 'Poor Man's Pudding and Rich Man's Crumbs,'" *Journal of American Studies*, Vol. 6, No. 1 (April 1972): 69–83; Jonathan A. Cook, "Christian Typology and Social Critique in Melville's 'The Two Temples,'" *Christianity and Literature* Vol. 56, No. 1 (Fall 2006): 5–33; James Duban, "Transatlantic Counterparts: The Diptych and Social Inquiry in Melville's 'Poor Man's Pudding and Rich Man's Crumbs,'" *The New England Quarterly*, Vol. 66, No. 2 (June 1993): 274–286; Maurice Lee, "Melville's 'Mistakes': Correcting the Politics of 'Poor Man's Pudding and Rich Man's Crumbs,'" *ESQ*, Vol. 41, No. 2 (1995): 153–175.

[54] Paul Giles, *Virtual Americas: Transnational Fictions and the Transatlantic Imaginary* (Durham: Duke University Press, 2002).

Though the two objects [referring to the "two temples"] did by no means completely correspond, yet this partial inadequacy but served to tinge the similitude not less with the vividness than the disorder of a dream. (326; cited in Giles 68)

As Giles notes, "this juxtaposition becomes almost surreal," always occurring in the second-half of the two-paneled stories, "where conceptual matrices of heaven and hell are superimposed on two quite different sets of circumstances, linked only by the accident of gender exclusivity" (Ibid.), class, or geographic location. Here, in this final section, I want to briefly focus upon the political aspect of this intertextual strategy by considering the object of Melville's critique in these moments of "inverted similitude." On a related note, and looking ahead to my final chapter, this notion of "inverted similitude" is, I will suggest, very similar to what Tony Tanner calls "reversibility," where "all things are potentially double, paradoxically mixed, oddly reversible" (*The American Mystery*, 77). I will examine this concept in more detail later in this study.

Before doing so, one crucial target that may need further explanation is "American exceptionalism," mentioned earlier in this study. This term denotes a "logic taken to the New World by the first Puritan migrants," according to Deborah Madsen, that entailed belief that they

> were charged with a special spiritual and political destiny: to create in the New World a church and a society that would provide the model for all the nations of Europe as they struggled to reform themselves (a redeemer nation). In this view, the New World is the last and best chance offered by God to a fallen humanity that has only to look at His exceptional new church for redemption. Thus, America and Americans are special, exceptional, because they are charged with saving the world from itself and, at the same time, America and Americans must sustain a high level

of spiritual, political and moral commitment to this exceptional destiny—America must be as "a city upon a hill" exposed to the eyes of the world (1–2).[55]

This mission or "errand in the wilderness" was something that the Puritan fathers never tired of reminding their people in a ritualistic sermon that Sacvan Bercovitch has charted and called "the American Jeremiad," which, as discussed above, chastises the New Israelites for their backsliding, warns of the wrath to come should they shirk their responsibilities, but also assures victory, restoring confidence in their mission. Father Mapple's sermon in *Moby-Dick* is surely Melville's clearest appropriation of this rhetoric, and my understanding of it owes much to Bercovitch's indispensable study, particularly in terms of Typology, which provided Melville with his main rhetorical strategy or technique for criticizing contemporary American society through his fiction of the mid-1850s, as illustrated above.

Another crucial term, "Typology," is, according to W. R. Owens,[56] a "method of interpretation of the Bible in which persons, events, and things in the Old Testament are regarded as 'types' or 'shadows' of persons, events, and things in the Christian dispensation, the latter being referred to as 'antitypes' or 'fulfilments' of the types." As such, it is an attempt by the Church fathers to legitimate the Christian Bible much as, later, the Puritan fathers attempted to read their own struggles in terms of the ancient Israelites. Melville was attempting to satirize, parody or otherwise subvert, undermine or demythologize

---

[55] Deborah L. Madsen, *American Exceptionalism* (Edinburgh: Edinburgh University Press, 1998).

[56] W.R. Owens, "Introduction" to John Bunyan's *The Pilgrim's Progress* (Oxford: Oxford University Press, 2003): xxv.

this aspect of American exceptionalism, through what we might call "renegade typology," particularly in the transatlantic work that directly compares and contrasts the "Old" and "New Worlds." American exceptionalism is a myth grounded upon an absolute break with Europe, in which the New World eclipses the Old by fulfilling its role typologically. Melville critiqued this view, as we shall see, and attempted in his transatlantic diptychs to show how, as he will later write, "Our New World bold/Had fain improved upon the Old/but the hemispheres are counterparts" (*Clarel*, 1876)—in other words, how *unexceptional* America really is. Let me begin with my readings of the three stories in order to illustrate this.

First published in the June 1854 issue of *Harper's*, "Poor Man's Pudding and Rich Man's Crumbs" begins with the poet Blandmour's assertion that "through kind nature, the poor, out of their very poverty, extract comfort" (291) and his experiment to verify this claim: the narrator will visit the impoverished Coulter family in order to taste for himself their meager supper of "Poor Man's Pudding." The couple—a farmer and his pregnant wife—are gaunt, exhausted, and joyless, yet despite the narrator's insensitivities (learning that the poor themselves do not actually use the phrase "Poor Man's Pudding," for example), he is treated most hospitably. Blandmour proves to be completely wrong: "Poor Man's Pudding," a "bitter and mouldy" stew of rice, milk, and salt (295), is in fact inedible, and the Coulter's "extract" no comfort from "kind nature" or from their poverty. The narrator flees the scene in shame.

In "Picture Second," the same narrator recalls his wanderings in London during the summer after his visit to the Coulters, at which time his acquaintance with a city official, who boasts of the city's "noble charities," provides him with an opportunity to observe them firsthand. The previous night, a royal assembly had gathered at the Guildhall for a sumptuous feast celebrating the victory over Napoleon at Waterloo; today, the city's beggars will be granted access to the leftovers. The only way for the narrator to enter the hall is to join this ragtag group of paupers, scrambling for crumbs while they are held in check by armed guards. The narrator witnesses a virtual stampede and retreats, once again, to a comfortable place far removed from the scene. The "and" of the title establishes not only the diptych, but also the doubling that occurs between the two panels: "for both the Coulters in rural America and the beggars in London, the lot of the poor man is to make his pudding from the rich man's crumbs." Here, Melville's strategy seems to be an ironic juxtaposition in which the notion of American moral superiority (or "American exceptionalism" more generally) is criticized, leaving the reader to ponder how different the two types of poverty really are. We must now look more closely at the specific moments of what Melville calls "inverted similitude."

The first, brief instance occurs near the beginning of "Picture Second," when the narrator enters the banquet hall and notes how "[t]he spot was as grimy as a back-yard in the Five Points," referring to a notorious slum district of New York City, and was "packed with a mass of lean, famished, ferocious creatures" (298). Melville is implying that the urban poor in both countries face the same, inhuman conditions—an idea he continues in the second moment, once again describing the poor in inhuman metaphors:

> It was just the same as if I were pressed by a mob of cannibals on some pagan beach. The beings around me roared with famine. For in this mighty London misery but maddens. In the country it softens. As I gazed upon the meagre, murderous pack, I thought of the blue eye of the gentle wife of poor Coulter. (298)

Here, on the surface, we can see Melville attempting to differentiate between the conditions of the poor in rural and urban areas, essentially between the poor in the Old and New Worlds; however, when we consider the allusion to the Five Points, cited above, and the pathos with which he described the misery of the Coulters in the first panel, which is much more fully developed and sympathetic than this scene in the Guildhall, the reader is left to wonder who, if either type of pauper, is really the better off. Moreover, taking into consideration the symbolism of Squire Teamster's sexual exploitation of Coulter's wife, a relation that is positively feudal, the ironic juxtaposition (and equivalence) of the two scenes becomes clear, as in the final instance of "inverted similitude," when the narrator exclaims at the end of the story:

> 'Now, Heaven in its kind mercy save me from the noble charities of London,' sighed I, as that night lay bruised and battered on my bed; 'and Heaven save me equally from the "Poor Man's Pudding" and the "Rich Man's Crumbs." (302)

The next diptych that I will consider, "The Paradise of Bachelors and the Tartarus of Maids," was first published in the April 1855 issue of *Harper's*, essentially reversing the geographic movement of "Poor Man's Pudding." In this story, the American narrator once again travels to London, but does so in the first half, returning home in the second. The diptych begins in London's temple district, where the narrator eats and drinks with a fraternity of lawyers. His entrance into this "paradise" is figured as a "mystic" journey through a "cool, deep glen" (316), carrying him far away from "the whole care-worn world." A reverie places the roots of the lawyers in the medieval Knights-Templar; however, in this case, they are bachelors living in monastic seclusion but devoted to no higher calling than pleasure. In a scene rivaling "A Squeeze of the Hand," chapter 94 of *Moby-Dick*, in terms of its erotic imagery, the narrator is so excited by the bachelor lifestyle that he exclaims to his host, "with a burst of admiring candor—'Sir, this is the very Paradise of Bachelors!'" (323).

The second picture, presenting by contrast the opposing world of "The Tartarus of Maids," which will be discussed in chapter two of this study, begins with the description of a journey that in some ways mirrors the opening of the first panel; however, instead of a delightful spring stroll that leads to an earthly paradise, the narrator now describes an arduous winter trek to a remote paper mill that more closely resembles a descent into the Inferno, taking him past a series of landmarks whose names suggest both the female body and gothic horror: "Woedolor Mountain," "Mad Maid's Bellow Pipe," "Black Notch," "Devil's Dungeon," and "Blood River." The narrator hopes to reduce the costs involved with his "seedman's business" by purchasing directly from the factory the paper envelopes he requires to package his seeds. He escapes the freezing wind only to be confronted by a hellish scene within the factory's walls, where the virginal Maids—"blank looking girls, with blank, white folders in their blank hands, all blankly folding paper" (328)—oversee the various stages of the paper's mechanized mass-production. After the narrator places his order, he asks for a guided tour of the factory, which climaxes in a famous scene standing before the "great machine" (331) that processes the pulp into paper. Here, the sexual symbolism becomes increasingly explicit, as the narrator, alternately horrified and fascinated by what he sees, becomes increasingly ill before eventually fleeing the scene. Melville seems to be taking aim at two central features of Adam Smith's Laissez-Faire economics: the division of labor and the so-called "invisible hand" of the free market, which have helped to produce this lopsided relation across the Atlantic (and across genders). Now, we must turn to a closer look at the moments of "inverted similitude."

The first occurs in a lengthy passage when the narrator comes upon the "large, white-washed factory," which reads as follows:

[T]hen something latent, as well as something obvious in the time and scene, strangely brought back to my mind my first sight of [...] Temple-Bar [...] and I said to myself, 'This is the very counterpart of the Paradise of Bachelors, but snowed upon, and frost-painted to a sepulchre [...] The inverted similitude recurred—'The sweet, tranquil Temple garden, with the Thames bordering its green beds,' strangely meditated I. But where are the gay bachelors? (326–7)

Here, Melville not only introduces the phrase, "inverted similitude," but also ironically juxtaposes the images of the bachelors' luxurious garden with the virgins' prison-like workplace, implying the necessary relation between the two.

The second moment occurs in the "rag-room" where the narrator learns that some of the recycled shirts to be used in the paper-making process come from overseas: "'Tis not unlikely, then," he asks, "that among these heaps of rags there may still be some old shirts, gathered from the dormitories of the Paradise of Bachelors" (330), which leads to a discussion of "Old Bach," the boss of the factory, himself a bachelor, and an intriguing passage describing what Marx called "alienated labor" ("Their own executioners; themselves whetting the very swords that slay them; meditated I").

The final instance occurs, once again, at the very end of the story, echoing the ending of "Bartleby, The Scrivener" (1853), as follows:

At the Black Notch I paused, and once more bethought me of Temple-Bar. Then, shooting through the pass, all alone with inscrutable nature, I exclaimed—Oh! Paradise of Bachelors! and oh! Tartarus of Maids! (335)

In both of these diptychs, we see a similar pattern emerge, which seems to point to the equivalence and interdependence of the Old and New Worlds; however, in the third, we will see a variation in which the Old World is actually shown to be superior to the New. This may in fact be one of the reasons that the story was unpublished in Melville's lifetime.

At any rate, of the three diptychs, "The Two Temples" (rejected for publication in May 1854), is the simplest in terms of structure, as pointed out by Winter. In the first panel, the narrator attends Sunday morning church services at a "marble-buttressed, stained-glass, spic-and-span new temple" in New York (303). His new coat being held onto, perhaps as collateral by his tailor, he is denied entry to the temple by a "fat-paunched, beadle-faced man" on the basis of his rather poor appearance. In this way he is made conscious of the class divisions in New York, and he complains that he is "defrauded of [his] natural rights" (305). Sneaking into the church through an unguarded side door to watch the service by climbing up inside the church tower, he finds himself locked in and, worse still, late for an appointment. He decides to ring the church's bell, which leads to his arrest. He flees New York, having committed no crime other than "humbly indulg[ing] in the luxury of public worship" (309).

In the second panel, the same narrator finds himself wandering the streets of "Babylonian London" (310), after accompanying a wealthy lady as her personal physician on a European tour. Unfortunately, he was "cavalierly dismissed" upon their arrival in England when she suddenly changed her plans. Bankrupted by the cost of the voyage, he seeks the solace of a "genial humane assembly" (311), but since it is Saturday evening he cannot attend church. When a working man offers him a theater ticket, he hesitates, for this would be the first charitable gift he has ever received. Swallowing his pride, and reversing what Melville had earlier written about Americans not accepting such alms, he enters the theatre, climbing to the "topmost gallery" of this second "temple," and feeling the same "dizzy altitude" as he did at the top of the church tower. The "bewildering and blazing spectacle" (313) of the play and the narrator's feeling of genuine communion with his fellow spectators throw him into a reverie, leading him to reflect on his earlier humiliation. As

Marvin Fisher notes, Melville detaches the "American Dream" of equality from the American nation-state as its "necessary locus [of] realization," thereby questioning "the self-styled role of America as the redeemer nation" (86). One way that he accomplishes this is through the strategy of "inverted similitude," which we have explored in the other two stories. We must now look at how it works in this final story to debunk the myth of messianic nationalism.

The first instance takes place when the narrator enters the "Temple Second," winding his way up the stairs, "whose boards much reminded [him] of [his] ascent of the Gothic tower on the ocean's far other side" and whose orchestral music "revived the memory of the organ-anthems [he] had heard while on the ladder of the tower at home. The next moment," he remarks,

> the wire-woven gauzy screen of the ventilating window in that same tower, seemed enchantedly reproduced before [him]. The same hot blast of stifling air once more rushed into [his] lungs. From the same dizzy altitude," he "stood within the topmost gallery of the temple. *But hardly alone and silently as before. This time [he] had company.* (313; emphasis added)

This last comment is crucial: the two sides of the Atlantic are not shown to parallel, depend upon, or otherwise support one another, as with the other diptychs. Here, the superiority of the English "temple" is clearly shown over the American, as we can see in the second moment of "inverted similitude:" "As at the tower, peeping into the transatlantic temple [by which he means the American church], so stood I here, at the very main-mast-head of all the interior edifice," whose "decorum" was such "that nothing objectionable was admitted within its walls." This ecstatic feeling extends to the "delight[ful]" occupants of the gallery, including a "ragged, but good-natured looking boy," clearly contrasted with the "beadle-faced man" back in New York. The boy is selling drinks, and asks the penniless narrator, "Ain't you a Yankee? [...] Well dad's gone to Yankee-land, seekin' of his fortin'; so take a penny mug of ale, do Yankee, for dad's sake" (314). This generous act revives the narrator's "drooping spirits" and he blesses the boy, and the temple, gazing upon them with "an unhurt eye of perfect love" (314), reflecting the true (Christian) charity he has received here, across the Atlantic. Of note, as well, in this second passage is Melville's use of the word, "transatlantic," which is repeated in this sketch, thus underscoring his point.

The story ends, as did the other two, with a final instance of "inverted similitude," in which the narrator reveals that

> I went home to my lonely lodging, and slept not much that night, for thinking of the First Temple and the Second Temple; and how that, a stranger in a strange land, I found sterling charity in the one; and at home, in my own land, was thrust out from the other. (315)

Thus, like the Biblical Ishmael—a parallel drawn quite clearly by Melville though his repeated use of the words "wandering" and "stranger" throughout this story—as well as the Ishmael of *Moby-Dick,* the narrator finds himself "thrust out" in the world's wilderness, yet "only [...] another orphan" (*Moby-Dick*, "Epilogue") who has realized that the American nation-state, and the myths upon which it attempts to legitimate itself, is as un-exceptional as any other.

In this chapter, we have seen how Hawthorne's influence upon Melville inspired him to transform *Moby-Dick* into a more profound tale, at the heart of which lies its "defiant sufferer," Ahab, and his bachelor-machine. This machine consists of Ahab, the *Pequod,* the ship's crew, and the various parts of dead whales and wrecked ships that have crossed its path. Ahab turns his machine away from the sun, away from land, from hearth and home, from conjugality and (re)oedipalization, and traces what Deleuze and Guattari call a "line of flight" that attempts to escape the nation-state. In his defiance, he constructs an interracial, interspecies, and most crucially for my purposes, a transnational machine that turns away and attempts to escape from the nation-state and its mythology. This critique of the nation-state, particularly the myth of "exceptionalism" that subtends the American imaginary, is echoed in several of the transatlantic fictions, as we have seen. In this context, the novel *Pierre* was discussed, if only briefly; in the following chapter, it will be the main focus, and I will show how Ahab's pattern of defiance is continued, in many ways repeated and deepened, then transformed, along with the author himself. To this task we now turn.

Chapter 2
Lost Sons (and Daughters); or, Escaping the Family

There is always betrayal in a line of flight. [...] We betray the fixed powers which try to hold us back, the established powers of the earth.

—Gilles Deleuze[57]

Melville's next novel, *Pierre; or, The Ambiguities* (1852), was perhaps begun "with an eye toward regaining his former popularity by appealing to female readers, the largest audience of his day, with what he perhaps disingenuously touted to English publisher Richard Bentley as 'a regular romance,' 'very much more calculated for popularity than anything you have yet published of mine'" (WHM 14: 226).[58] As is by now well-known, however, "regular" was "perhaps the last word that contemporary readers would apply to *Pierre*, which not only founded its plot on brother-sister (and, to a lesser extent, mother-son) incest but which from its opening pages committed the still graver literary sins of irreverence, morbidity, linguistic obscurity and abstruse philosophizing" (Ibid.). *Pierre* was in many ways, and as I will show in this chapter, a rewriting of *Moby-Dick*—in Robert Milder's words, "a Melvillean quest" featuring a defiant sufferer who probes "at the very axis of reality," as Melville in his "Mosses" review had described

---

[57] "On the Superiority of Anglo-American Literature," 40.
[58] Leon Howard, "Historical Note to *Pierre*," WHM 7: 365–79; qtd. in Milder, 35; for an example of the argument that Melville was aiming at female readers, see Brook Thomas, "The Writer's Procreative Urge in *Pierre*: Fictional Freedom or Convoluted Incest?" *Studies in the Novel*, Vol. 11, No. 4 (Winter 1979): 16–30.

Shakespeare's "darker" characters[59] —"recast ironically, even parodically, in a nightmarish subversion of sentimental romance and deconstructed with an unsparing, even cruel, intellectual and psychological acuity all the more painful because Pierre's family history (literally) and authorial career (figuratively) are visibly modeled upon Melville's own" (Ibid.)

Melville's "nightmarish subversion of sentimental romance" can perhaps best be seen by closely examining the tangled web of "family" relations in this overheated novel. I cannot improve upon William C. Spengemann's pithy description of what he calls the novel's "labyrinth of untethered kinships" (xii), which runs (in his "Introduction" to the Penguin Classics edition of *Pierre*) as follows:

> Pierre calls his mother "Sister," takes his sister (if that's what Isabel is) to wife, and makes a cousin of his jilted fiancée [Lucy]. A nameless orphan, Isabel makes Glendinning [Pierre's father] her father, makes the guitar her mother, and takes the name inscribed therein for her own. Pierre's mother disowns him. He disowns his father. Delly's parents [Delly is Pierre's servant-girl] disown her when her seducer decamps and she delivers a stillborn child. Lucy's mother disowns her. Pierre kills both his mother and [his cousin] Glen Stanly, who is his own boyhood lover-brother. Isabel causes the death of her "sister" Lucy, assists the suicide of her brother-husband, Pierre, and poisons herself. (Ibid.)

As Milder has pointed out, *Pierre* is a "fascinating study of betrayal and madness" that functions as "the pivot of Melville's career, both artistically and professionally" (36). "One must understand [*Pierre*] before all others," E.

---

[59] WHM 9: 244; qtd. in Milder, 50.

L. Grant Watson remarked long ago, in order to understand Melville.[60] It is difficult, if not impossible, to tease out all of the possible biographical references embedded in the text. Regardless of Melville's motivation in writing it, "the book's publication was," as Milder asserts, "a disaster from which Melville's career as a novelist never quite recovered":

> Previously, hostile reviewers had found Melville furtively subversive; now, responding to his numerous provocations in this latest novel, nearly all reviewers were hostile, pronouncing him "sick," immoral, and possibly insane. The diseased *Pierre* was set against the "healthy" *Typee*, and Melville was advised to "diet himself for a year or two on Addison" and leave morbidity and metaphysics alone.[61] (36)

And Melville did just that, or gave the appearance of doing so. He turned to writing short stories, luckily enough, just as two new periodicals emerged—*Harper's New Monthly Magazine* (1850) and *Putnam's Monthly Magazine* (1853)—that welcomed his contributions and were willing to pay him their highest rate ($5 per page). This was not enough to provide for his growing family, as Watson points out, nor allow Melville to repay some of his mounting debts, but it did allow for him to "continue as a working author" while he recovered from the "psychological ordeal" of writing *Pierre* and the

---

[60] E. L. Grant Watson, "Melville's *Pierre*," in *Critical Essays on Herman Melville's "Pierre; or, The Ambiguities,"* ed. Brian Higgins and Hershel Parker (Boston: Hall, 1983), 183; qtd. in Ibid..

[61] Fitz-James O'Brien, "Our Young Authors—Melville," in Higgins and Parker, *Critical Essays on "Pierre,"* 75–76; qtd. in Ibid. Even Hawthorne, years later, would use the term "morbid" to describe Melville ("his writings, for a long while past, have indicated a morbid state of mind"); see WHM 15: 628 for a reprint of Hawthorne's journal entry of November 20, 1856, when they met, for the final time, in England.

"critical ordeal" of its publication and reception (Milder 37). I would like to now turn to some of the tales before diving into *Pierre* in depth.

The Isle of Shoals

It seems that in 1852–1853, Melville wrote and "was prevented from printing" (WHM 14: 250) a narrative entitled "The Isle of the Cross," based upon the story of a Nantucket woman named Agatha Hatch Robertson (exhaustively detailed, though with a great deal of conjecture and ungrounded speculation, by Hershel Parker in his Melville biography).[62] Melville was now experimenting with the tale or sketch, a genre that forced him to write for a popular audience while, at the same time, allowing him to continue his explorations into the metaphysical. For Milder, while *Pierre* had been an explicit challenge to "piety and convention," the magazine sketches of 1853–1856 "subtly insinuated theirs" (37), as Marvin Fisher has noted in his important study,[63] in essence pointing the way toward what Melville would, much later in life, call "inside narrative[s]" (the subtitle of *Billy-Budd, Sailor*, published posthumously, in 1924, but a phrase that could easily be applied to any of Melville's tales or sketches of the mid-1850s). These included "Benito Cereno," a harrowing exploration of race and slavery, "Poor Man's Pudding and Rich Man's Crumbs," and "The Paradise of Bachelors and the Tartarus of Maids," discussed earlier, and perhaps his masterwork in the form, "Bartleby, the Scrivener: A Story of Wall-Street."

---

[62] See his *Herman Melville: A Biography, Volume 2, 1851–1891* (Baltimore: The Johns Hopkins University Press, 2002): 136–161.

[63] See his aptly titled *Going Under: Melville's Short Fiction and the American 1850s* (Baton Rouge: Louisiana State UP, 1977).

Melville published fourteen tales and sketches between 1853 and 1856 (as mentioned above, "The Two Temples" was rejected by *Putnam's* as offensive to the sensibilities of churchgoers), along with *Israel Potter*, a serialized historical novel, which appeared in book form the year before five of the *Putnam's* stories were collected and published as *The Piazza Tales* (1856). Reviews were generally favorable, but Melville's financial situation improved little: his combined income from the magazine pieces of 1853–1856 was less than $1,400.[64] "In the aftermath of *Pierre* and with financial burdens pressing more heavily on him as notes on Arrowhead came due and a third child was born in 1853, a fourth in 1855" (Milder 38–39), Melville was clearly in desperate straits. However, the economy with which he was forced to write in order to please his magazine editors and audience lent itself to the creation of the episodic novel—the last to be published in his lifetime—*The Confidence-Man: His Masquerade* (1857), which is the main focus of chapter three of this study. Before addressing that text, however, in the following chapter, I will discuss *Pierre*, followed by several "minor" works in which female characters—quite rare up to this point in Melville's career—figure prominently, beginning with a moment when Melville is languishing, in Wyn Kelley's phrase, "in the shoals," stranded and abandoned by his friend, Nathaniel Hawthorne.[65] In fact, before turning to *Pierre; or, the Ambiguities*, we must continue our examination of the Hawthorne-Melville encounter, which takes a crucial turn at the time of *Pierre's* publication. This was when Melville had proposed a collaborative project—the so-called "Agatha" story,

---

[64]   See Merton M. Sealts' detailed "Historical Note" to WHM 9: 494.
[65]   "Hawthorne and Melville in the Shoals: 'Agatha,' the Trials of Authorship, and the Dream of Collaboration," in Argersinger and Person, eds., *Hawthorne and Melville*, 173–195.

which may or may not have been completed by Melville. There has been a great deal of scholarly speculation as to what Melville possibly did with material given him by lawyer John Henry Clifford in 1852. However, three letters to Hawthorne—as Kelley notes, "urging him to write the story, outlining scenes, supplying documentation, and suggesting approaches that Hawthorne, ultimately, decided not to take up—and that Melville possibly did" (173)—are all that have thus far emerged.

Although biographer Hershel Parker is convinced that Melville completed and was somehow "prevented from" publishing the "Agatha" story in novel form—perhaps it had been rejected, for example—as Kelley reminds us, no manuscript has ever been located, so perhaps the tale lives on only in scattered traces among other texts:

> References in the Melville family correspondence to another narrative written in 1853—possibly titled *The Isle of the Cross*—imply that Melville may have expanded the "Agatha" tale and given it that title, though no manuscript evidence exists; details in Melville's later works suggest that *The Isle of the Cross* could also have served as an early version of some other narrative. (Ibid.)

Regardless, Melville never published *The Isle of the Cross*. Parker's main evidence for his conjecture is what Kelley refers to as "an enigmatic letter to *Harper's* in November 1853" in which Melville "wrote of 'the work of which I took to New York last Spring, but which I was prevented from printing at that time'" (WHM 14: 250; November 24, 1853; qtd. in Ibid.). Be that as it may, the "Agatha" story has long been understood as significant. Melville's "epistolary account of a woman abandoned by her shipwrecked sailor-husband, with its haunting evocation of a lonely shoreline, a decaying postbox to which no letter arrives, and a woman's undaunted courage in the face of this hopeless situation has been viewed as the germ of such later fiction as

'Bartleby, the Scrivener' and 'The Encantadas'" (Ibid.). It is certainly the most interesting story that Melville may never have actually written.

As Kelley notes, "[l]ess attention has been paid to the fact that 'Agatha' may be one of the most interesting stories that *Hawthorne* never wrote" and even less to the fact that it is "the most remarkable story Melville and Hawthorne never wrote *together*" (173–4; emphasis in original). This project—story or novel, Hawthorne's or Melville's or both authors' work—has rightly been framed as

> an outgrowth of their friendship, and "Agatha" has been taken to reflect the psychological, erotic, and literary dimensions of their mutual influence from the time they met in August 1850 in the Berkshires until whatever endpoint seems most significant: Hawthorne's move, out of Lenox, in November 1851; his departure for Liverpool in the summer of 1853, to take up the consulship awarded him by President Franklin Pierce [his friend from their days at Bowdoin College]; the final meeting of Hawthorne and Melville in England in November 1856; the year 1864, when Hawthorne died and Melville may have written the poem "Monody" for him; or even as late as 1876, when Melville almost certainly included his old friend as a character ("Vine") in his long, still-misunderstood poem, *Clarel: A Poem and Pilgrimage in the Holy Land*. (174)

But what makes the "Agatha" story so intriguing, and why I dwell upon it at length, is the fact that it is also "the closest that Melville ever came to collaborating professionally with another author, even if all that remains of that would-be collaboration resides in his letters and in Hawthorne's journal" (Ibid.). As Kelley points out, this "dream of collaboration" likewise "coincides with a shift in the way both authors were thinking of their work" during what she calls "the annus horribilis of 1852;" in other words, "when, after the completion of Melville's *Pierre* and Hawthorne's *The Blithedale Romance*, an election season converged with changes in their literary fortunes to make them both consider leaving authorship and taking political posts under the new administration" (174–5). It would seem that the "Agatha" project was indeed a turning point (Kelley) for both authors, in that Hawthorne soon took up a US consulship in England, courtesy of his classmate and friend, Franklin Pierce, while Melville turned his attention from writing novels to publishing magazine fiction, after he, himself, had failed to secure a consular post.

Kelley makes several important points in her essay, including one especially germane to this study: the fact that the sailor-husband who abandons Agatha, a man named Robertson (in real life; Melville seems to have either mistakenly referred to him or perhaps dubbed him "Robinson" in his letters to Hawthorne), is "a thriving American type," a "cosmopolitan" or transnational type who "travels freely from one country to another," thus, bearing "no particular allegiance to America" (179). In this way, Kelley argues, "Robinson" prefigures Melville's "confidence man;" I would add to this suggestion the idea that he also reflects Ahab, in his cosmopolitan or transnational dimension (discussed in the previous chapter). More importantly, however, is the "cosmopolitanism" of Agatha, herself: despite the scant (extant) record Melville left behind, there is persuasive evidence that Agatha lived "within no essential boundaries," as Kelley phrases it; in other words, that she was not bound by geography or nationality. Walking along the beach, awaiting the arrival of her sailor-lover, young Agatha gazes out over a vast sea that reminds her of this fact: "There is no land," Melville writes, "over against this cliff short of Europe & the West Indies" (WHM 14: 235). "Her America," according to Kelley, is "but an open border to the world" (180). Similarly, in *Moby-Dick* (much like the remarkable passage in Hawthorne's *Scarlet Letter*, quoted at the beginning of this study) Melville speaks of the Nantucket whalemen as knowing no limits to their sovereignty: "thus have these naked Nantucketers, these sea hermits, issuing from their anthill in the sea, overrun and conquered the watery world like so many Alexanders" (WHM 6: 64). Thus, the "cosmopolitan" Agatha, in Melville's imaginary, mirrors her transnational lover, "Robinson," and to some extent repeats the figure of Ahab (among his multinational, multiracial crew) and prefigures the confidence-man.

Kelley's most intriguing insight, however, concerns the resonance—at once literary, artistic, "democratic" and even erotic—of the concept of "collaboration" in this anomalous joint-project, which brings us back to Hawthorne. "In *Moby-Dick*," as Kelley reminds us, "Melville had suggested the erotic nature of collaborative labor in his extraordinary chapter, 'A Squeeze of the Hand' (chapter 94)—'Squeeze! squeeze! squeeze! all the morning long; I squeezed that sperm till a strange sort of insanity came over me; and I found myself unwittingly squeezing my co-laborers' hands in it'" (WHM 6: 416; qtd. in Kelley 182)—and his earlier "Hawthorne and His Mosses" essay could also be characterized as an ecstatic tribute to community and collaboration, drawing as it does upon the tradition of Renaissance drama. As Kelley remarks, critics and historians of Renaissance collaboration have long argued that the dream of literary co-authorship is powerfully erotic. To these critics, "the world of Renaissance drama represents a lost Eden, a precapitalist male subculture (not unlike the democratic, homoerotic universe Robert K. Martin describes in *Moby-Dick*) where author-ity rests not in the hands of a single genius but in the clasped hands of the many" (183).[66] Along with Shakespeare, Kelley adds, "[Francis] Beaumont and [John] Fletcher recur periodically in Melville's writing from 1849–54," including the

---

[66] Kelley is referring to Robert K. Martin's *Hero, Captain, and Stranger: Male Friendship, Social Critique, and Literary Form in the Sea Novels of Herman Melville* (Chapel Hill: University of North Carolina Press, 1986).

aforementioned "Hawthorne and His Mosses," as "emblems of literary and bodily commingling" (Ibid.). She also points to references to the two authors in *Mardi* and *White-Jacket*, as well as to Melville's documented purchases (and subsequent heavy marking in the margins) of Beaumont and Fletcher's plays while in London in 1849, just before he composed the "Mosses" essay, and even a quotation from their work in an epigraph in one of the "sketches" of "The Encantadas." This all strongly supports the idea that, with the "Agatha" story, then, we have a glimpse of what Robert K. Martin and Leland S. Person identify as the ways "Hawthorne and Melville sought to express their desires textually, or sometimes to repress them" through their common labors: Kelley argues for the way in which the examples of Shakespeare, Beaumont, Fletcher and other Renaissance dramatists offered a model for Melville to understand and express male-male desire.

Apparently, Hawthorne took Melville's idea to heart, and began work on the text during a vacation near the Isles of Shoals, which straddle New Hampshire and Maine (discussed in Kelley 186–190). He only gave up on the project, according to Kelley, when Franklin Pierce called upon him to serve as US Consul in Liverpool—not due to "homosexual panic," which Edwin H. Miller and other biographers have speculated was the cause of his "estrangement" from Melville. Whether or not Melville was disappointed by Hawthorne's ultimate response, he seems to have taken on the project single-handedly from this point, asking permission to use the title Hawthorne had considered, "Isle of Shoals" (Kelley 190). The name itself, as Kelley notes, "reflects the 'shallowly expansive' waters Melville mentioned in *Pierre* and his own sense, shared with Hawthorne, that he, and elite literary authorship in general in America, had arrived in a secluded cove" (Ibid.). However, "Hawthorne was afraid of drowning in the shoals, [while] Melville seems to have crossed them to new literary waters [...] produc[ing] fourteen short stories, the novella *Israel Potter*, a collection titled *The Piazza Tales*, and his novel *The Confidence-Man* before his and Hawthorne's final meeting in Liverpool" (Ibid.). Hawthorne, to the contrary, confessed that "the more I use a pen, the worse I hate it" (qtd. in Ibid.) It may be the case that Melville ultimately ended up using the title *The Isle of the Cross*, but perhaps this refers less to some type of crucifixion (as Parker would have it)[67] and more to his crossing paths—and then parting ways with, even being abandoned by— Hawthorne in "the isle of shoals," as Kelley eloquently argues. Before turning to a discussion of the abandoned figures (mainly female, itself a rarity in Melville's male-centric fiction) that proliferate in this period of Melville's career, however, we must look more closely at *Pierre*, a transitional, even pivotal work that shows Melville's transformation of the "defiant sufferer" character, thus bridging the gap between Ahab's "madness" and the confidence man's "masquerade." This time, however, Melville's (anti-) hero will wage a "war against domesticity" (in Rogin's words, discussed below).

The Avenging Dream: Pierre; or, the Ambiguities

Hawthorne had left Lenox on November 21, 1851; as Miller points out in his biography, it was about this time that Melville began his new novel—and as was the case with the composition of *Moby-Dick*, once again Melville imprisoned himself in his study and wrote "with his usual fury and dedication" (224). Around the Christmas holiday, his neighbor (Mrs. Morewood) informed Duyckinck that "I hear that [Melville] is now engaged in a new work as frequently not to leave his room till quite dark in the evening— when he for the first time during the whole day partakes of solid food—he must therefore write under a state of morbid excitement which will soon

---

[67]   See Hershel Parker's Melville biography, Volume 2, 146–7.

injure his health—I laughed at him somewhat and told him that the recluse life he was leading made his city friends think that he was slightly insane—he replied that long ago he came to the same conclusion himself" (qtd. in Miller 223). On March 1, 1852, Elizabeth Melville's physician wrote to Melville's father-in-law, Judge Shaw, that his daughter's "husband, I fear, is devoting himself to writing with an assiduity that will cost him dear by & by" (Ibid.). On January 21 Melville's brother Allan was arranging a contract with Harper and Brothers for the publication of *Pierre*, and on February 20 Melville received an advance of $500. In February, Herman (or perhaps Allan) wrote to Richard Bentley about English publication. Bentley was unwilling to make an advance payment because he had sustained losses from the last four books and he proposed that profit be tied to sales of *Pierre*. Meanwhile, Melville worked at the new novel with his customary passion. The book was finished about the end of March, and on April 16 he sent a set of proofs to Bentley, accompanied by a letter rejecting the publisher's financial scheme. "My new book," he wrote, possesses "unquestionable novelty, as regards my former ones,—treating of utterly new scenes & characters; —and, as I believe, very much more calculated for popularity than anything you have yet published of mine—being a regular romance, with a mysterious plot to it, & stirring passions at work, and withal, representing a new & elevated aspect of American life" (qtd. in Miller 224).

According to Miller, "Melville was either deliberately inaccurate or was indulging himself in a 'wicked' joke" (Ibid.). By any definition, *Pierre* is far from "a regular romance." Miller (among myriad other critics and biographers) has, for the most part, an extremely low opinion of *Pierre*: it is, according to him, "an arrogant but frighteningly narcissistic projection of [Melville's] own despair. The cosmos is shriveled to reflect his own self-evaluation: 'I am nothing,' and "Pierre is neuter now!' This is an infantile whine for sympathy" (232). Miller also asserts that *"Pierre* is disjointed like the life it records. It violates fictional structure, shifts points of view at will, takes a comic attitude toward noncomic matters like incest, and introduces a cacophony of styles scarcely conceivable to the ordinary writer or reader but justifiable to *Pierre*. The style is Pierre [sic]" (Ibid). Yet, he does grudgingly admit that "in a crazy kind of way the book is a virtuoso performance. For despite the narrator's understandable confusion as to whether he is an objective observer, a stand-in for Pierre, or Melville's voice, there is real control of the disorderly materials and an underlying logic" (Ibid.). He also praises it for succeeding by means of "camouflage," subversively covering its scathing critique of contemporary society. But in the end, for Miller, the story of *Pierre* is also the story of Herman Melville, "reflect[ing] his anger as well as his guilt" (Ibid.). And it is, "[i]n final analysis," an "unattractive, sometimes repellant romance" (233), which reflects Melville's own life—with his wife and mother, his father and brothers, and, most crucially for my purposes, with Hawthorne. Miller is overstating the Oedipal undercurrent in *Pierre*, to be sure, but he was certainly correct to discern in the novel some reflection of how Hawthorne had recently "betrayed" Melville (Ibid.). To this highly contentious issue we now turn.

The "dream of collaboration," the so-called "Agatha" project, discussed earlier, which Kelley so admirably described, somehow runs aground: as a result, scholars are divided in their opinion of the Hawthorne-Melville collaborative project, as they are concerning the possible cause(s) of the demise of Hawthorne and Melville's friendship. One school of thought contends that the two gradually drifted apart, as people are wont to do, and that Hawthorne was simply maintaining his characteristic restraint and silence, whereas the excitable, even manic Melville was more emotional about the entire affair, in keeping with his own personality. However, the more dominant interpretation, which subscribes to the so-called "estrangement theory," first advanced by Charles N. Watson, Jr.,[68] falls into two broad camps: those who believe that the overzealous Melville somehow precipitated the estrangement through some sort of aggressive, most likely sexual, behavior (gesture, action, or attitude) directed toward the more conservative (possibly more "repressed") Hawthorne, and those who do not. Critics who attack this thesis, which is taken to its furthest extreme by Miller (cited above) in his highly speculative, psychosexual biography of Melville (building as it does upon Watson's essay and Arvin's more subtle biography, also cited above), are by and large much more conservative in their readings of Melville, political or otherwise, and perhaps are revealing more about their own attitude toward homosexuality and homosexual desire than about Melville's.[69]

In the following section, I will therefore primarily draw upon the "estrangement theory" and assume that there was some sort of overture on Melville's part, sexual or not (it hardly matters—and we will probably never know, in any case), that did not necessarily *repel* Hawthorne (perhaps by revealing to him his own deeply repressed desires or otherwise causing him to flee in what Sedgwick called "homosexual panic"), but did in fact have some type of cooling effect, so to speak, on their formerly warm friendship. It seems likely that we shall never know what "really" happened between the two men, or solve the mystery of this supposed "estrangement." In the end, perhaps that matters less than what effect the friendship's cooling or dissolution had on Melville's writing. As Deleuze has argued, the search for the "dirty little

---

[68] "The Estrangement of Hawthorne and Melville," *The New England Quarterly*, Vol. 46, No. 3 (September, 1973): 380–402.

[69] Parker's work is perhaps the most egregious example; see Martin and Person's and Argersinger and Person's helpful introductory essays for detailed accounts of this type of reading.

secret" often takes away from more important, indeed more vital and productive questions,[70] and so I will accordingly focus upon the texts produced during this period, themselves, always with an eye on Hawthorne—and all that he had come to mean to Melville.

On the face of it, *Pierre* would seem an odd choice for Melville's next novel. A gothic tale of incest, betrayal and violent retribution, it pushed the conventions of "domestic fiction"—melodramas, essentially, that were calculated to appeal to the growing, predominantly female readership of popular fiction in the mid-nineteenth century United States—to their absolute limit. So much so, in fact, that to this day there remains a sharp division among Melville scholars as to whether *Pierre* was originally one manuscript or, as we have seen in the case of *Moby-Dick*, an amalgam of multiple drafts, eventually cobbled together and published. Once again, Hershel Parker is at the heart of this debate and he has claimed that *Pierre* was begun in all sincerity as a domestic fiction, taking Melville's letter to Sophia Hawthorne (Nathaniel's wife) to be decisive in this regard, devoid of irony (or the patronizing tone Melville almost always adopted when writing to women): "my next work," he assured her, "will be a rural bowl of milk." Parker likewise draws upon Melville's letter (cited above)—once again, highly dubious due to the various possible levels of irony—to his English publisher, Richard Bentley, to whom he promised to deliver a "romance [...] calculated for popularity." On the basis of this rather scanty evidence, Parker bases his argument that Melville had in all earnestness begun writing a domestic melodrama "calculated for popularity" but then, after the decidedly mixed

---

[70] See "On the Superiority of Anglo-American Literature," in *Dialogues II*, trans. Hugh Tomlinson and Barbara Habberjam (New York: Columbia University Press, 2002): 46–49.

reviews and poor sales of *Moby-Dick*, greatly altered the novel, adding chapters concerning the publishing world ("Young America in Literature," in particular) and transforming Pierre into a writer. Though this is entirely plausible, Parker takes great liberties with Melville's work when he follows this thesis to its logical conclusion when he published what he calls "The Kraken Edition" of *Pierre*: an abridged text, which Parker claims is the novel as Melville "originally intended" it to be published, with the chapters or passages dealing with Pierre as an author, the literary marketplace, "Young America in Literature," and so on expurgated.[71] The justification for this abridgment, the details of which lie far beyond the scope of this study, was first made in an essay co-authored by Parker and Higgins.[72]

Surely this is going too far. If Melville had "originally intended" to publish a novel without these chapters or passages, then why did he not attempt to "correct" the manuscript on his own during the nearly four decades of his life that followed *Pierre's* original publication? And the opening segment of the novel, the chapters dealing with Pierre's idyllic life at Saddle Meadows, his ancestral manor and birthright, are so overwrought and clumsy that a writer of Melville's considerable talents could not possibly have intended them as anything other than parodic. Several scholars have argued as much (including critics as diverse as Miller, Milder and Spanos) and I am

---

[71] New York: HarperCollins, 1997.
[72] Brian Higgins and Hershel Parker, "The Flawed Grandeur of Melville's *Pierre*," in *New Perspectives on Melville*, ed. Faith Pullin (Edinburgh: Edinburgh University Press, 1978): 162–96.

going to follow suit in what follows.[73]

Parker is correct, however, in at least one respect. Melville did in fact refer to *Pierre* as a "kraken" in a famous letter of November 1851 to Nathaniel Hawthorne, in which he stated that "Leviathan is not the biggest fish;—I have heard of Krakens" (WHM 14: 213). In other words, this is to say that Melville had high hopes for this novel, which followed close on the heels of *Moby-Dick*, his greatest accomplishment to date. My question concerns why Melville chose to return to land (so to speak) at this point, why he decided to write "domestic fiction" (parodic or not), especially when we consider that everything he had written up to this point (1851–52) had been about escaping the domestic sphere, avoiding precisely this setting. As a result, the work up to this point had likewise been almost entirely devoid of female characters. So why did Melville choose at this point to bring his "defiant sufferer," now styled a "heaven assaulter," onto dry land?

There are various schools of thought on this issue, as one might imagine. Some scholars maintain that Melville had simply exhausted his own personal experiences, from which he had up to this point drawn upon for his fiction,[74] while others, including Parker, argue that Melville had set out to write a sincere domestic melodrama in order to make a living as a professional author, but that something had caused him to greatly miscalculate his

---

[73] For more detailed critiques of the Higgins and Parker "Kraken" thesis, see, for example: Michael S. Kearns, "Interpreting Intentional Incoherence: Towards a Disambiguation of Melville's 'Pierre; Or, The Ambiguities,'" *The Bulletin of the Midwestern Language Association*, Vol. 16, No. 1 (Spring, 1983): 34–54; and Nicola Nixon, "Compromising Politics and Herman Melville's *Pierre*," *American Literature*, Vol. 69, No. 4 (December 1997): 719–741.

[74] The early biographers, Weaver and Mumford, mentioned in the previous chapter, fall into this category, as do more recent ones, like Arvin, Miller and Delbanco.

chances[75] —either he was unaware that the themes of incest, madness and murder/suicide would prove shocking to his (largely female) readers' sensibilities and taste (though this hardly seems likely), or while writing and/or revising the manuscript, something happened to him that greatly altered either his vision of or enthusiasm for the project (some, like Parker, argue that he was depressed or angry over the critical and commercial reception of *Moby-Dick*, while others, most notably Renker, claim—on the basis of family anecdotes—that he had begun a fairly rapid descent into mental illness).[76]

I agree that "something happened" during the composition of *Pierre*, but I contend that it was in fact the cooling of Melville's friendship with Hawthorne that most disturbed him during this period. There have been other scholars who either suggest or support this thesis, including the aforementioned essay by Martin and Person, who persuasively argue that Melville's *Pierre* and Hawthorne's *The Blithedale Romance* (1852) are each heavily influenced by the friendship between the two authors (and its demise), but scholars have largely neglected to look at how this parting effected *Pierre* in terms other than personal, by which I mean "biographical;" in other words, dealing with Melville's life which, it is argued, is closely reflected in the novel. To put it yet another way, we need to look at ways in which not only the man Hawthorne but also what he had come to represent or embody for Melville—collaborator, friend or brother, "American [literary] Shiloh," embodiment of

---

[75] Howard, in his biography of Melville, maintains this view, as do James E. Miller, Jr. in *A Reader's Guide to Herman Melville* (New York: Noonday Press, 1962) and Brook Thomas in "The Writer's Procreative Urge in *Pierre*," cited above.

[76] Elizabeth Renker, *Strike Through the Mask: Melville and the Scene of Writing* (Baltimore: The Johns Hopkins University Press, 1996); see, also, Paul McCarthy, *The Twisted Mind: Madness in Herman Melville's Fiction* (Iowa City: University of Iowa Press, 1990).

the genius of American culture and democracy—is expressed in this still-shocking work. After examining *Pierre* in more detail, in keeping with this goal, I will again turn to the "minor" work at the end of this chapter, looking at the numerous figures of abandonment, isolation, and abjection (most of them female characters), in some of the shorter fiction that followed. It is my intention, in the following section, to show how *Pierre* is in fact less a documentary account of Melville's madness or despair, and much more a calculated assault on the domestic sphere, meaning not only the dynamics of the family,[77] meaning filiation, genealogy, property and inheritance, but also, through the particular family Pierre/Melville is assaulting—his distant relatives, the Van Rensselaers (the largest landowners at that time in New York state), as well as his closer relatives, the Ganesvoorts (to a lesser extent)—the larger American society, including its relation to the past via its monuments and public memory.

For Pierre, like Ahab, has built a kind of "bachelor machine," which he then directs against several targets—perhaps too many, which may account for the sense that one gets, as one reads *Pierre*, that Melville had somehow strained himself, that he had spread himself too thin, and that the material, in the end, had gotten the better of him. Most scholars agree that *Pierre* was a falling off from *Moby-Dick*, but many are at a loss when it comes to explaining in what aspects Melville had "failed" in the work. It would seem that there is consensus among scholars in locating some points of Melville's

---

[77] However, it must be noted from the outset that my intention is certainly not to "reoedpialize" Melville; see Michael Paul Rogin's *Subversive Genealogy: The Politics and Art of Herman Melville* (Berkeley: University of California Press, 1985) for the most sophisticated, nuanced and persuasive, yet deeply flawed attempt at this to date.

critique: the family; writing and the literary marketplace; property and inheritance; and what Nietzsche (and later, Foucault) called "monumental history."[78] Very few, however, have brought these concerns together in a satisfactory way,[79] so in the section that follows, I will attempt to do so, thereby contributing to this ongoing conversation in Melville scholarship, and bettering our understanding of this enigmatic and important, yet neglected and largely misunderstood novel. Before doing so, however, we must first look closely at a point that Rogin made in *Subversive Genealogy*:

> George Washington Peck excoriated [*Pierre*] for nine pages in the *American Whig Review* [in which he wrote that] *Pierre* "strikes with an impious... hand, at the very foundations of society." These foundations, *Pierre*'s subversion made perfectly clear, lay in the family. A democratic age suspicious of institutional coercion excepted only the family. It was the single refuge from antebellum social anxiety, and Peck was right to see *Pierre* as a declaration of war against domesticity. (160; ellipsis in original)

This idea of *Pierre* amounting to Melville's "declaration of war against domesticity" is the starting point of my investigation. In my reading, I will

---

[78] Michel Foucault, "Nietzsche, Genealogy, History" in *Language, Counter-Memory, Practice: Selected Essays and Interviews*, ed. and trans. Donald F. Bouchard (Ithaca: Cornell University Press, 1977): 161.

[79] Here, I would single out the work of Rogin and Spanos as the very strongest to date. Rogin, in *Subversive Genealogy* (chapter 6), sees *Pierre* as a "bourgeois family nightmare," critiquing property and class, while Spanos, in *Herman Melville and the American Calling* (chapter 2), reads *Pierre* as a critique of hegemony, more specifically the triumphant, and "monumentalist," antebellum discourse of the 1850s, in light of Heidegger, Althusser, Said and Foucault.

attempt to trace exactly how Melville wages this war, following the course of Pierre's "bachelor-machine" while keeping an eye on the series of sister-lovers that trail along and bolster or support him in his struggle. The war against domesticity is one simultaneously against the mother (and father), against property and inheritance, and as Peck was correct to point out, "the very foundations of society." Rogin further explains this idea, and in the process clearly and concisely sums up the plot of the novel (which I will quote in full), as follows:

> Pierre Glendinning, scion of an ancient American family, discovers on the eve of his wedding that his father had an illegitimate daughter. Pierre determines to befriend his half-sister, Isabel, and redress the paternal wrong. Allegedly to protect his dead father's reputation, and to preserve his mother's image of her husband, Pierre keeps Isabel's identity secret. He abandons his betrothed, pretends to marry Isabel, and takes her with him to the city. But by the time Pierre leaves his ancestral home, he has become conscious of his sexual attraction to Isabel. Not altruism has motivated him, but rather incestuous desire for his lost half-sister, and rage against the family he has known. Pierre's actions leave his family, and the ideal of American domesticity, in ruins. (160–161)

We must now turn to a more detailed examination of the text. Looking at the remarkable Book (Chapter) I of *Pierre*, entitled "Pierre Just Emerging from His Teens," we notice that much of what is at stake in the novel is laid out for us: the themes of family and genealogy, property and inheritance, the supposed differences between the "New World" and the "Old," as well as incest, undoubtedly the most disturbing aspect of this highly unusual text (even shockingly so, no doubt, for Melville's contemporary readers). In the following section, I want to closely read *Pierre* by focusing upon what the protagonist, "heaven assaulting Pierre," is attacking: first, the institution of the family, particularly what Deleuze and Guattari call "conjugality" (which we can think of as hetero-normative sexual union, recognized by the state, assuring the continuance of the bloodline and property rights) and "Oedipal incest," directed at his mother, which Pierre transforms into "schizo-incest," aimed at his (half-) sister, Isabel; through this assault, Pierre is also attacking the notion of property and inheritance, which raises the issue of landownership and the context of the "Anti-Rent Wars" which raged in the Hudson Valley, directed against the Van Rensselaer family, to which Melville was related and from which he apparently drew inspiration for Pierre's wealthy landowning family, the Glendinnings;[80] this, in turn, leads me to a discussion of what William Spanos has called, following the work of Nietzsche and Foucault, "monumentalism" or "monumental history,"[81] and Pierre's assault upon the larger society through his attempt to escape the family and conjugality—in Peck's words, cited above, "the very foundations of society."

In other words, Pierre not only attempts to escape and de-legitimize the family, by creating a parody of "conjugality" in the heterotopic space of New York City (which involves his lover, Lucy Tartan, along with his halfsister Isabel, as his "wife," Delly Ulver, a Hester Prynne-like figure who has been cast out of Saddle Meadows for adultery, and the odd bachelor-like characters called "the Apostles," who live in a commune-like arrangement with Pierre and his women, his "sisters"), but also, in so doing, he assaults the very

---

[80] For studies that examine precisely this, see: Samuel Otter, "The Eden of Saddle Meadows: Landscape and Ideology in *Pierre*," *American Literature*, Vol. 66, No. 1 (March 1994): 55–81; Roger Hecht, "Rents in the Landscape: the Anti-Rent War in Melville's *Pierre*," *ATQ*, Vol. 19, No. 1 (March 2005): 37–51; and Jeffory A. Clymer, "Property and Selfhood in Herman Melville's *Pierre*," *Nineteenth-Century Literature*, Vol. 61, No. 2 (September 2006): 171–199.

[81] See chapter 2 of *Herman Melville and the American Calling* for a full elaboration of this subject.

foundations of his society, the "Hindooish" (Brahmin-led or caste-like) aristocracy that rules the Hudson Valley. Melville makes this clear by his repeated references to monuments and statues, and the (official or sanctioned) history to which they refer—the story of the Glendinnings, especially that of Grand Old Pierre, his grandfather, who established Saddle Meadows and began the genealogical line, as well as Pierre's father, the memory of whom Mrs. Glendinning attempts to whitewash or sterilize, even as she attempts to keep Pierre a "docile" boy. In this way, *Pierre* is also a critique of the ways that memory and history are put to political purposes, not only through "monumentalism"—the erecting of statues and monuments to mark certain events, episodes or "heroes," while burying others—but also through writing. My final point will concern Pierre's status as a writer, an aspect of the novel that proves so troubling to Parker and other orthodox Melville scholars. I end by speculating on this element of the novel, before turning to a discussion of Melville's increasing interest in what he calls "the vanquished" in this period of his writing, most notably female characters (up to this point, as mentioned earlier, quite rare in his fiction).

As discussed above, in Book I of *Pierre*, at the very beginning of the narrative, we are introduced to Pierre and his youthful, widowed mother, whose blatantly Oedipal relationship is described thus (in a long passage that needs to be quoted in full):

> But a reverential and devoted son seemed lover enough for this widow Bloom; and besides all this, Pierre when namelessly annoyed, and sometimes even jealously transported by the too ardent admiration of the handsome youths, who now and then, caught in unintended snares, seemed to entertain some insane hopes of wedding this unattainable being; Pierre had more than once, with a playful malice, openly sworn, that the man—gray-beard, or beardless—who should dare to propose marriage to his mother, that man would be some peremptory unrevealed

agency immediately disappear from the earth. This romantic filial love of Pierre seemed fully returned by the triumphant maternal pride of the widow, who in the clear-cut lineaments and noble air of the son, saw her own graces strangely translated into the opposite sex. There was a striking personal resemblance between them [...] In the playfulness of their unclouded love, and with that strange license which a perfect confidence and mutual understanding at all points, had long bred between them, they were wont to call each other brother and sister. (5)

We are told that his birthright, the manorial Saddle-Meadows, "a name likewise extended to the mansion and the village" (6), had been established by Pierre's paternal great-grandfather, who died on the spot during the earliest years of the colony, battling Native Americans, and had been defended by his grandfather during the Revolutionary War. "All the associations of Saddle-Meadows," we are told, "were full of pride to Pierre. The Glendinning deeds by which their estate had so long been held, bore the ciphers of three Indian kinds, the aboriginal and only conveyancers of those noble woods and plains." This, we are instructed, was "the background of [Pierre's] race" (6)—the last being a resonant word of which we must take note. However, besides this blatant "Oedipal-incest," illustrated in the lengthy passage quoted above, there are already hints of another form of incest—which Deleuze and Guattari call, in their iconoclastic study of Kafka, "schizo-incest"[82] —brewing beneath the surface at this early point in the novel: "He who is sisterless, is as a bachelor before his time. For much that goes to make up the deliciousness of a wife, already lies in the sister. 'Oh, had my father but had a daughter!' cried Pierre" (7). This will be developed in much greater length later in the novel.

---

[82] *Kafka: Toward a Minor Literature*, trans. Dana Polan (Minneapolis: University of Minnesota Press): 67.

Section three (iii) is perhaps the most interesting and important, however, of the six that make Book I. In this portion of the narrative, we are told more about Pierre's "race," as mentioned above, a term that should immediately alert us to the significance of Pierre's genealogy and its possession of the land, and the aristocracies of England and America, the "Old" and "New Worlds," are compared and contrasted. The following passage makes this clear:

> The monarchical world very generally imagines, that in demagoguical America the sacred Past hath no fixed statues erected to it, but all things irreverently seethe and boil in the vulgar cauldron of an everlasting uncrystallizing Present. This conceit would seem peculiarly applicable to the social condition. With no chartered aristocracy, and no law of entail, how can any family in America imposingly perpetuate itself? (8)

The narrator goes on to "compare pedigrees with England" (9), to which the United States seems to come up wanting; however, it is quite another story when we are asked to "consider those most ancient and magnificent Dutch Manors at the North [like the Glendinnings'], whose perches are miles—whose meadows [and we must note the deliberate use of this word, as in "Saddle-Meadows"] overspread adjacent counties—and whose haughty rent-deeds are held by their thousand farmer tenants, so long as the grass grows and water runs" (10–11).[83] We must note the use of the word, "haughty," which will be used repeatedly throughout the novel to describe Pierre's mother, "sister

---

[83] Here, we must note the repetition of this phrase, which Melville most certainly meant ironically, as Samuel Otter has pointed out, recalling Andrew Jackson's broken promises to Native Americans; see Otter's *Melville's Anatomies* (Berkeley: University of California Press, 1999): 200–202.

Mary." Melville then continues: "These far-descended Dutch meadows [repeated] lie steeped in a Hindooish haze; and eastern patriarchalness sways its mild crook over pastures, whose tenant [another conspicuous repetition] flocks shall there feed, long as their own grass grows, long as their own water shall run [repeated]. Such estates seem to defy Time's tooth" we are told. "But our lords, the Patroons, appeal not to the past, but they point to the present. One will show you that the public census of a county, is but part of the roll of his tenants [repeated]. Ranges of mountains, high as Ben Nevis or Snowdon, are their walls; and regular armies, with staffs of officers, crossing rivers with artillery, and marching through primeval woods, and threading vast rocky defiles, have been sent out to distrain upon three thousand farmer-tenants of one landlord, at a blow. A fact most suggestive two ways; both whereof shall be nameless here" (11). Here, we must note the conspicuous repetitions, the ironic (and thus deeply subversive) tone and the multiple levels of meaning that Melville employs in this passage.

The narrator continues in this vein, noting with characteristic Melvillean irony the paradox of such feudal remnants in the middle of a modern democracy—"But whatever one may think of the existence of such mighty lordships in the heart of a republic, and however we may wonder at their thus surviving, like Indian mounds, the Revolutionary flood; yet survive and exist they do" (Ibid)—before drawing an explicit parallel, which Melville will further develop in his "transatlantic fiction" (examined at length in the previous chapter), between England and America, Old World and New: "our America will make out a good general case with England in this short little matter of large estates, and long pedigrees" (Ibid.). For now, it is important to note how Melville is drawing together the notions of genealogy and history, blood and soil, in the person of Pierre Glendinning. At the end of this rather remarkable opening chapter, Pierre is commanded by his "lover-like" (16) mother, "sister Mary," to "always think of [his] dear perfect father" so that he

[Pierre] will "never err" (19). Spanos has read this section of Book I, in which the term "docile" (or variations thereof) is repeated no fewer than a dozen times in the space of a single page, and has focused our attention upon the manner in which Pierre is being molded or shaped by his mother's (and his genealogy's) discipline: "docility" of course being a term which, as Spanos has decisively shown, practically invites a Foucaultian reading and provides us with the perfect example of the "docile body."[84]

More important for my purposes, however, is the function of the portraits in *Pierre*, beginning with the one of Pierre's grandfather. "The grandfather of Pierre measured six feet four inches in height [...] Pierre had often tried on his military vest, which still remained an heirloom at Saddle Meadows, and found the pockets below his knees [...] Never could Pierre look upon his fine military portrait without infinite and mournful longing [...] The majestic sweetness of this portrait was truly wonderful in its effects upon any sensitive and generous-minded young observer. For such, that portrait possessed the heavenly persuasiveness of angelic speech; a glorious gospel[85] framed and hung upon the wall, and declaring to all people, as from the Mount [again, we must note this deliberate word-choice on Melville's part, to be given an added depth later], that man is a noble, god-like being, full of choicest juices; made up of strength and beauty" (30).

However, there are two other portraits that have an even stronger

---

[84] See chapter 2 of *Herman Melville and the American Calling: The Fiction after* Moby-Dick, *1851–1857* (Albany: SUNY Press, 2008), especially 23–24.

[85] We should note that this is the first instance of this word, "gospel," which will take on a deeper significance later in the novel, when Pierre vows to "gospelize the world anew;" see Spanos for an analysis of this term in his *Herman Melville and the American Calling*, 34–35.

effect upon Pierre. The first is the one of his father that is approved of—was, in fact, commissioned—by his mother, which shows the elder Pierre Glendinning in middle age, in a dignified and noble manner; the second is a rather crude oil painting of the same man, which has about it an air of mystery, apparently made by a cousin, in secret, in order to capture the expression on Pierre Sr.'s face after clandestine visits to a beautiful French émigré with whom he had fallen in love in a moment of youthful indiscretion. "Sister Mary" loathes this portrait, but when an elderly Glendinning aunt bequeaths it to young Pierre, she is powerless to do anything about it. Pierre practically keeps it hidden in his upstairs study, while the larger, "approved" portrait is given pride of place in the manor, occupying "the most conspicuous and honorable place on the wall" (72) in the downstairs drawing-room. I will return to these two portraits in a moment; first, however, I want to briefly look at two moments that lead up to the revelation, within the narrative of *Pierre*, of the two portraits. These moments involve Pierre turning away or escaping from the idyllic life at Saddle-Meadows, though they happen a bit prematurely and are frustrated. However, they foreshadow what is to come, when Pierre begins his assault on his mother (and father: at least, the false father captured in the "approved" portrait cherished by his mother) and all that she represents.

The first involves Pierre's glimpse of a lovely, lonely, "immemorial" face, "where Anguish had contended with Beauty" (47)—that of Isabel, who he sees for the first time working a needle at a makeshift workshop for recently arrived emigrants set up at one of the Glendinnings' tenants' homes. Pierre stares at Isabel, then averts his gaze. The narrator tells us that:

> Recovering at length from his all too obvious emotion, Pierre *turned away* still farther, to regain the conscious possession of himself. A wild, bewildering, and incomprehensible curiosity had seized him, to know something definite of that face. To this curiosity, at the moment, he

entirely surrendered himself; unable as he was to combat it, or reason with it in the slightest way [...] But at length, as [...] he was crossing the room again [to get closer to this mysterious stranger], he heard his mother's voice, gaily calling him away; *and turning*, saw her shawled and bonneted. He could now make no plausible stay, and smothering the agitation in him, he bowed a general and hurried adieu to the company, and went forth with his mother. (47; emphasis added)

Here, we see Pierre turning away, quite literally (again, noting how Melville repeats this phrase or word, as he had with Ahab) in fact, from his mother and her world, but then he is called back by her, and at this stage of the narrative, he obeys. He will not continue to do so for much longer, as we shall soon see. After receiving a letter from this mysterious stranger, who calls herself Isabel, his half-sister who has just arrived from Europe, Pierre is directly addressed by the narrator:

Ay, Pierre, now indeed art thou hurt with a wound, never to be completely healed but in heaven; for thee, the before undistrusted moral beauty of the world is forever fled; for thee, they sacred father is no more a saint; [...] and now, now, for the first time, Pierre, Truth rolls a black billow through thy soul! [...] And as the mariner, shipwrecked and cast on the beach, has much ado to èscape the recoil of the wave that hurled him there; so Pierre long struggled, and struggled, to escape the recoil of that anguish, which had dashed him. (65)

We should note in passing that the "black billow" that rolls through Pierre's soul, as well as the references to "mariner[s]," "shipwreck[s]," and "wave[s]" strongly recall scenes from *Moby-Dick*. To make this repetition of the previous novel even clearer, Melville then has Pierre deliver a soliloquy worthy—and certainly reminiscent—of Ahab:

"Myself am left, at least," he slowly and half-chokingly murmured, "With myself I front thee! Unhand me all fears, and unlock me all spells! Henceforth I will know nothing but Truth; glad Truth, or sad Truth; I will know what *is*, and do what my deepest angel dictates [...] Isabel,—sister,—brother,—me, *me*—my sacred father! [...] I will lift my hand in fury, for am I not struck? [...] Thou Black Knight, that with visor down, thus confrontest me, and mockest at me; Lo! I strike through thy helm, and will se they face, be it Gorgon!—Let me go, ye fond affections; all piety leave me;—I will be impious, for piety hath juggled me, and taught me to revere where I should spurn. From all idols, I tear all veils; henceforth I will see the hidden things; and live right out in my own hidden life!" (65–66; emphasis in original)

Here, we must take note of the striking similarities between Pierre's monologue and Ahab's "strike though the mask" speech, cited in chapter one, as well as the confusion that Pierre experiences when Isabel is abruptly introduced into his genealogy—the categories "sister," "brother," "father" and even the self ("me") become confused.

As if to underscore precisely this point, the chapter that immediately follows, Book IV, "Retrospective," takes a look back at the "marble" shrine which had "long stood" "in the fresh-foliaged heart of Pierre," the "one-pillared temple of his moral life," within which stood a central pillar that had a carved likeness, a "perfect marble form," of his departed father: "without blemish, unclouded, snow-white, and serene" (68). Now, "in one night," Pierre had been "stripped [of] his holiest shrine," and the marble statue "of the saint," his "perfect" father, had been "buried [...] beneath the prostrated ruins of the soul's temple itself" (69). Pierre seems to recall his father calling out, in the final fever of his death agony, for a "daughter" (70–71), which inspires him to look more closely at the oil portrait of his father, the mysterious one that his mother abhors.

In the following section, we are introduced to the two portraits, first to the crude one of Pierre Sr. in his youth, followed by the approved one. At the same time, the narration shifts to Pierre's interior monologue, and the young man spends a restless night debating with himself what is true and what is illusion, and considering a course of action. In the next chapter (V, "Misgiving and Preparations"), Pierre reverses the oil portrait hanging in his room and declares, "I will no more have a father" (87). He then "remove[s] the picture wholly from the wall, and the closet; and conceal[s] it in a large chest [...] and locked it up there" (Ibid.). This chapter has been the subject of much scrutiny, most notably by Spanos. We might add to his analysis by noting the similarities between the language of this chapter and that of *Moby-Dick*: "Not only was the long-cherished image of his father now transfigured before him from a green foliaged tree into a blasted trunk [the same image is used to describe Ahab], but every other image in his mind attested to the universality of that electrical light [which certainly stretches back to Ahab and the scene involving St. Elmo's Fire, then forward to Isabel and her strange "electricity," particularly in the music she plays with her guitar, dubbed "mother"] which had darted into his soul." (88) This is the passage that Spanos has shown to be absolutely crucial to the novel, Pierre's "extraordinary emergency" (89). Once again harkening back to *Moby-Dick*, the narrator makes the analogy plain: Pierre feels himself "orphan-like" and "driven out an infant Ishmael into the desert, with no maternal Hagar to accompany and comfort him" (Ibid.).

Another parallel is drawn to *Moby-Dick*, this time between Father Mapple's sermon—"Delight is to him, who gives no quarter in the truth, and kills, burns, and destroys all sin though he pluck it out from under the robes of Senators and Judges" (54)—and Pierre's oath, which it reverses while retaining the same meaning: "Welcome then be Ugliness and Poverty and Infamy, and all ye other crafty ministers of Truth, that beneath the hoods and rags of beggars hide yet the belts and crowns of kings" (90). Yet another repetition occurs in section three (iii) of the same chapter, in which Pierre, suffering from insomnia, joylessly awaits the sunrise, something that used to brighten his soul: "The one small window of his closet looked forth upon the meadow [repeated], and across the river, and far away to the distant heights, storied with the great deeds of the Glendinnings. Many a time had Pierre sought this window before sunrise, to behold the blood-red [invoking genealogy], out-flinging dawn, that would wrap those purple hills as with a banner. But now the morning dawned in mist and rain, and came drizzlingly upon his heart. Yet as the day advanced, and once more showed to him the accustomed features of his room by that natural light, which, till this very moment, had never lighted him [echoes of Ahab, and through him, of Milton's Satan: "this lovely light, it lights not me," from Chapter 37, "Sunset," of *Moby-Dick*, 182] but to his joy; now that the day, and not the night, was witness to his woe; now first the dread reality came appallingly upon him. A sense of horrible forlornness, feebleness, impotence, and infinite, eternal desolation possessed him" (92–93). The parallel here to Ahab should be clear.

A drastic change has come over Pierre, which his mother quickly notices: "'What haggard thing possesses thee, my son? Speak, this is incomprehensible! [...] speak, speak, my darling boy!' 'My dear sister,' began Pierre. 'Sister me not, now, Pierre;—I am thy mother.' 'Well, then, dear mother, thou art quite as incomprehensible to me as I to—' 'Talk faster, Pierre [...] Thou art my son, and I command thee [...] consider well before thou determinest upon withholding confidence from me. I am thy mother. It may prove a fatal thing. Can that be good and virtuous, Pierre, which shrinks from a mother's knowledge? Let us not loose hands so, Pierre; thy confidence [repeated] from me, mine goes from thee'" (95–96). Here, we must note how Mrs. Glendinning no longer wishes to be called "sister;" instead, she insists upon being recognized as Pierre's mother, demanding that he not withhold "confidence" from her—a word that takes on a much deeper resonance if we look ahead to *The Confidence-Man*, which is organized around a series of explorations of this concept, foreshadowed here, in *Pierre*. Most crucially, however, we must recognize this as Pierre's mother's attempt to forestall Pierre's "schizo-incest" and re-impose the Oedipal variety, thereby "reoedipalizing" her son.

In this same chapter, Ned, one of the Glendinnings' servants, who apparently has seduced Delly Ulver, another servant (despite already being a husband and father), is discussed and it is determined by Mrs. Glendinning that he will be dismissed, and Delly (with their illegitimate child) expelled from Saddle-Meadows along with him. There is an obvious parallel to Pierre Sr., his lover, the beautiful Frenchwoman, and Isabel, also born out of wedlock and cast out like the Biblical Ishmael; Pierre Jr., who is privy to this secret history, takes great offence at his mother's—and her would-be suitor, the Reverend Falsgrave's—harsh judgment on the matter. He attempts to defend Delly (while agreeing with the others in their low opinion of Ned), and this scene at the breakfast table with his mother and would-be father, Falsgrave, marks the beginning of Pierre's open rebellion. The fact that this happens as a result of the web of family relations—in other words, reoedipalization—must be kept in mind.

Pierre has another confrontation with his mother, yet again at the breakfast table; once more, his mother attempts to reinforce the Oedipal relation, what Deleuze and Guattari, as mentioned above, call "reoedipalization," denying the playful and subversive "schizo-incest" seen earlier, in which the two had referred to one another as "brother" and "sister:" "'I have been quite an absentee, sister Mary,' said [Pierre], with ill-affected pleasantness. 'Yes, Pierre. How does the coffee suit you this morning? It is some new coffee.' 'It is very nice; very rich and odorous, sister Mary.' 'I am glad you find it so, Pierre.' 'Why don't you call me brother Pierre?' 'Have I not called you so? Well, then, brother Pierre,—is that better?' 'Why do you look so indifferently and icily upon me, sister Mary?' 'Do I look indifferently and icily? Then I will endeavor to look otherwise. Give me the toast there, Pierre.' 'You are very deeply offended at me, my dear mother.'" Here, we can see that Pierre is being reoedipalized successfully in this scene, brought back into his position as the son in this relation. It continues thus: "Not in the slightest degree, Pierre. Have you seen Lucy lately?" Mrs. Glendinning continues in this vein, trying to remind Pierre of his conjugal duty, to marry his betrothed, Lucy Tartan.

Pierre then says, "You are too proud to show toward me what you are this moment feeling, my mother.' Mrs. Glendinning slowly rose to her feet, and her full stature of womanly beauty and majesty stood imposingly over him." Here, we may note a striking similarity between this scene and Kafka's "The Judgment," in which the father rises up from his bed and stands "imposingly" over the cowering son. "Tempt me no more, Pierre. I will ask no secret from thee [...] Beware of me, Pierre. There lives not that being in the world of whom thou hast more reason to beware" (130), the mother warns. Pierre then "quitted the table, and the room, and the mansion" (Ibid.), thus foreshadowing his final departure from Saddle-Meadows. Mrs. Glendinning seems to intuit this, and she throws her fork in a fit of rage: not by chance does it pierce her own portrait, hanging next to the "approved" one of her late husband, Pierre Sr. Her son, Pierre Jr., that "nobly-striving but ever-shipwrecked character" (136), for his part, "plunge[s] deep into the woods" and seeks comfort or guidance in the so-called "Memnon Stone" (132), a heavy boulder that is precariously balanced. Like the son in Kafka's "The Judgment," Pierre seems to be following the guilt-laden "Oedipal-incest" of his mother to its conclusion, tempting suicide, practically begging the rock to crush him, as Kafka's protagonist leaps to his death.

Alternately, we could say that Melville here seems to be once again pointing to what Spanos has called (following Nietzsche and Foucault) "monumentalization," which I will discuss in a moment, after quickly pausing on yet another structural parallel to *Moby-Dick*. In part viii of Book VII, the section immediately following the Memnon Stone episode, Pierre thinks back upon the oil portrait, and has a moment of realization that is worded almost exactly as a scene in *Moby-Dick*, when the *Pequod* passes through the lightning-storm and Ahab harnesses St. Elmo's Fire. It is said in that chapter ("The Candles," Chapter 119) that "God's burning finger has been laid on the [*Pequod*]" and "His 'Mene, Mene, Tekel, Upharsin' has been woven into the shrouds of the cordage" (549). Here, in Book VII of *Pierre*, Melville offers us the same image, taking it even further: "[H]ow could [Pierre] fail to acknowledge the existence of that all-controlling and all-permeating wonderfulness, which, when imperfectly and isolatedly recognized by the generality, is so significantly denominated The Finger of God? But it is not merely the Finger, it is the whole outspread Hand of God" (139). Melville continues in this manner, drawing an analogy between the forest in which Pierre now finds himself and the sea:

> Still wandering through the forest, his eye pursuing its ever-shifting shadowy vistas; remote from all visible haunts and traces of that strangely willful race, who, in the sordid traffickings of clay and mud, are ever seeking to denationalize [I will return to this deliberate word-choice in a moment; again, Pierre follows Ahab in this respect] the natural heavenliness of their souls; there came into the mind of Pierre, thoughts and fancies never imbibed within the gates of towns; but only given forth by the atmosphere of primeval forests, which, with the eternal ocean, are the only unchanged general objects remaining to this day, from those that originally met the gaze of Adam. (139)

Immediately following this section, there is the passage that Spanos has once again decisively read, in which Pierre realizes that life has "no proper endings," but instead "imperfect, unanticipated, and disappointing sequels (as mutilated stumps)" (141). In *The Errant Art of Moby-Dick*, Spanos shows how Ishmael "unnames" the white whale (which Ahab has attempted to make "practically assailable" by naming it "Moby Dick"), thereby refusing to reify or domesticate its "nameless horror," which may in part account for why he, alone, survived the destruction of the *Pequod*.[86] Here, in *Pierre*, we see something very similar happening with the eponymous protagonist, a young author who had, up until this point in the narrative, believed in the reality of plots and endings, in the type of philosophy espoused by Plotinus Plinlimmon's pamphlet on "Horologicals" and "Chronometricals"—in other words, human or terrestrial versus divine or celestial time—and in the ability of mortal man to live up to such divine standards, such as his father has been elevated or apotheosized by his mother. However, like the Memnon Stone, this "perfect" image of Pierre, Sr.—now suspected of being false—threatens to crush the young man.

We can see yet another clear parallel between *Moby-Dick* and *Pierre* in the person of Isabel, who, like Ahab, seems possessed by the spirit of fire: "She lifted her dry burning eyes of long-fringed fire to him" (149). When she begins playing her guitar, also named "Isabel," the instrument's strings quiver with the lightning flashing outside, and the girl summons the spirit of her mother, much as Ahab did with the "spirit of fire" in the critical scene described earlier ("The Candles"). The "deep oaken recess" of the guitar seems to Pierre the "vestibule of some awful shrine," and the scene, we are told, is "softly illuminated by the mild heat-lightnings and ground-lightnings, that wove their wonderfulness without, in the unsearchable air of that ebonly warm and most noiseless summer night" (149–150). As Isabel summons her mother's spirit, the strings begin to quiver, until the girl's hair sweep over them, and "strange sparks—still quivering there—caught at [Isabel's] attractive

---

[86] See, especially, 127–131 for an elaboration of this "unnaming" of the whale.

curls; the entire casement was suddenly and wovenly illumined; then waned again; while now, in the succeeding dimness, every downward undulating wave and billow [another analogy to the sea] of Isabel's tossed tresses gleamed here and there like a tract of phosphorescent midnight sea;[87] and, simultaneously, all the four winds of the world of melody broke loose" (150). We are then told that "Pierre felt himself surrounded by ten thousand sprites and gnomes, and his whole soul was swayed and tossed by supernatural tides" (Ibid.), thus continuing the sea-imagery in this passage, and strengthening the connection to "The Candles" chapter of *Moby-Dick*, as well as to schizo-incest, which is connected to sound, as we shall see, rather than to portraits (which are connected to Oedipal-incest).

As if this were not clear enough, Melville pauses and dwells upon this "preternatural" scene in the next section (iii) of the same chapter: "[A]ltogether, these things seemed not at the time entirely produced by customary or natural causes. To Pierre's dilated senses Isabel seemed to swim in an electric fluid; the vivid buckler of her brow seemed as a magnetic plate [...] he could not help believing [that this was because of] an extraordinary physical magnetism in Isabel. And—as it were derived from this marvelous quality thus imputed to her—he now first became vaguely sensible of a certain still marvelous power in the girl over himself and his most interior thoughts and

---

[87]   Once again, we see Melville repeating imagery and language from *Moby-Dick*: in this case, Chapter 119, "The Candles," to which I have been drawing attention in terms of Ahab harnessing the corpusants; here, Isabel can also be likened to the crew, whose eyes, teeth and tattoos glow with the blue flames of the ball-lightning, as in the following sentence: "While this pallidness was burning aloft, few words were heard from the enchanted crew; who in one thick cluster stood on the forecastle, all their eyes gleaming in that pale phosphorescence, like a faraway constellation of stars" (506). Note the word, "phosphorescen[t/ce]" repeated in both scenes.

motions [...] a power which [...] seemed irresistibly to draw him toward Isabel" (151), much as Ahab is drawn like a magnet to Moby Dick—or, we could say, as Melville claimed he was drawn to Hawthorne (in his references to "magnets" in his letter, cited above). Isabel, we are told, has "bound [Pierre] to her by an extraordinary atmospheric spell," during this "first magnetic night," in which "the physical electricalness of Isabel seemed reciprocal with the heat-lightnings and the ground-lightnings" outside their room, "the sparkling electricity in which she seemed to swim" (Ibid.). "She seemed molded from fire and air," the narrator concludes, "vivified at some Voltaic pile of August thunder-clouds heaped against the sunset" (151–152). Though far removed from the raging Typhoon and wild storm at sea in *Moby-Dick*'s pivotal "Candles" chapter, during which Ahab harnesses the corpusants, the ball-lightning known to sailors as "St. Elmo's Fire," earlier described, to consecrate not only his specially forged harpoon but also the oath sworn by his "pagan" crew and extinguish all remaining fears among them, Isabel's more "feminine," "gentle" and "soft" ground-lightning and heat-lightning scene is strikingly similar in meaning, if not in intensity.

Not by accident, then, does the next chapter of *Pierre*, immediately following this scene, begin with the image of "minds forever lost, like undiscoverable Arctic explorers" who have entirely lost "the directing compass of [their] mind[s]; for arrived at the Pole, to whose barrenness only it points, there, the needle indifferently respects all points of the horizon alike" (165). We will recall that in *Moby-Dick*, it is at precisely this point that Ahab dashes his quadrant to pieces and tramples it in a fit of anger. Like Pierre irresistibly drawn to the "magnetic" Isabel, Ahab is being pulled toward the White Whale, and therefore needs no compass or quadrant to tell him where he is: all that matters for him, as for Pierre, is where he will be, where he is heading. Like Ahab, Pierre tramples his former guide, though it is not a compass or quadrant—for Pierre, as we shall soon discover, has hitherto been guided by literature, and he now tears to shreds two books that had served him up to this point: Dante's *Inferno* and Shakespeare's *Hamlet*. With no more books to guide him, he finds himself torn between "impossible adjuncts," Isabel and his mother; or, in other words, Oedipal-incest and schizo-incest, which "once brought together" will "mutually expire" (171). And it is not by chance that the most crucial scene in the narrative comes next, in this chapter (Book X) entitled "The Final Resolution of Pierre" and the one following it, "He Crosses the Rubicon" (Book XI). For everything has been leading up to this moment, when Pierre finally turns away from "Home and Mother" (in D.H. Lawrence's words), once and for all, and embarks upon his "avenging dream."

The very wording of the phrase, "avenging dream," which appears at a key juncture in the crucial passage that concludes Book X (section iii), should alert us to the importance that Melville attaches to both Pierre's vengeance—what I am calling, following Melville himself, Pierre's "assault on heaven;" in other words, his Ahabian defiance—and to his dreams, particularly the "dream of Enceladus," which will occur precisely at the novel's climax, and which I will discuss later in this chapter. Before doing so, however, we must first look more closely at the passage in question, which Melville placed just before Pierre "crossed the Rubicon"—a familiar expression, no doubt, but one that nonetheless should recall Lawrence's (and Deleuze's) comment concerning Melville "crossing the horizon" and escaping (quoted in the Introduction):

> There is a dark, mad mystery in some human hearts, which, sometimes, during the tyranny of a usurper mood, leads them to be all eagerness to cast off the most intense beloved bond, as a hindrance to the attainment of whatever transcendental object that usurper mood so tyrannically suggests. [...] We think we are not human; we become as immortal bachelors and gods. (180)

This is the key not only to *Pierre* but also to understanding Melville's major phase: specifically, this phrase "immortal bachelors and gods," which should bring to mind Melville's various "defiant sufferers" and "heaven-assaulters," each of whom builds a kind of machine, a "bachelor-machine," as it were, then turns away and flees or escapes. Melville continues, stating that "[w]eary with the invariable earth, the restless sailor breaks from every enfolding arm, and puts to sea in height of tempest that blows off shore." This imagery should recall Bulkington—later transformed into Ahab—and "The Lee Shore" chapter of *Moby-Dick*, discussed in chapter one. "But in long night-watches at the antipodes," Melville warns, "how heavily that ocean gloom lies in vast bales upon the deck; thinking that that very moment in his deserted hamlet-home the household sun is high, and many a sun-eyed maiden meridian as the sun." Not by chance does Melville repeat the sun imagery in this passage, echoing the same "sun" from which Ahab turned and fled. And like Ahab, Pierre "curses Fate; himself he curses; his senseless madness, which is himself"—here, we should recall Ahab's cursing his "forty years of making war on the horrors of the sea," his "guinea coast slavery of solitary command," to Starbuck, and likewise his phrase, "I am madness maddened!" Yet another parallel is drawn between these two great novels. In any case, the passage continues: "For whoso once has known this sweet knowledge, and then fled it; in absence, to him the avenging dream will come. Pierre was now this vulnerable god; this self-upbraiding sailor; this dreamer of the avenging dream" (181). Pierre, Ahab and, I will argue, Melville himself, are likewise "vulnerable god[s]," "self-upbraiding sailor[s]," and "dreamer[s] of the avenging dream." In this way, all three are heirs or successors of Bulkington. This crucial scene in Pierre echoes, repeats and deepens the still-mysterious Bulkington chapter (23) of *Moby-Dick*, "The Lee Shore," to which I referred earlier but will here quote at length. In that chapter, we must recall, Bulkington

> unrestingly push[es] off again for still another tempestuous term. The

land seemed scorching to his feet. Wonderfullest things are ever the unmentionable; deep memories yield no epitaphs; this six-inch chapter is the stoneless grave of Bulkington. Let me only say that it fared with him as with the storm-tossed ship, that miserably drives along the leeward land. The port would fain give succor; the port is pitiful; in the port is saftety, comfort, hearthstone, supper, warm blankets, friends, all that's kind to our mortalities. But in that gale, the port, the land, is that ship's direst jeopardy; she must fly all hospitality; one touch of land, though it but graze the keel, would make her shudder through and through. With all her might she crowds all sail off shore; in so doing, fights 'gainst the very winds that fain would blow her homeward; seeks all the lashed sea's landlessness again; for refuge's sake forlornly rushing into peril; her only friend her bitterest foe! Know ye, now, Bulkington? Glimpses do ye seem to see of that mortally intolerable truth; that all deep, earnest thinking is but the intrepid effort of the soul to keep the open independence of her sea; while the wildest winds of heaven and earth conspire to cast her on the treacherous, slavish shore? But as in landlessness alone resides the highest truth, shoreless, indefinite as God—so, better is it to perish in that howling infinite, than be ingloriously dashed upon the lee, even if that were safety! For worm-like, then, oh! who would craven crawl to land? Terrors of the terrible! is all this agony so vain? Take heart, take heart, O Bulkington! Bear thee grimly, demigod! Up from the spray of thy ocean-perishing—straight up, leaps thy apotheosis! (106–107)

Pierre follows in Bulkington's footsteps, or (perhaps more precisely) takes his place, as does Ahab (and Melville, in "real life"). They manage to "keep the open independence of [their] sea[s]" but then "perish in that howling infinite." In this way, Pierre—again, like Ahab—is a kind of "apotheosis" of Bulkington: Bulkington come back to life, with much the same grandeur and majesty, yet nursing the profoundest woe, akin to Milton's Satan. They are not meek or submissive, like Starbuck or Jonah, but defiant instead, indomitable, "unsurrendered." We must also note the way that this crucial section of *Pierre* ends, echoing that statement in the "stoneless grave," the "six inch chapter" that memorializes Bulkington in *Moby-Dick*, yet "yield[s] no epitaph": "But here we draw a vail. Some nameless struggles of the soul can not be painted, and some woes will not be told. Let the ambiguous procession of events reveal their own ambiguousness" (181).

It is once again in section iii of a chapter of *Pierre* (Book XII, "The Portrait") that a crucial scene appears: in this case, Pierre's destruction of the oil portrait of his father. Pierre arrives at the Black Swan Inn after leaving Saddle-Meadows and gazes upon the portrait, which he had taken with him. This scene may recall Ishmael, arriving at the Spouter-Inn, in which he spies a "boggy, soggy, squitchy, picture truly, enough to drive a nervous man distracted. Yet there was a sort of indefinite, half-attained, unimaginable sublimity about it that fairly froze you to it, till you involuntarily took an oath with yourself to find out what that marvelous painting meant" (MD 12–13). Pierre is confronted with a similarly "sublime" painting. "Face up" in his traveling chest, we are told, "it met him with its noiseless, ever-nameless, and ambiguous, unchanging smile" (P 196). He is now shocked by what he takes to be the striking likeness it bears to Isabel, and he lifts it "in his own two hands, and held it averted from him." Here, we should take note of how he turns away from the portrait, from the gaze of his father. "It shall not live," he exclaims, "Hitherto I have hoarded up mementoes and monuments of the past [another resonant word, 'monuments']; been a worshiper of all heir-looms" but now, after realizing that his formerly "perfect" father in fact led a secret life, he vows to "never more [..] play the vile pigmy, and by small memorials after death, attempt to reverse the decree of death, by essaying the poor perpetuating of the image of the original" (197–198).

"Let all die, and mix again!" he exclaims, while "detaching and dismembering [echoing another crucial word from *Moby-Dick*: Ahab's own 'dismembering'] the gilded but tarnished frame" in order to stoke his room's wood-fire, upon which he then throws the portrait. At one point, while the canvas is burning, he imagines that "the upwrithing portrait stared at him in beseeching horror," so he thrusts his hand into the fire in order to rescue the "imploring face" (198). However, he "swiftly drew back his scorched [...] burnt and blackened" hand, before "seizing repeated packages of family letters, and all sorts of miscellaneous memorials in paper" (Ibid.), which the likewise commits to the flames. "[N]ow all is done, and all is ashes!" he declares; "Henceforth, cast-out Pierre hath no paternity, and no past" (199).

We must pause and take note, here, of Deleuze and Guattari's insight, in their study of Kafka, pertaining to the function of the portrait and how it is deeply tied to "Oedipal incest," which we clearly see on display in Pierre's fixation on his father's portraits and his mother's attitudes toward them. Deleuze and Guattari write that "Oedipal incest is connected to photos, to portraits, to childhood memories, a false childhood that never existed but that catches desire in the trap of representation, cuts it off from all connections, fixes it onto the mother to render it all the more puerile or spoiled, in order to have it support all the other, stronger interdictions and to prevent it from identifying itself as part of the social and political field."[88] Is this not the very same "false childhood" that Pierre now realizes he has experienced, and that his mother (who styles herself "sister Mary," we must always remember) would perpetuate if given the chance? And does this portrait, the "official" one, so to speak, sanctioned by his mother, and the false childhood that it represents, not attempt to "prevent [Pierre's desire] from identifying itself as part of the social and political field"? To illustrate this latter point, all we need do is point to Pierre's radical (relative to his mother's, or the Reverend Falsgrave's) views on Delly and her illegitimate child, or to his sympathy for the tenant-farmers, more precisely the serfs, of Saddle Meadows: the "unofficial" portrait of Pierre, Sr., the one his mother loathes, is precisely what

---

[88]   *Kafka* 67.

sparks an interest in these radical thoughts—which is then repeated in the face of Isabel and, eventually, her haunting music: all of which calls Pierre away from the mother, from Oedipal incest and domesticity, from "the very foundations of society," while drawing him deeper into the labyrinth of the city and the "social and political field" (represented by the "Young America in Literature" passages, which we can see are absolutely crucial, contra Parker).

The alternate portrait, which has led Pierre away from his father's "official" portrait and the memory enshrined by his mother, leads him to Isabel, eventually to her mysterious music, mentioned above, which is played on a guitar that she resonantly named "Mother." Deleuze and Guattari point out that this is, in fact, precisely how "Schizo-incest"—diametrically opposed to "Oedipal incest"—functions:

> Schizo-incest, in contrast [to Oedipal incest], is connected to sound, to the manner in which sound takes flight and in which memory-less childhood blocks introduce themselves in full vitality into the present to activate it, to precipitate it, to multiply its connections. Schizo-incest with a maximum of connection, a polyvocal extension, that uses as an intermediary maids and whores [in Kafka, for Deleuze and Guattari, but, as we shall see later in this chapter, in Melville as well] and the place that they occupy in the social series—in opposition to neurotic [Oedipal] incest, defined by its suppression of connection, its single signifier, its holding of everything within the limits of the family, its neutralization of any sort of social or political field. (Ibid.)

The question of Isabel's music will be discussed later, during a crucial scene in which Melville in several ways repeats a key moment in *Moby-Dick*; for now, it must suffice to point to the absolute difference between "Oedipal-" and "Schizo-incest," and how our understanding of the two are crucial in recognizing Melville subversive "art of escape" in *Pierre*. After leaving Saddle Meadows, with his ragtag entourage of sisters, in a sense precisely the "maids and whores" that people so much of Kafka's fiction and to which Deleuze and Guattari referred above, Pierre heads to New York City, in search of forming new connections, escaping the "limits of the family," in some ways building his own society (of brothers and sisters, no doubt). He eventually accomplishes this, at great expense, when he joins forces with the mysterious cult known as "the Apostles," and connects his own series of "sisters," "maids and whores" to this odd assortment of bachelors; however, before looking at these moments in the narrative, we should examine his initial thwarted attempts, upon reaching New York.

When Pierre, now accompanied by Isabel and Delly Ulver, enters the city, in search of refuge with his cousin, Glen Stanly, he finds himself instead cast out, literally, and then in a precinct jail. In the chapter entitled "First Night of Their Arrival in the City" (Book XVI), Melville deliberately paints the scene much as Milton does in *Paradise Lost*, describing the fallen angels:

> The sights and sounds which met the eye of Pierre on re-entering the watch-house [after depositing Isabel and Delly there, for safekeeping, while he rushed to Glen Stanly's home to make arrangements, before being thrown out], filled him with inexpressible horror and fury. The before decent, drowsy place, now fairly reeked with all things unseemly. Hardly possible was it to tell what conceivable cause or occasion had, in the comparatively short absence of Pierre, collected such a base congregation. In indescribable disorder, frantic, diseased-looking men and women of all colors, and in all imaginable flaunting, immodest, grotesque, and shattered dresses, were leaping, yelling, and cursing around him [...] words and phrases unrepeatable in God's sunlight, and whose very existence was utterly unknown, and undreamed by tens of thousands of the decent people of the city; syllables obscene and accursed were shouted forth in tones plainly evincing that they were the common household breath of their utterers. The thieves'-quarters, and all the brothels, Lock-and-Sin hospitals for incurables, and infirmaries and infernos of hell seemed to have made one combined sortie, and poured

out upon earth through the vile vomitory of some unmentionable cellar. (240–241)

This Miltonian section immediately precedes a crucial chapter, called "Young America in Literature" (Book XVII), which forms a pair or diptych with the next, with which it is thematically linked, "Pierre, as a Juvenile Author, Reconsidered" (Book XVIII). As Spanos has shown in *Moby-Dick*, Melville often pairs chapters (or, later, short stories, such as those Jay Leyda dubbed "diptyches," which I discussed in the previous chapter) intentionally, back-to-back as it were, in order to achieve a certain effect.[89] In *Pierre*, as I will show, he does this not once, but twice: here, with two chapters concerning literature, and then, more crucially for my purposes, later, at the narrative's climax, when Pierre has his "dream of Enceladus" (Book XXV, which begins, significantly, with "Pierre at His Book;" in other words, Pierre attempting to finish his novel, which would "gospelize the world anew"), followed by a chapter detailing a dizzying visit to an art gallery, in which a "foreign portrait" that bears a striking similarity to the oil painting of his father, earlier destroyed at the Black Swan Inn, and a brief but momentous voyage at sea (Book XXVI, which ends with the death of Lucy, Pierre and Isabel).

Book XVII begins with Pierre stating that he "write[s] precisely as [he] please[s]" (244), which Parker and other scholars focused upon Melville's "original intentions" in writing this novel (or any text) would like to challenge, before moving on to a curious passage describing the manufacturing of paper, made from shreds of cloth, which Melville will take up again in his story "The Tartarus of Maids" (discussed in the pervious chapter). This is, in turn,

---

[89] See 121–131 of *The Errant Art of* Moby-Dick, in which Ahab's naming and Ishmael's unnaming of the white whale is the focus of analysis.

followed by a section discussing Pierre's distaste for lecturing, which would (with unintentional irony, no doubt) foreshadow Melville's own, real-life (and utterly disastrous) stint as a lecturer, and then a meditation on the theme of "Timonism," which is taken up later in *The Confidence-Man* (and which I will discuss in the next chapter). Finally, there is a crucial passage in which Pierre turns away, once and for all, from "the unsatisfactoriness of all human fame" and burns all of his remaining reminders of his former life, all of "the letters of his Biographico and other silly correspondents" (255), oddly enough mirroring Melville's own penchant for burning correspondence (such as that from Hawthorne, mentioned previously). Once more, in this passage at the end of Book XV, there is an allusion to Pierre being "Timonized" (Ibid.), an odd turn of phrase to which Olson drew readers' attention in *Call Me Ishmael*, particularly in the context of the friendship with Hawthorne—a phrase to which, and not by chance, Melville will return later in *The Confidence-Man*.

Book VXIII begins with a metaphor concerning the "temple" that Pierre had constructed out of the "fine marble" of Saddle-Meadows: his birthright, his "double Revolutionary inheritance" or glorious genealogy, his sentimental education and the inspiration for his art. Melville is here continuing the theme of "monumentalism" and stone, something that will return, later, with Israel Potter and the Bunker Hill Monument or with Bartleby perishing in The Tombs—but, more immediately, with Pierre (literally "the rock") ending his tale of woe, as did Bartleby, in a stone prison cell. However, the most provocative and in many ways enigmatic passage in this chapter concerns the narrator's meditation on "originality," a theme (once again) repeated later in *The Confidence-Man*. "The world is forever babbling about originality;" he informs us, "but there never yet was an original man" (259). In this passage, Melville invokes Milton, as well, calling his Satan, from *Paradise Lost*, a true "original," and thereby providing us with a strong hint as to why he returned so often to this character in his own work. Yet another moment where *Pierre* seems to be foreshadowing or giving way to *The Confidence-Man* is in the following, well-known passage: "[F]ar as any geologist has yet gone down into the world, it is found to consist of nothing but surface stratified on surface. To its axis, the world being nothing but superintended superficies. By vast pains we mine into the pyramid; by horrible gropings we come to the central room; with joy we espy the sarcophagus; but we lift the lid—and no body is there!—appallingly vacant as vast is the soul of a man!" (285). Here, we are fast approaching the end of *Pierre*, and the horrible meaning of its "ambiguities": the idea that identity is groundless, a play of masks, phantoms or simulacra. But before this is made clear, Pierre's body begins to fail him, perhaps paralleling Melville's own frail health of this period.

Indeed, in Book XXV, while working himself to exhaustion upon his novel, Pierre's eyes rebel against him, much as Melville's did him, literally "roll[ing] away from him [and from his attempts to focus upon the blank sheets of paper in front of him] in their orbits" (341; rpd. on 342). Here begins one of the most intense passages of the novel (340–347):

> [A] special corporeal affliction now descended like a sky-hawk [itself a resonant image, bringing to mind *Moby-Dick*'s final scene] upon him. His incessant application told upon his eyes. They became so affected, that some days he wrote with the lids nearly closed, fearful of opening them wide to the light. Through the lashes he peered upon the paper, which so seemed fretted with wires. Sometimes he blindly wrote with his eyes *turned away* from the paper;—thus unconsciously symbolizing the hostile necessity and distaste, the former whereof made of him this most unwilling states-prisoner of letters. (340, emphasis added)

Pierre begins walking around the city now, to escape from his prison-cell (his writing desk), and masochistically enjoys being pummeled by wind, rain, and hailstones, "till one night as he paused a moment previous to turning about for home, a sudden, unwonted, and all-pervading sensation seized him. He knew not where he was; he did not have any ordinary life-feeling at all. He could not see; though instinctively putting his hand to his eyes, he seemed to feel that the lids were open. Then he was sensible of a combined blindness, and vertigo, and staggering" (341). He then passes out, and awakes "lying crosswise in the gutter, dabbled with mud and slime" (Ibid.). After the fit passes, he returns to his writing desk, resumes his labors and vows to avoid walking such desolate streets in future. "But if that terrible vertigo had been also intended for another and deeper warning," we are told, Pierre "regarded such added warning not at all; but again plied heart and brain as before." Now, however, he loses control over his eyes:

> But now at last since the very blood in his body had in vain rebelled against his Titanic soul; now the only visible outward symbols of that soul—his eyes—did also turn downright traitors to him, and with more success than the rebellious blood. He had abused them so recklessly, that now they absolutely refused to look on paper. He turned them on paper, and they blinked and shut. The pupils of his eyes rolled away from him in their own orbits. (341)

The next morning, he tries again to write, but "again the pupils of his eyes rolled away from him in their orbits" (342). We must take note of how this turning or rolling away is repeated here, precisely when a strange dream overtakes him: "During this state of semi-unconsciousness, or rather trance, a remarkable dream or vision came to him," a familiar sight, recalled from his idyllic youth in Saddle-Meadows, "the phantasmagoria of the Mount of the Titans," a natural rock formation situated not far from his "ancestral manor" (342). Not by coincidence does this dream begin with the tenant-farmers "petition[ing] their lady-landlord," Pierre's mother, "for some abatement in their annual tribute," due to the "immortal amaranth" which annually spreads, robbing their cattle of grazing-lands and costing them dearly. "[F]ree us from the amaranth, good lady," they plead, "or be pleased to abate our rent!" (343). Their pleas, we may safely assume, fall on deaf ears.

This is likewise the point where the crucial dream of Enceladus begins, a dream that the narrator recounts by directly addressing the reader for the first and only time ("you"): "You saw Enceladus the titan, the most potent of all the giants, writhing from out the imprisoning earth;—turbaned [Ahab is also 'turbaned'] with upborne moss he writhed; still, though armless, resisting with his whole striving trunk, the Pelion and the Ossa hurled back at him;—turbaned [repeated] with upright moss he writhed; still turning his unconquerable front toward that majestic mount eternally in vain assailed by him, and which, when it had stormed him off, had heaved his undoffable incubus upon him, and deridingly left him there to bay out his ineffectual howl" (345). Here, Melville refers to the rock-formation as "this American Enceladus," "not unworthy to be compared with" the famous statue at Versailles, and at one point he describes it as an "impotent Titan" (346), a phrase that will be recalled later, in *The Confidence-Man*, when a Pierre-like character appears ("the invalid Titan"). But first, we are told

> [s]uch was the wild scenery—the Mount of Titans, and the repulsed group of heaven-assaulters, with Enceladus in their midst shamefully incumbent at its base; such was the wild scenery, which now to Pierre, in his strange vision, displaced the four blank walls, the desk, the camp-bed, and domineered upon his trance. But no longer petrified in all their ignominious attitudes, the herded Titans now sprung to their feet; flung themselves up the slope; and anew battered at the precipice's unresounding wall. Foremost among them all, he saw a moss-turbaned, armless giant, who despairing of any other mode of wreaking his immitigable hate, turned his vast trunk into a battering-ram, and hurled his own arched-out ribs again and yet again against the invulnerable

steep. "Enceldaus! it is Enceldaus!"—Pierre cried out in his sleep. That moment the phantom faced him; and Pierre saw Enceladus no more; but on the Titan's armless trunk, his own duplicate face and features magnifiedly gleamed upon him with prophetic discomfiture and woe. (346)

The myth of Enceladus and the Mount of Titans, which surely recalls Ahab's titanic rage, reveals itself as follows: "Old Titan's self was the son of incestuous Coelus and Terra, the son of incestuous Heaven and Earth. And Titan married his mother Terra, another and accumulatively incestuous match. And thereof Enceladus was one issue. So Enceladus was both the son and grandson of an incest" (347), which may recall Pierre's own genealogy, and the theme of incest with which Melville has been playing all along in this novel; and, like Enceladus "even thus, there had been born from the organic blended heavenliness and earthliness of Pierre, another mixed, uncertain, heaven-aspiring, but still not wholly earth-emancipated mood; which again, by its terrestrial taint held down to its terrestrial mother, generated there the present doubly incestuous Enceladus within him; so that the present mood of Pierre—that reckless sky-assaulting mood of his, was nevertheless on one side the grandson of the sky" (Ibid.). Like Enceladus—and recalling not only Milton's Satan but also the chapter on Bulkington in *Moby-Dick*, concerning the necessity of leaving the safety of shore and standing tall in the "howling gale"—Pierre must "storm heaven." As Melville phrases it: "For it is according to eternal fitness, that the precipitated Titan should still seek to regain his paternal birthright even by fierce escalade. Wherefore whoso storms the sky gives best proof he came from thither! But whatso crawls contented in the moat before that crystal fort, shows it was born within that slime, and there forever will abide" (347). Pierre, like Ahab, will take his bachelor-machine and set it on iron rails.

First, however, Pierre "wrestle[s] with the strange malady of his eyes, this new death-fiend of the trance, and this Inferno of his Titanic vision" (Ibid.) and resolves himself to act cheerfully and propose that Lucy and Isabel take a walk with him outdoors. And here, at the end of this crucial passage and chapter, Melville once more repeats the amaranth imagery, encountered earlier in the narrative when the question of rent came up between his mother the her tenants, as follows: "And even so, to grim Enceladus, the world the gods has chained for a ball to drag at his o'erfreighted feet;—even so that globe put forth a thousand flowers, whose fragile smiles disguised his ponderous load" (Ibid.). But Pierre (as Enceladus) is compelled to "strike through the mask," as was Ahab, "even if there is naught beyond" the "fragile smiles" of these flowers that "disguise" the reality of the situation. Pierre is now ready to tear the veil, represented by the flowers associated with his mother, even if there is "naught beyond," as Ahab found out.

In the final chapter (Book XXVI), Pierre decides to walk to the ocean, to refresh himself with the sea air and "get on some other element than earth" for he has "sat on earth's saddle till [he is] weary" (348). The three—Pierre, Isabel and Lucy—walk toward the water, but along the way stop in at a gallery to see paintings, "newly imported from Europe, and now on free exhibition preparatory to their sale by auction" (Ibid.). A portrait entitled *"No. 99. A stranger's head, by an unknown hand"* catches his eye. It turns out to be "the resurrection of the one [of his father] he had burnt at the Inn" (351), a fact that Isabel also notices. Pierre tells her that they must "keep eternal silence" (352) and the three abruptly leave. Pierre then falls into a reverie:

> How did he know that Isabel was his sister? [...] -how did he *know* that Isabel was his sister? Nothing that he saw in her face could he remember as having seen in his father's. The chair-portrait, *that* was the entire sum and substance of all possible, rakable, downright presumptive evidence,

which peculiarly appealed to his own separate self. Yet here was another portrait of a complete stranger—a European; a portrait imported from across the seas, and to be sold at public auction, which was just as strong an evidence as the other. Then, the original of this second portrait was as much the father of Isabel as the original of the chair-portrait. But perhaps there was no original at all to this second portrait. (353)

Here, in this last sentence, we can see Melville moving ever more closely toward the idea of the simulacrum, the copy without original, that he will more fully explore in *The Confidence-Man* (to be discussed in the next chapter). But first, there is a crucial series of sea-related images, beginning with the following:

With such bewildering meditations as these in him, running up like clasping waves upon the strand of the most latent secrecies of his soul, and with both Isabel and Lucy bodily touching his sides as he walked; the feelings of Pierre were entirely untranslatable into any words that can be used. (353)

Pierre begins to doubt Isabel's entire story, including her claim that, though she had crossed the Atlantic in her childhood, "upon Pierre's subsequent questioning of her, she did not even know that the sea was salt" (354). "In the midst of all these mental confusions they arrived at the wharf" and board a ship for a cruise of the bay. Isabel begins to behave strangely, claiming to recognize the motion of the waves, a distant memory from her childhood crossing of the ocean. She then cries, "Don't let us stop here! Look, let us go through there!" pointing to the horizon; "out there upon the blue! yonder, yonder! far away—out, out!—far, far away, and away, and away, out there! where the two blues meet, and are nothing!" Like Melville, who is perhaps expressing his own, innermost desires in this passage, Isabel wants to flee, to "escape" (recalling Deleuze's quotation from D.H. Lawrence): "Yes, I will go yonder—yonder; out there! I will, I will! Unhand me! Let me plunge!" (355).

They manage to stop Isabel from plunging into the deep, and killing herself, but only to return to shore, where cousin Glen Stanly waits with Lucy's brothers for Pierre. Pierre rushes to confront them, and murders Glen Stanly, "his own hand [...] extinguish[ing] his house in slaughtering the only unoutlawed human being by the name of Glendinning" (360), and he is quickly apprehended. "That sundown," we are told, "Pierre stood solitary in a low dungeon of the city prison," where, it should be noted, his life in the metropolis both began and now will end. "The cumbersome stone ceiling almost rested on his brow; so that the long tiers of massive cell-galleries above seemed partly piled on him," thus fulfilling the prophecy contained in the dream of Enceladus, who is likewise crushed under a heavy load of stone. "His immortal, immovable, bleached cheek was dry; but the stone cheeks of the walls were trickling," which provides a curious image, confusing the stone walls and Pierre's face, somehow intermixed or intermingled, both now turned to stone. And like Enceladus (and Ahab), Pierre remains unmoving, unswerving and defiant to the end: "I will mold a trumpet of the flames, and, with my breath of flame, breathe back my defiance!" (360) he cries. In this final scene, the three "lovers"—Pierre, Lucy and Isabel—all die, and the last scene is indeed a bloody one, filled with corpses.

In the previous scenes, leading up to the frenzy of violence that marks the climax of the novel, we watch in increasing horror as Pierre attempts to grasp the meaning of his father's portrait, which, like the white whale in *Moby-Dick*, acts as a "floating signifier," always escaping him, his understanding or comprehension, his grasp. He can never know his father's true character or identity, or whether or not Isabel is his sister, particularly at end of the novel, in the powerful chapter in which the aforementioned portrait from Europe, entitled "*No. 99. A stranger's head, by an unknown hand*," is encountered, or, immediately following this scene, when the strange "family" of sibling-lovers head toward the water and find themselves "lost in the infinite series of the sea" (as Melville phrases it in "The Mast-Head" chapter of *Moby-Dick*). As discussed above, the picture bears an uncanny resemblance to his father, to the other portrait which his mother had tried to suppress or hide, and Pierre absolutely loses his moorings—which also happens to Isabel once the trio leave the shore and she gazes upon the ocean. It now seems that nothing is certain, nothing retains its former solid foundations: for Pierre, the idea dawns upon him that perhaps there are several copies of this same portrait all over Europe and that it is not, in fact, a picture of his father; for Isabel, she experiences a kind of vertigo when faced with the "infinite series" of the waves, and the absolute indeterminancy of the sea and sky, which meet and blend into one another at the horizon. This idea—very close to the concept of the simulacrum, a copy without original—will be further developed in *The Confidence-Man*, which is the focus of the third chapter of my study.

Pierre and Isabel are here experiencing a kind of vertigo due to an overturning of hierarchies in their understanding of the world. Up until this point, their lives have been ruled by what we could call Mimesis and the order of Representation: for Pierre, in particular, living up to the model of his esteemed father, becoming a copy or faithful resemblance of him, as it were, has been his task in life, one in which his mother has been in deadly earnest in supervising or overseeing. However, in the city, all such hierarchies or genealogies are overturned or thrown into confusion; the doomed lover-siblings encounter nothing but simulacra, a series of copies of undiscernible or nonexistent origin. We may pause here to recall that, as Michel Foucault has taught us, the simulacrum is in fact very different from a simple or straightforward copy. In his study of René Magritte, Foucault asserted that the painter had

> dissociated similitude from resemblance [...] Resemblance has a 'model,'

an original element that orders and hierarchizes the increasingly less faithful copies that can be struck from it. Resemblance presupposes a primary reference that prescribes and classes. The similar develops in series that have neither beginning nor end, that can be followed in one direction as easily as in another, that obey no hierarchy [...] Resemblance serves representation, which rules over it; similitude serves repetition, which ranges across it. Resemblance predicates itself upon a model it must return to and reveal; similitude circulates the simulacrum as an indefinite and reversible relation of the similar to the similar. (44)

Before moving to that discussion, however, we must first look more closely at the abandoned figures, the series of "sisters," "maids and whores" or abject women that populate the fiction of this period of Melville's work. To this task we now turn.

The Vanquished: Melville's Female Characters

Melville's oeuvre does not feature many female characters, so focusing upon them may prove fruitful, simply due to their novelty or relative scarcity. However, a more important question concerns why they appear at this point in Melville's career; in other words, why Melville, in the wake of his passionate but ultimately disappointing friendship with Hawthorne, begins focusing upon these female figures of abjection, abandonment, sterility or virginity. Up to this point, Melville had been concerned with "immortal bachelors and gods," employing the phrase from *Pierre* cited above; in and through the writing of *Pierre*, with its strange series of sister-lovers, something changes and Melville is transformed: he now begins writing about what he will call, in "The Encantadas" (1854; reprinted in 1856), one of the texts under scrutiny in this final section of chapter two, "the vanquished." Our task in what follows is to explore the possible reasons why this occurs at this point.

One possibility is that Melville is here, once again, conforming to the pattern of what Deleuze and Guattari have called "schizo-incest," a concept examined earlier in this chapter. Specifically, Melville seems to be approaching what Kafka, according to Deleuze and Guattari, had accomplished in his fiction through his sister-like "maids and whores." As they describe it, in Kafka "this genre of women with dark, sad eyes" (much, we should note, like Isabel in *Pierre*, or Hunilla, as we shall see, in "The Encantadas") function as "connectors" of desire, presenting a blend of roles, "part sister, part maid, part whore," and as such are "anticonjugal and antifamilial" (*Kafka* 64). This "ensemble," as Deleuze and Guattari phrase it, of "sister-maid-whore" (66), can be first seen in *Pierre* in the form of Isabel, Delly and Lucy, but it is repeated in what I am calling the "minor fiction" which follows. The "connective function" of these women becomes apparent if we consider the ways in which Isabel "connects" the mystery of Pierre Sr.'s portrait to a past hitherto unimagined by Pierre Jr., and to a crumbling or deconstruction, so to speak, of the "false childhood" and "perfect" genealogy of the Glendinning "race." Delly Ulver connects Pierre to this alternate past through her act of adultery, of having a child out of wedlock to a married man, in a way repeating Isabel's illegitimate origin, in addition to opening onto the question of the servants, the tenant-farmers or, or to put it another way, "the working class" of Saddle Meadows, by her very status. Lucy Tartan, for her part, begins as a connection to conjugality, and thus "reoedipalization," but ends as something vastly different: after leaving her family and joining Pierre and Isabel in a kind of ménage à trios, she more or less becomes a kind of "sister-maid-whore" in one character, once she enters their New York City home. She offers to act as Pierre and Isabel's servant, while slaving away at "her crayon art" portraits in order to earn money for this odd household, attending to both Isabel's domestic needs and, presumably, to Pierre's libidinous desires. But the three cannot function without one another, as Deleuze and Guattari have argued of this "ensemble" (Ibid). In this way, they are inextricably joined together and, as such, as an ensemble, they join the final element (after, we must recall, the music of Isabel's guitar, which displaces the portraits of Pierre Sr.) of "schizo-incest:" "a homosexuality of doubles, of brothers or of bureaucrats" (68), which has in fact been present to some extent in Melville's work all along, but becomes markedly pronounced in the character of Glen Stanly and in the various "minor" works—stories like "Bartleby" or "Jimmy Rose," the serialized novel *Israel Potter*, even the poems—that follow *Pierre*.

In his "Mosses" essay, Melville famously wrote that "[f]ailure is the true test of greatness."[90] We may assume that he was speaking of the artist's need to risk defeat by constantly reaching beyond his horizons, attempting more demanding and original projects. For Melville, as R.W.B. Lewis long ago pointed out,[91] had always honored the daring failure over the safe success: "If it be said," he contended, "that continual success is a proof that a man wisely knows his powers, it is only to be added that, in that case, he knows them to be small" (*PT* 248; qtd. in Lewis, 7). Melville must have sensed his own powers to be great: he was at that very moment in the midst of his most powerful work (and spectacular critical failure to date, it must be remembered),[92] *Moby-Dick*. But just as he had come to demand such overreaching artistic efforts, Melville likewise began to develop a notable relation, even obsession, with defeat, a preference in his fiction that seems to mirror his own life—particularly, as I have been arguing, his friendship with

---

[90] "Hawthorne and His Mosses" (1850), WHM 9: 248.

[91] See his magisterial "Introduction" to *Herman Melville: A Laurel Reader* (New York: Dell, 1962), upon which I heavily draw in what follows.

[92] He would outdo himself, in terms of garnering critical opprobrium, with his next novel, *Pierre* (1852), as discussed above.

Hawthorne, now grown cold. "Praise be to God for the failure!" is the motto of one of his weaker stories of this period ("The Happy Failure," 1854), and in "The Encantadas" he located his symbol of praiseworthy humanity "not in the laurelled victor, but in this vanquished one," Hunilla, the Chola (mestiza) widow.

As Lewis noted, when Melville wrote in "The Encantadas" that he worshipped humanity not in the figure of the victor but in the figure of "the vanquished," he was "giving precise statement to the tragic sense that possessed him in this period of his life. It is a sense that communicates more directly, perhaps, to our own age of wreckage, anxiety and defeat than it did to the more confident America of Melville's time" (Ibid.)—the culture of triumphalism that Spanos, for example, has shown Melville to have critiqued in works such as *Moby-Dick*, *Pierre*, *Israel Potter*, *The Piazza Tales* and *The Confidence-Man*. For Melville, like Thomas Pynchon in our own time, found human dignity in the "Preterite" (Pynchon's term), the passed-over or forgotten; not among the powerful and successful, in other words, but among the oppressed, the afflicted, the defeated or vanquished. In the characters of Captain Ahab and Pierre, Melville had offered readers titanic images of magnificent defeat; but in the tales that followed, as I will show in this brief concluding section of chapter two, the focus was instead on the touching or forlorn, particularly female characters—Mariana, for example, "a pale-cheeked," "lonely girl, sitting at a lonely window;" Hunilla, who stoically endures her many trials, a "heart of yearning in a frame of steel;" or the blank-looking girls in the hellish paper mill of "The Tartarus of Maids," with their tormented, pallid faces and "pale virginity," to which we shall now turn.

We begin our brief exploration of "the vanquished" by looking back at a story discussed earlier, "The Tartarus of Maids," part of a "diptych" that stands in stark contrast to its companion-piece, "The Paradise of Bachelors." Rogin called this tale a "sketch of working-class life," and discusses it in a chapter entitled "Class Struggles in America;"[93] while humanist critics have read it as Melville's "anguished cry [...] for improved working conditions" in factories,[94] such as the paper mill he actually visited in Dalton, Massachusetts in the winter of 1851. Whereas the gay, "immortal bachelors" are truly "gods"—or, at the very least, leading a god-like existence at Temple Bar—as described in "The Paradise of Bachelors," the pale virgins slaving away in the paper mill, turning the discarded, ragged shirts of the bachelors into blank sheets of paper in a place aptly named the Devil's Dungeon, are truly among the damned. Philip Young, in many ways extending the work of several scholars who illustrated *Pierre*'s debt to the *Inferno*,[95] a text that is mentioned alongside *Hamlet* in a crucial scene in Melville's novel (as discussed above), pointed out the connection between "Melville's Inferno" and Dante's:

> The Maids of Tartarus, though spoken to, do not in the tale speak. They are Dante's "shades," which is to say spirits of the dead inhabiting hell. Sentenced to more than maidenhood, they are [...] Melville's version of the first spirits Dante encountered at the entrance to the underworld (Canto III) who, as Virgil explains, "of death / No hope may entertain." (218–219)

These blank-looking wraiths, whom the narrator wishes to somehow save or

---

[93] Rogin, *Subversive Genealogy*, 201–204.

[94] Ray B. Browne, *Melville's Drive to Humanism* (Lafayette: Purdue University Studies, 1971): 227; qtd. in Milder, 53.

[95] G. Giovannini, "Melville's *Pierre* and Dante's *Inferno*," *PMLA*, Vol. 64, No. 1 (March 1949): 70–78; Nathalia Wright, "*Pierre*: Melville's *Inferno*," *American Literature*, Vol. 32, No. 2 (May 1960): 167–181; and Rita Gollin, "*Pierre*'s Metamorphosis of Dante's *Inferno*," *American Literature*, Vol. 39, No. 4 (January 1968): 542–545.

protect, much like younger sisters—but, failing that, finds himself "reverencing" for their virginity, before nearly fainting, much like Dante in the *Inferno*, when he imagines that he sees their faces in the roll of foolscap they are producing—are, quite literally, "maids," though perhaps not in the sense that Deleuze and Guattari intended the term (looking at the servant-girls that people Kafka's texts). Nonetheless, these pale virgins share the function of serving or otherwise laboring for the bachelor-figure(s) in the story, much as the "maids" do in Kafka's work. They are barred, however, not only from speech but also from sexuality. This is something that "Agatha" does not share with them, though she will not be as sexualized as her later incarnation, Hunilla.

Looking at the "Agatha" story, once again, we must first note that it is not by chance a story that is, simultaneously, one about abandonment and, at the same time, itself an abandoned or aborted story, the virtual enactment of Melville's own abandonment by Hawthorne, the failure of and disappointed hopes for his dream of collaboration with Hawthorne—perhaps even the very possibility of literary greatness in America (or the world) "holding hands," as he put it in his "Mosses" review. Returning to the circumstances of its creation, we see that Melville had been occupied with it during the winter of 1853, after first hearing of it from a New Bedford lawyer while visiting Nantucket Island with his father-in-law, Judge Lemuel Shaw in July, 1852. On the following August 13, he wrote to Hawthorne, then living in Concord (after having moved from Lenox, close by Melville's farm, Arrowhead, in Pittsfield), enclosing a memorandum that the lawyer had sent him. A "regular story," he thought, might be based on the "striking incidents" recounted in the memo; however, Melville added, such a tale seemed to him more suited to Hawthorne than to himself.

The lawyer, Melville explained, had first told him of Agatha Hatch (Robertson) to illustrate "the great patience, & endurance, & resignedness of the women of the island in submitting so uncomplainingly to the long, long absences of their sailor husbands" (WHM 14: 232). The letter proceeds to give the details of Agatha's abandonment by an unfaithful mate who had left her with child and bigamously married two other women. In the facts of her situation, Melville felt, lay "a skeleton of actual reality to build about with fullness & veins & beauty. And if I thought I could do it as well as you, why, I should not let you have it" (WHM 14: 237). On October 25, Melville wrote again to offer another "little idea" for the story, in case his friend had "thought it worth while to write" about Agatha, but when he visited the Hawthornes at Concord early in December, Hawthorne "expressed uncertainty" about undertaking the project and urged Melville himself to do so. Writing from Boston after their discussion, Melville reported his decision to "begin it immediately" upon returning to Pittsfield after the Christmas holidays and asked Hawthorne to return the lawyer's memo to him with any further suggestions he might have for treating "so interesting a story of reality." Had Hawthorne "come to this determination at Concord," Melville added, the two authors "might have more fully and closely talked over the story, and so struck out new light."[96]

This was Melville's last known contact with Hawthorne until their brief reunion in England nearly four years later, in late-1856, when Melville was on his way to the Mediterranean and Hawthorne was American consul at Liverpool. If Melville wrote the story of Agatha during the winter months of 1853 "with Hawthorne's vein and style predominantly in mind," as Henry A. Murray has suggested, the lost manuscript may very well have constituted "a

---

[96]   See Harrison Hayford, "The Significance of Melville's 'Agatha' Letters," *ELH: A Journal of English Literary History*, XIII (December, 1946), 299–310, and Melville's *Letters*, 153–163; qtd. in Milder, 56.

step or transition, one might say, toward the Hawthornesque symbolism of [Melville's] later short stories." However, "since no such story was ever published or found in manuscript form, the chances are it was destroyed, [possibly] burnt by Melville himself."[97] Whatever the physical fate of the manuscript itself may have been, there are most certainly echoes of "the patience, & endurance, & resignedness" that Melville associated with Agatha in much of the fiction he was to write over the next three years: Bartleby and Israel Potter immediately spring to mind, as does the destitute Merrymusk family in "Cock-A-Doodle-Doo!" and, perhaps above all, Hunilla the "Chola widow" in the eighth sketch of "The Encantadas," published in April of 1854.

  The story of Hunilla is, as Herbert F. Smith long ago observed, "closely connected to the sensibility of an Agatha-character,"[98] and one can easily make the same case for Bartleby or other "abandoned" figures. Turning finally to how the "Agatha" story resurfaces in Melville's "minor" work of this period, we must briefly examine the figures of Hunilla and Mariana (whose story, "The Piazza," will be discussed in more detail in chapter three). Hunilla, the first and perhaps clearest reincarnation of "Agatha," is the central character in "Sketch Eight" of "The Encantadas," entitled "Norfolk Isle and the Chola Widow." During the narrator's visit to the Encantadas, his ship stopped at Norfolk Isle for two days to capture tortoises. As they were leaving, a sailor standing on a windlass saw a white object being waved from an inland rock. The captain gazed through his spy-glass and spotted a human figure. He launched a boat and picked up Hunilla, a "Chola"—a mestiza or "half-

---

[97] See the "Historical Note" to *The Piazza Tales* (483) for details on this possibility, as pointed out in Milder, 60.

[98] "Melville's Master in Chancery and His Recalcitrant Clerk," *American Quarterly*, XVII (Winter 1965), 737; qtd. in Ibid.

breed Indian"—from Payta, Peru. She then related her woeful tale.

Three years earlier, she and her husband Felipe and her only brother, Truxill, were left on the island by a French sea captain, to boil out tortoise oil. He said he would return for them in four months, but like Agatha's lover, he never returned. To make matters worse, Felipe and Truxill one day built a raft and went fishing, unaware of their desperate situation, and capsized. They were drowned, while Hunilla helplessly looked on from a cliff. Only Felipe's body was recovered, and Hunilla dutifully buried it on shore. On and on she waited for the ship to return, then for any ship. On a hollow cane she recorded the passing days, but after one hundred and eighty had passed, she stopped counting and lost track—though many more followed. When the narrator's captain presses her for an explanation, she would not explain, but gradually let on that she had been raped by vicious sailors who had landed on the island, and then once more abandoned. In the end, of course, she was rescued, but the image of this abject creature, though solemnly dignified and almost Christ-like—"last seen," we are told, "passing into Payta town, riding upon a small gray ass; and before her on the ass's shoulders, she eyed the jointed workings of the beast's armorial cross" (WHM 9: 162)—haunts us in very much the same way as does "Agatha," or perhaps even Melville himself, abandoned by Hawthorne. This brings us back full-circle, as it were, to Melville's "Mosses" essay and his farewell to Hawthorne in the short story, "The Piazza," which will be discussed in greater detail in chapter three. At this point, and as a way of concluding this chapter, we will briefly look at Marianna, the female character encountered in this short story.

Marianna, like Hunilla, seems to be a reincarnation of "Agatha." As Dryden has shown, in many ways, "The Piazza" is in dialogue with

Hawthorne's "The Old Manse" (1846).[99] But Melville, as Dryden makes clear, "does not recall the magic spell of Hawthorne's fairy land and its earlier effect on him in order to celebrate unambiguously the positive aspects of such enchantments;" instead, "his experiences on the piazza duplicate those of the Old Manse" taking "the form of a new, more negative reading of Hawthorne's text" (55). A "dark aspect of enchantment"—suggested, but never developed by Hawthorne—"troubles the text of 'The Piazza'" (56). Here, we may see this "dark aspect" reflecting Melville's own "enchantment" with Hawthorne, and with their mutual dream of collaboration. This is nowhere made clearer in fact than in the figure of Marianna.

The narrator of "The Piazza" sees "the fairy queen sitting at her fairy window," and as Dryden notes, "she recalls the deserted and isolated figure of Tennyson's poem 'Mariana'"—or, we might add, the deserted and isolated figures of Agatha or Hunilla. Like Tennyson's Mariana, Melville's "sits alone in an isolated, dilapidated, dreary house and laments her weary existence" (57). Unlike the enchanted ground of Hawthorne's "The Old Manse," Marianna's surroundings possess no "slumberous influence" ("The Old Manse" 39), for she is tormented by "weariness and wakefulness together," and even the picturesque moss of Hawthorne's sketch proves here, in Melville's, yet another sign of decay ("This old house is rotting. That makes it so mossy."). The world of Marianna, as Dryden points out, is one of "enigmatic shadows that lead not to essential forms but to other shadows" (57). For Marianna, "shadows are as things," her only companions; in fact, "the friendliest one,"

---

[99]   Edgar A. Dryden, "From the Piazza to the Enchanted Isles: Melville's Textual Rovings," in *After Strange Texts: the Role of Theory in the Study of Literature*, Gregory S. Jay and David L. Miller, eds. (Tuscaloosa: The University of Alabama Press, 1985): 46–68.

"the shadow of a birch" tree "that used to soothe [her] weariness so much," was "taken from [her], never to return," for it had been "struck by lightning" and was cut into pieces by her brother, for whom she waits in vain. Like him, the shadow of the birch "is flown, and never will come back, not ever anywhere stir again" (WHM 9: 11)—much like Hawthorne, now "flown" from Melville's life.

In this chapter, we have seen how Hawthorne's "abandonment" of Melville and their "dream of collaboration" resulted in the transformation of *Pierre* from a "romance calculated for popularity" to an all-out "declaration of war on domesticity." Pierre's bachelor-machine, which includes a series of female "connectors" that help it escape from the confines of the family and conjugality, is turned against "the very foundations of society," as early reviewers like Peck had intuited and feared. In his defiance, Pierre, the "heaven assaulter," constructs a "schizo-incestuous" machine made up of an assemblage of siblings—brothers, sisters, maids and whores—who attack the notions of genealogy, filiation, property and inheritance, and "monumental history." These female "connectors" are repeated in several of the "minor" texts that follow Pierre, as we have seen; however, in the last "major" work of the period under scrutiny in this study—in other words, *The Confidence-Man* (1857), the main focus of the following chapter—this idea of repetition is taken to its furthest limit, where it is transformed into something new. To this we now turn.

Chapter 3
An (Un)Holy Ghost; or, Escaping the Subject

In fleeing everything, how can we avoid reconstituting both our country of origin and our formations of power, our intoxicants, our psychoanalyses and our mummies and daddies?

—Gilles Deleuze[100]

Set on a Mississippi riverboat, ironically named *Fidèle*, on April Fools' Day, *The Confidence-Man* is perhaps Melville's most "American" book in terms of its setting, characters, and cultural references. We could also say, along with Milder, that it is his most "postmodern" work, exploring the instability of the notion of "confidence," or faith, in the reliability of nature, God, man, knowledge and, as I will show in the following chapter, in the stability of the self or subject (Miller 39). Melville had thought, at one point, to serialize it in *Putnam's* (Ibid.), but regardless of his original intentions, *The Confidence-Man* is a deeply troubling, subversive, and challenging novel. Indeed, its "very language"—"dense, allegorical, self-reflexive"—"challenges the reader to such an extent that Melville almost seems," as Milder points out, "to have been writing to himself, perhaps as an exercise, without any intention of conveying or communicating anything to his reader" (Ibid.) In the end, of course, this unread, unloved novel may as well have been written to himself alone: "the novel was barely noticed in America," where, according to Milder, Melville "had ceased to be recognized as a writer of the highest order, and English reviewers, while generally more sympathetic and thoughtful, were completely baffled" (Ibid.). *The Confidence-Man* was published on April

---

[100] "On the Superiority of Anglo-American Literature," 38.

Fools' Day in 1857, while Melville was abroad, by Dix, Edwards & Co., which—in a final, ironic twist—went bankrupt by the end of the month (Ibid.).

The Sand Dunes

Melville was at that time on what would turn out to be a seven-month journey to Europe and the Near East, paid for by his father-in-law, Judge Shaw, "in response to family anxieties about his state of mind" (Milder 40). Hawthorne met Melville in November 1856 in Liverpool (where Hawthorne was now American consul), and wrote that he found him "looking much as he used to do (a little paler, and perhaps a little sadder)" but genial enough for the men to resume "pretty much [their] former terms of sociability and confidence."[101] Melville stayed with Hawthorne for three days (he would visit again—the final meeting of their lives—just before sailing home in May) and during a memorable, now-famous walk on the Southport dunes, Hawthorne recorded in his journal, "Melville, as he always does, began to reason of Providence and futurity, and of everything that lies beyond human ken," informing Hawthorne that "he 'had pretty much made up his mind to be annihilated'" (Milder 40), a significant comment to which I will return at the end of this chapter. Hawthorne then provides what is perhaps the most sensitive and astute diagnosis of Melville's mental state:

It is strange how he persists—and has persisted ever since I knew him,

---

[101] Nathaniel Hawthorne, *The English Notebooks, 1856–1860*, the Centenary Edition of *The Works of Nathaniel Hawthorne*, vol. 12, ed. Thomas Woodson and Bill Ellis (Columbus: Ohio State University Press, 1997). 163; qtd. in Ibid.

and probably long before—in wandering to-and-fro over these deserts, as dismal and monotonous as the sand hills amid which we were sitting. He can neither believe, nor be comfortable in his unbelief; and he is too honest and courageous not to try to do one or the other. If he were a religious man, he would be one of the most truly religious and reverential; he has a very high and noble nature, and better worth immortality than most of us.[102]

From Liverpool, Melville sailed to the Mediterranean, where he visited some of the legendary Greek islands and Constantinople. The heart of the journey was four weeks in Egypt and Palestine, including stays in Cairo and Jerusalem, excursions to the Pyramids, and a three-day circuit through the Judean desert to the River Jordan, the Dead Sea, the Mar Saba monastery high in the mountains, and Bethlehem, a trip that would serve as the geographical basis for the pilgrims' ten-day journey in the epic poem, *Clarel: A Poem and Pilgrimage in the Holy Land*, published twenty years later (in 1876, after Melville had given up hope of earning a living through writing, lecturing or being posted at a consulate abroad, and had entered the Customs House in New York City, where he was appointed a deputy inspector—a position he held from 1866 to 1885). Returning to America in May 1857, a month after *The Confidence-Man* fell stillborn from the press, as it were, Melville resolved that he was "not going to write any more at present," as reported (with much relief) by his brother-in-law Lemuel Shaw, Jr. (Melville Log II: 580).

Miller asserts that the "despair and depression that gnaw at *Pierre* and suffuse 'Bartleby, the Scrivener' seem to reach their nadir in *The Confidence-Man*, on the surface a grim parable or dark joke which plays diabolical games around the words 'trust' and 'confidence'" (271). In his

---

[102] Ibid.

concise summary, the novel presents readers with

> [a] cross-section of Americans in the 1850s from all classes and professions—beggars, students, preachers, swindlers, intellectuals—are aboard a ship ironically named *Fidèle*, which sails from St. Louis down the Mississippi River. Although the narrator (perhaps himself some type of confidence man) speaks of his "variety of characters," the passengers—despite surface differences in class and education—are for the most part an undifferentiated mass, not even accorded the dignity or individuation a name bestows. (Ibid.)

However, this is not an artistic failure, as Miller has argued in his psychobiography of Melville,[103] but instead a deliberate strategy or style, an approach to characterization that illustrates Melville's discovery during this trying period of his life: what Tony Tanner called a shift from "reversibility" to "interchangeability," a shift that I will argue occurs midway through *The Confidence-Man*, which has gone unnoticed in the literature on this perplexing work, and which I will discuss at greater length later in this chapter.

"Quite an Original": *The Confidence-Man: His Masquerade*

The motley cross-section of American frontier society that makes up the bulk of passengers we meet on board the *Fidèle* is united in one great "monomania"—self-interest, as Miller rightly points out[104]—and it is into this milieu that the confidence man will arrive, assuming many disguises or masks, manipulating the passengers to his will as successfully as Ahab manipulates

---

[103] Edwin Haviland Miller, *Melville: A Biography*, 271.
[104] Ibid. (additional references to Miller will be cited parenthetically in this section)

the crew of the *Pequod*. But where Ahab by virtue of his position, the force of his will, charisma, and rhetoric imposes a unity of purpose upon the sailors, the confidence man instead "exacerbates and ultimately exploits the disunity or fragmentation in the lives of those aboard the *Fidèle*" (Ibid.). The setting of the novel, according to Miller, recalls Melville's own experiences in 1840, when he went West, to visit an uncle in Galena, Illinois, traveling as far as the Mississippi River. "At that time," as Miller rightly points out, Melville was "an ex-clerk, ex-teacher, a one-time sailor, and a former student of surveying. He had neither a livelihood nor the prospect of one" (272). He was, as Miller pointedly phrases it, "a nobody" (Ibid.). On that trip, Melville visited his father's brother, Thomas Melvill, a charming eccentric who could give the young man neither a job nor a model of confidence: for Uncle Thomas, it turns out, lived a confidence man-like existence, something hidden from his family back East, and young Herman returned to New York, in Miller's words, "still a nobody" (Ibid.). Dependent upon his maternal relatives for support, yet again, but now afflicted with the "hypos," as he famously phrased it in *Moby-Dick*, Melville signed aboard a whaling ship at the end of the year, "an act of desperation" (Miller) which would eventually result in his masterwork.

The Confidence-Man, which brings this period of intense creativity full circle, initiated by Melville's whaling epic and his encounter with Hawthorne, itself opens "At sunrise on a first of April," or, in others words, at the birth of the day and of spring. In his biography of Melville, Miller notes how the pilgrims in *The Canterbury Tales* assemble in the same season ("Whan that Aprille with his shoures soote/The droghte of March hath perced to the roote"; 272). Some of Chaucer's pilgrims are hypocrites or medieval confidence men who crassly exploit for their ends those who naively or superficially trust in God and His institutions; however, their machinations are balanced by portraits of those who live lives of virtue. "In Chaucer's world

God still lives, and social or religious orders bind men together," Miller argues, while "[i]n Melville's world God is dead, the unity of self-interest separates and estranges, and the 'pilgrims' move not toward light or enlightenment but toward darkness or death" (Ibid.). The apparent "looseness" of the (episodic, seemingly meandering) narrative, on which I will have more to say, may also reflect the influence of Chaucer—and, as Miller notes, of Sebastian Brandt's Ship of Fools (273)—but, despite the fact that one tale could easily be substituted for another or the order of events altered, the "looseness" is in fact deceptive. For, as in the seeming chaos of *Pierre*, or—as Spanos has shown[105] —in the "errant art" of *Moby-Dick*, the book is under the firm control of an artist in full command of his powers. On one level, the book centers on suspicious "get rich quick" schemes, the kind that post-Bernie Madoff Americans may feel are eerily prescient or proleptic, yet beneath this layer is a profound examination of confidence or trust on a personal, psychological, even spiritual level. It is also, as we shall see in what follows, a deconstruction of the subject or individual.

The confidence man himself, as Miller notes, is "truly one of Melville's most dazzling creations, blending God and Satan, Ishmael and Ahab"—perhaps even the white whale, as well. Or we could say, with Miller, that he is "a dazzling cipher," a kind of mask behind which nothing exists, since he has no identity of his own: he assumes eight, perhaps nine disguises, ostensibly in order to expose the hollowness of society and man, but more crucially to illustrate Pierre's horrifying insight, cited earlier, that the world is "nothing but surface stratified upon surface" (*Pierre* 285). This parade of avatars or masks results in the fleecing of greedy passengers through various "get-rich-quick" schemes and worthless "medicine" to those who are

---

[105]   *The Errant Art of Moby-Dick*, 180–181.

desperately ill or hypochondriacs. It begins in St. Louis with the arrival of the confidence man, as a youth boards the *Fidèle*. "In appearance," Miller points out, "he is not unlike Melville's other handsome sailors, or even Billy Budd: 'His cheek was fair, his chin downy, his hair flaxen, his hat a white fur one, with a long fleecy nap.' He is accompanied neither by porter nor by friend. 'It was plain' we are informed, 'that he was, in the extremest sense of the word, a stranger'" (274). Miller asserts that the "very language that Melville employs foretells that this is to be, in some ways, the most estranged of all of Melville's 'Ishmaels'—Tomoo, Taji, Redburn, White-Jacket, Ishmael himself or Pierre," for "they at least bear names, even assumed ones or nicknames in some instances" (Ibid.). Worse still, this unnamed, mysterious youth is mute and must write enigmatic slogans on boards, which turn out upon examination to be biblical texts. "The passengers shrink from his petitions and questions, and even suspect that he uses the Bible for his own purposes," Miller tells us; they "answer his pleas for guidance with hostility, by projecting their suspicions and distrust upon him" (Ibid.).

The mute, "like an infant lacking the power of speech," in Miller words, "cannot even voice his pain" (Ibid.). When the confidence man later (re)appears as a man with a wooden leg, Melville has thus given visual form to his pain, and accordingly the man articulates the mute's despair in an angry outburst: "You fools!... you flock of fools, under this captain of fools, [in] this ship of fools!" In his rage, the man with the wooden leg points out "the fact that neither captain nor officers are in evidence, and that the *Fidèle* is, as it were, without authority or control" (Ibid.). For the first time in Melville's novels, Miller rightly points out, there is no father figure, no leader or tyrant who "at the very least provides a form of stability, even if it is a parody of familial structure or order" (Ibid.). The "Ishmael" figures in the earlier works often "define themselves in their rebellions against authority," but in *The Confidence-Man* "there is no way of achieving self-definition" (Ibid.). This is a key point, since Melville is here purposely withholding the comfort of a stable self, a sense of subjectivity or identity. As Melville writes of one of his characters, in this text the author himself "ponders the mystery of human subjectivity in general" (129). Black Guinea, a legless beggar (actually the confidence man in another disguise) epitomizes and underscores the situation at the very outset of the novel when he humbles himself according to grossly stereotyped language, "Oh sar, I am der dog widout massa" (10; qtd. in Ibid.). But in this and other instances of pidgin language he reveals a wisdom that eludes the others on board the *Fidèle*: they are not aware that they, too, are "widout massa," without a system of beliefs or any organizing principle that will produce confidence in themselves, in the world around them, in their fellow human beings, or in their own sense of identity. This "groundlessness," so to speak, is an important point, to which I will return.

Soon seemingly older and attired like the other passengers, the confidence man engages in polemical discussions and tricks the foolish passengers into self-damaging admissions, in a Socratic style, which several scholars have noted.[106] To take one example, in an exchange with a student who "ostentatiously displays a copy of Tacitus," the confidence man "turns his attack upon the author into a commentary upon the modern age":

> "Without confidence himself, Tacitus destroys it in all his readers. Destroys confidence, paternal confidence, of which God knows that there is in this world none to spare. For, comparatively inexperienced as you are, my dear young friend, did you never observe how little, very little, confidence there is? I mean between man and man—more particularly

---

[106] See, for example, Merton M. Sealts, Jr., "Melville and the Platonic Tradition," in *Pursuing Melville: 1940–1980* (Madison: University of Wisconsin Press, 1982): 326–327.

between stranger and stranger" (Ibid.)

The student proves too vain to understand the confidence man's point. Later, in conning a suspicious miser out of his money, the confidence man plays upon the man's greed so artfully that, "falling back now like an infant," the elderly miser finally cries out like a child: "I confide, I confide; help, friend, my distrust!" (Ibid.). This regression to an infantile state, noted by Miller, continues in several of the other swindles: as the "Natural Bone-Setter," for example, or in the role of the Herb Doctor, the confidence man offers his most acute diagnosis of the malaise afflicting the passengers aboard the *Fidèle*: "gladly seek the breast of that confidence begot in the tender time of your youth, blessed beyond telling if it returns to you in age." The passenger who wants a bottle of medicine to relieve his bodily pain, not a prescription for his psychic well being, makes the common-sense reply—"Go back to nurse again, eh? Second childhood, indeed. You are soft" (Ibid.). But he is unaware that what the confidence man is doing, what Melville is doing through this character, is reversing the roles of parent and child, the very order of time and chronology itself, thereby attacking one of the pillars of subjectivity.

Although on the surface it might seem a contradiction for the confidence man himself to be the one who attempts to establish bonds of mutual trust, understanding and friendship among the strangers aboard the ship (as Miller points out, particularly in the second half of the novel, when he is known as "the cosmopolitan"), it is in fact part of Melville's deeper purpose for this "masquerade." In two scenes, "the cosmopolitan" (here named "Charlie Noble") attempts to establish comradely relationships—first, with a character named Frank Goodman, who some critics have identified with Hawthorne, and later with a young philosopher called Egbert, who is said to be a fictional portrait of Henry David Thoreau (along with his master, Mark Winsome, said to be a caricature of Emerson). In both episodes, as Miller notes, Noble alone reveals emotion: "with longing eyes," "eying him in tenderness," and "lovingly leaning towards him" (276). "Although he may be counterfeiting sentiment, his tender advances" should remind us of those of "Tommo to Marnoo, for example, or Redburn to Bolton and Carlo, Ishmael to Queequeg, or Pierre to Glen Stanly" (Ibid.). But it appears that the time for such "fraternal familiarities of youth" (as Melville had earlier phrased it) has passed: in each case the relationship collapses when Noble or Egbert (and Winsome) reveal their true intentions or feelings. "Rosy boys," as Miller rightly points out, "have now become suspicious men" (Ibid.)—or, perhaps more accurately, "con men." In one of the reported tales embedded within the larger narrative, a character named Orchis (Greek for "testicle," we should note) convinces a younger friend, China Aster, to invest in spermaceti tallow for his candles—both of which should be deeply resonant to readers of *Moby-Dick*, particularly its remarkable, homoerotic "Squeeze of the Hand" sequence—and gives him money for this purpose, promising him that it can be repaid "whenever it is convenient." "But Orchis turns out to be a crafty money-lender," in Miller's words, "and eventually forces China Aster into bankruptcy and ruin" (Ibid.).

This tortured, extended treatment of the theme of friendship in *The Confidence-Man* should take on a much deeper resonance when we consider it against the backdrop of Melville's "estrangement" (dramatic or not) with Hawthorne, an important point emphasized in Miller's biography. Beginning in 1839, there are pictures of successful friendships between "brothers" in *Typee*, *Redburn*, and *Moby-Dick*, or even between "fathers and sons" in *Omoo*, *Mardi*, and *White-Jacket*. The theme—following Miller, who employs a phrase from Melville, "fraternal familiarity"—achieves its fullest, happiest development in the so-called "honeymoon" of Ishmael and Queequeg. However, as Miller notes, there then comes an abrupt change. In *Pierre* for the first time friendship "turns to ashes" in Glen Stanly's betrayal, which first takes place in the hellish metropolis; Bartleby "prefers not to" accept the lawyer's advances; and the "friendship" between Benito Cereno and his slave Babo is of course, as Miller aptly phrases it, "a brutal fraud" (Ibid.). Israel Potter fares no better, and is betrayed by almost everyone with whom he comes in contact—most significantly by Benjamin Franklin. Finally, in *The Confidence-Man* there are—again, as Miller points out—"no real connections, only charades" (Ibid.). Perhaps here, the reality of his situation—his utter isolation, his desperate circumstances—was becoming plain to Melville, and this, it can safely be assumed, is somehow reflected in his work.

Accordingly, in Miller's analysis, after *Moby-Dick*, Melville's foundlings or orphans are "truly orphaned" (277), which seems to lend support to the theory that Hawthorne's departure from the Berkshires upset Melville to a great extent, driving a final nail into the coffin of his career as a public author (it must be noted, of course, that he tried his hand at lecturing, then poetry, before resigning himself to the fact that he would never again be considered a successful, working writer). It has been suggested, though poorly supported, that Orchis, who drives China Aster into bankruptcy through his betrayal, is a fictional portrait of Hawthorne. Miller claims that, since China Aster dies shortly after his business failure "with a wandering mind," not unlike Allan Melvill in 1832, the tale "may also substantiate the thesis that Hawthorne's 'betrayal' replicated" Melville's father's (277). Whether Orchis or Noble is inspired by Hawthorne will remain speculative; however, Miller's point that the name of the ship of fools in Melville's final novel "recalls a Hawthorne tale" which Melville found "deep as Dante," and from which, in that review he wrote after their meeting in 1850, "Hawthorne and His Mosses," he quoted a passage that "in some respects reverberates throughout *The Confidence-Man*" is an important one: "'Faith!' shouted Goodman Brown, in a voice of agony and desperation; and the echoes of the forest mocked him, crying—'Faith! Faith!' as if bewildered wretches were seeking her all through the wilderness." In fact, Melville will further develop this theme—"bewildered wretches [...] seeking for [Faith] all through the wilderness"—in his epic poem, *Clarel*, published in 1876. And it is not by chance that this late work also features a character that seems clearly inspired by Hawthorne ("Vine").

The last scene of *The Confidence-Man*—which is also the last joke in this darkly humorous novel—occurs at night on the same day (April Fool's) that the story had begun, in a cabin in which an old man sits at a white marble table, while in the bunks about the room other passengers sleep. The man, a retired farmer, is spotlighted by "a solar lamp [...] whose shade of ground glass was all round fancifully variegated, in transparency, with the image of a horned altar" (278). The lighting creates "a halo" about the man as he sits reading the Bible. The confidence man enters and soon is confounding (or conning) the old gentleman with quotations from the (apocryphal) Ecclesiasticus, "which advise distrust of, rather than confidence in, mankind" (Ibid.). "After the farmer recovers from this unexpected attack upon the authority and consistency of the Bible," in Miller's summary (Ibid.), the two find themselves in agreement that, as the old man puts it, "to distrust the creature, is a kind of distrusting of the Creator"—which is, of course, a reinterpretation of the biblical passages that soon becomes hypocrisy when a "juvenile peddler" enters carrying "a miniature mahogany door." Melville is here, as Miller shows us, "cluttering the scene with parodies of biblical passages" (Ibid.). "Go thy ways with thy toys, child," the old man says to the youth, but soon he is conned into buying one toy after another, since his trust in mankind is "purely verbal rather than genuine"—first, the peddler sells a lock to keep thieves out; then, a money belt, which in appearance resembles a truss. As a "gift" the youth hands the old man a "*Counterfeit Detector*," a book that will supposedly protect him against con-men. "Go, child—go, go!" the farmer orders; "Yes, child,—yes, yes," the boy replies in "roguish parody." "The old man has the naivety of youth, and the child the wisdom of age, in yet another Melvillean reversal" (278), as Miller aptly phrases it, that repeats the subversion of time and chronology we saw in the opening scene of the novel. The two—child and old man—are as one, however, in one aspect: their lack of confidence, with the boy at least being "the more honest of the two about the matter" (Ibid.). This doubling is precisely, as will be shown later in this chapter, what Tanner means by "reversibility"—taken to its absolute limit in *The Confidence-Man*, where it is transformed into what Tanner calls "interchangeability." I will turn to these concepts after finishing this summary of the text.

Some critics, as Miller notes, have devised elaborate allegorical explanations of this final scene, "describing the old man as the Past, the Old God or the Modern Christian, and the youth as Young America, Prometheus, or a latter-day Christian who accepts the death of God;" however, for Miller, this scene is a "cruel reduction ad absurdum [...] an endlessly repeating cycle of the same terrifying masquerade [...] an endless cycle of nothingness" (279). I read this "endlessly repeating cycle" in a very different way, as will become clear later in this chapter, but must credit Miller with bringing our attention to this phenomenon. He also makes a very important point, concerning the depersonalized language Melville employs in this novel, in the following observation: "The suggestiveness of this last episode [...] is reinforced, as is generally the case in Melville's writing, by the style itself. Here in *The Confidence-Man* there are no rococo flourishes, stylistic involutions, and parodistic literary cadences such as one finds in *Pierre*. Absent too are the exclamation points which reflect the overstated, overanxious idealism and despair of [...] *White-Jacket*." Likewise, he argues that the "noncharacters" (meaning the parade of avatars and masks, both perpetrators and victims) in *The Confidence-Man* are "denied the grandeur accorded to Ahab even in his maddest flights of self-aggrandizement." "Instead," Miller claims, "the sentences and paragraphs often resemble a lawyer's brief, studded with precedents from the past and twisting in short units to make logical what at bottom is illogical or playing upon words and meaning supposedly for the sake of clarification but actually for purposes of obfuscation." To illustrate this point, Miller then quotes the following paragraph, which "is not uncharacteristic":

> Which animation, by the way, might seem more or less out of character in the man in gray, considering his unsprightly manner when first introduced, had he not already in certain after colloquies, given proof, in some degree, of the fact, that, with certain natures, a soberly continent air at times, so far from arguing emptiness of stuff, is good proof it is there, and plenty of it, because unwasted, and may be used the more effectively, too, when opportunity offers. What now follows on the part of the man in gray will still further exemplify, perhaps somewhat strikingly, the truth, or what appears to be such, of this remark. (CM 38)

As Miller points out, the style is "unwarmed by compassion," or, to phrase it in terms of Melville's deliberate strategy or style, it is as cold, depersonalized, anonymous and detached as are the "strangers" aboard the ship. Although Richard Chase has argued that the style and the book are unified in "a dialectical movement of ideas,"[107] the Socratic or "dialectical movement" in fact breaks down midway through the narrative, with the arrival of the cosmopolitan. And the impersonality of the style and the intrusions of the narrator at intervals to comment upon the nature of fiction and art— intrusions or "insertions" that I argue are important, and will examine later in this chapter, but which critics like Miller, Branch or Parker wish to either

---

[107] "Melville's Confidence Man," *The Kenyon Review*, Vol. 11, No. 1 (Winter 1949): 137; qtd. in Miller, 280.

explain away or completely expunge—create the impression that the author is a confidence-man, if not in fact "the Confidence-Man" of the title.

Miller's reading is also highly instructive in that it is representative in terms of its efforts to "reoedipalize" Melville (in other words, explaining his fiction by recourse to his biography and "repressed" childhood memories), as the following comment makes clear: "The parable he [the narrator] tells is not fiction so much as autobiography in fictional form," with the death of Allan Melvill "cheat[ing] Herman of the paternal blessing and conned him of confidence" (280). Miller also draws upon a passage that Melville rejected, titled "The River," which is then (yet again) read in terms of parricidal wish-fulfillment, oedipal rivalry and betrayal. Miller even goes so far as to argue that the final scene is "an enactment of the oedipal drama," which he points out "occurs at the very hour at which Allan had died in 1832" (281). It is also read as "an attack upon an audience which had rejected him," which very well may be true to a certain extent, but the way that Miller links the final scene involving the chamber-pot, which the old man carries, and other scenes related to the buttocks or posterior in Melville's other work goes too far, as is the case with his highly questionable readings of the words "behind" and "rear" in selected passages of *The Confidence-Man* (281–282). For Miller, this signifies Melville's coming full circle, from the queen showing her buttocks to the French in *Typee*, Melville's first novel, to the old man and his bedpan in this final scene and chapter of *The Confidence-Man*, Melville's final novel—all symbols associated with "disease, dysfunctioning, and death" (282), which he [Miller] links to Melville's repressed homosexuality, "self-hatred" and unresolved Oedipal issues. In other words, how his love—of Jack Chase, of Hawthorne and of his father, Allan Melvill—turned into a self-defensive aggression and "hatred," which culminated in *The Confidence-Man*—and with Melville himself coming, in 1856, very "close to self-annihilation" (283). In the section that follows, I argue against this reading, drawing upon Parker, who has noted Melville's peculiar choice of word, "annihilation," in his seemingly off-hand remark to Hawthorne, which surely echoes Milton, particularly given the two authors' familiarity with and admiration of his work. Before doing so, however, I will first examine the structure of the novel, followed by an analysis of the three "intrusions" by the narrator on the subject of writing and of "originality" in fiction. I will then conclude by discussing Melville's enigmatic remark to Hawthorne in their final meeting, and show how this helps us make sense of Melville's later work, especially the poetry.

Melville, as stated at the outset of this chapter, had most likely been inspired to write *The Confidence-Man* after reading about the exploits of a real-life swindler, one active in New York City in the summer of 1849 (while Melville was there, composing *Redburn* and *White-Jacket*) and then, once again, in the Albany-area six years later, where he was dubbed the "Original Confidence Man." Articles about this man, who had called himself "Samuel Willis" while in Albany, had begun reappearing in both Albany and Springfield (Massachusetts) newspapers in 1855, while Melville was living in Pittsfield, roughly halfway between the two cities.[108] As Branch points out, there are several ways in which Melville's fictional character resembles the real-life confidence man—the most obvious example being his practice of asking his prospective dupes, "are you disposed to put any confidence in me?" before requesting money—and it seems highly probable that Melville based his novel, at least in part, on the exploits of this "original confidence man," all of which were well-reported in the newspapers of the time.[109]

---

[108] Watson G. Branch, "The Genesis, Composition, and Structure of The Confidence-Man," *Nineteenth-Century Fiction*, Vol. 27, No. 4 (March, 1973): 426–7; also noted by Bergmann and Foster: see Branch, n. 8 and 9, page 427.

[109] See Branch, 427–8.

But Melville of course improved on "real life" by having his confidence man appear in a series of avatars, first announced by a beggar named "Black Guinea," himself one of the avatars, and then establishing a pattern of relatively brief encounters between them and their victims, all of which significantly deepened the allegorical meaning of the text. That he intended all the avatars to be manifestations of the confidence man becomes clear when the reader, remembering that the novel is subtitled, "His Masquerade," notes that each avatar replaces his predecessor (usually following Black Guinea's list), that no two avatars appear together, and that one avatar frequently uses double entendres to suggest his identity with the others. According to Branch, "Melville in the first part of the book was focusing sharply on the transitions between the avatars and on the intricately worked connections—thematic, narrative, structural, verbal—among them;" however, "[n]ear the middle of the book the pattern begins to break down, and it completely collapses in the second part when the cosmopolitan enters" (429). Branch argues, rather unconvincingly, for a four-part structure to the novel, claiming that Melville "abandon[ed] the original structural pattern midway in *The Confidence-Man*" and "made his usual late insertions of generally extrinsic material, which is not fully integrated into the story" (Ibid). However, as with Parker, Bryant and other critics searching for the Ur-text (which would somehow reflect Melville's "original intentions" in writing these texts, prior to "his usual late insertions") by trying to recreate the chronological order in which the manuscript was composed, we may disagree with Branch's highly speculative account, and instead follow the lead of H. Bruce Franklin[110] and other scholars who see *The Confidence-Man* as, in fact, a tightly structured, two-part or diptych-like

---

[110] H. Bruce Franklin, *The Wake of the Gods: Melville's Mythology* (Stanford: Stanford University Press, 1963).

narrative—a structure that, we should recall, Melville had used before to great effect, as discussed earlier.

Indeed, it is not difficult to discern an overall pattern or structure to this text, and to see that the central figures in the successive chapters, the various avatars of the confidence man, are as follows: (1) in chapter one, the deaf-mute, promoting biblical charity; (2) in chapters two and three, Black Guinea, begging for money; (3) in chapters four and five, "the man with a weed," John Ringman, in mourning and soliciting aid from strangers; (4) in chapters six through eight, the man in a gray coat and white hat, representing the Seminole Widow and Orphan Asylum and promoting the World's Charity; (5) in chapters nine through fifteen, the man with a book, John Truman, president of the Black Rapids Coal Company, who encourages speculative investments; (6) in chapters sixteen through twenty-one, the herb-doctor, promoting his "Omni-Balsamic Reinvigorator" and "Samaritan Pain Dissuader"; and to close the first half of the narrative, in chapters twenty-two and twenty-three, "the man with a brass plate," representing the Philosophical Intelligence Office ("P.I.O.") and promoting faith in the goodness of man. The second half of the narrative follows the exploits of "the cosmopolitan," Frank Goodman, who promotes trust in and love of one's fellow man on all levels—perhaps cynically, perhaps sincerely, it is not clear—and who is, in an important role reversal, duped by various characters on board the *Fidèle*. My main focus, in what follows, will be placed upon the two-part structure of the novel and Melville's "insertions" concerning writing. These will in turn help support my readings of the "minor" work of this period of Melville's career, shedding light as well on the still-misunderstood poetry of his later years.

As Franklin describes it, "at the end of Chapter 23, which marks the exact center of the forty-five chapters in *The Confidence-Man*, there is a 'cordial slap on the shoulder,' and a voice 'sweet as a seraph's'" announces the entrance of "the cosmopolitan," whose appearance "divides [the novel] precisely into two halves" (164). The entire movement of the text is reversed at this point, as this final avatar of the confidence man "gives away two shillings and receives no money from anyone." In other words, he goes from swindler to victim. Goodman, also known as "the cosmopolitan," seeks to expose the true nature of his interlocutors and their philosophies of life. He asks for nothing, expects no money, yet engages in debate and even confronts the various confidence man who attempt to swindle him and other passengers. As Branch notes, "Melville had," in the first part of the book, "closely connected the avatars;" whereas, here, "in the second part he closely connected the cosmopolitan's interlocutors" (435). For Branch, this is an error on Melville's part, since it is "confusing" for the reader, representing a "breakdown in the book's initial structural pattern of maintaining a sequence [based upon Black Guinea's list] of avatars" (436). For Franklin, on the other hand, *The Confidence-Man* is Melville's "most nearly perfect work," most of all in its structure, which Melville carefully mapped out, without a "wasted or misplaced word" (153)—in sharp contrast, for example, to his earlier "major" novels, *Moby-Dick* or *Pierre*, which are marked by digression and puzzling (to critics like Branch, Bryant and Parker) "insertions" like "The Town-Ho's Story" or "Young America in Literature." If we examine the structure a bit more carefully, we will in fact find that Franklin's reading is much more productive.

The episodes at the end of the novel (when the cosmopolitan encounters, first, the barber, who appeared at the very start of the story, and then the old man and the boy peddler) are balanced by the episode at the beginning (in which the mute confronts the crowd), thereby forming a frame for the narrative. In chapter one, with its "advent," the mute, appearing at sunrise "suddenly as Manco Capac" boards the *Fidèle* and displays a slate with quotations about charity from I Corinthians 13: "charity" is a principal theme in the novel and is the ideal preached (and preyed upon) by the confidence man to set up his victims. In chapter forty-five, with its "apocalypse," the cosmopolitan, dispensing "a sort of morning through the night," enters the cabin like a "bridegroom" (241) and reads from Ecclesiasticus the warnings not to trust men, even friends: friendship and trust are the principal themes of the cosmopolitan's debates throughout the second half of the book but are now made cast under a dark, even ironic shadow. The novel ends ambiguously, with the old man and boy peddler either victims or swindlers of the cosmopolitan—perhaps even both. We must also note the barber episodes, which likewise frame the narrative, placed as they are at the beginning and end of the novel (noted above and by Branch 437), and the manner in which the cosmopolitan becomes, through his brilliant colors and motley dress, the veritable sum of all his previous appearances or incarnations: "the stranger sported a vesture barred with various hues, that of the cochineal predominating, in style participating of a Highland plaid, Emir's robe, and French blouse; from its plaited sort of front peeped glimpses of a flowered regatta-shirt, while, for the rest, white trousers of ample duck flowed over maroon-colored slippers, and a jaunty smoking-cap of regal purple crowned him off at top" (131). In this finery, in other words, the cosmopolitan announces the universality of his nature, describing himself thus: "A cosmopolitan, a catholic man; who, being such, ties himself to no narrow tailor or teacher, but federates, in heart as in costume, something of the various gallantries of men under various suns. Oh, one roams not over the gallant globe in vain. Bred by it, is a fraternal and fusing feeling" (132). We must also recognize the fact that the novel begins "[a]t sunrise" (3), "on a first of April," (significantly, noted only in this first chapter and in the final one), and ends in darkness: chapter forty-five begins with a description of a "solar lamp" which had not been extinguished because "the commands of the captain required it to be kept burning till the natural light of day should come to relieve it" (240), but it ends with Goodman, the cosmopolitan, "extinguish[ing]" it (251).

Outside the arc of this narrative, sketched above, there are three unusual moments in *The Confidence-Man* where Melville pauses to reflect upon the craft of writing and the concept of originality, particularly in terms of characterization. These reflections, even digressions (or, as Branch or Parker would no doubt have it, "insertions") are contained in three chapters with unwieldy, exceedingly enigmatic titles—14 ("Worth the consideration of those to whom it may prove worth considering"), 33 ("Which may pass for whatever it may prove to be worth"), and 44 (best known as "Quite an original," though the full title is, in fact, quite a mouthful: "In which the last three words of the last chapter ['quite an original'] are made the text of discourse, which will be sure of receiving more or less attention from those readers who do not skip it"). These meta-fictional commentaries are indeed jarring, in terms of tone and voice (with the narrator or author addressing, even criticizing or mocking the reader directly) as well as pacing, since they interrupt the flow of the story, and one is tempted to see them as "late insertions," otherwise extraneous musings that have little to do with the narrative arc. Indeed, they seem to detract from the artistry of the work, overall, and one wonders why Melville felt the need to include them. As with the reflections on "Young America in Literature," Hershel Parker sees them in entirely negative terms, and argues that they be stricken from this already fragmented novel, much as he had argued (and done) with *Pierre*. In the brief section that follows, I want to address the significance of these meta-textual asides and show, contrary to Parker, how they are in fact deeply significant, in a sense helping him to formulate his discovery concerning the nature of subjectivity, while helping us better understand this late-phase of Melville's "middle period," pointing as they do toward the later work (especially Melville's still-poorly understood poetry).

In the first meditation (chapter 14), Melville considers the "problem" of inconsistency in characterization. He begins by discussing a character in the previous chapter, one of the dupes of the confidence man—"He may be thought inconsistent, and even so he is"—before asking, "But for this, is the author to be blamed?" "True," he continues,

> "it may be urged that there is nothing a writer of fiction should more carefully see to, as there is nothing a sensible reader will more carefully look for, than that, in the depiction of any character, its consistency should be preserved. But this, though at first blush, seeming reasonable enough, may, upon a closer view, prove not so much so. For how does it couple with another requirement—equally insisted upon, perhaps—that, while to all fiction is allowed some play of invention, yet, fiction based on fact should never be contradictory to it; and is it not a fact, that, in real life, a consistent character is a *rara avis*?" (69)

Here, Melville is arguing for fiction mirroring the inconsistencies and irrationality of "real life," which seems ordinary enough; however, he continues by saying that "[i]f reason be judge, no writer has produced such inconsistent characters as nature herself has. It must call for no small sagacity in a reader unerringly to discriminate in a novel between the inconsistencies of conception and those of life" (70), before recounting the famous example of the duck-billed "beaver" (platypus) of Australia, which confounded naturalists in England when it was discovered, since it belonged to no known species or classification. Melville then makes a parallel argument concerning "a studious youth" who has been "poring over the best novels professing to portray human nature"—an example that should call to mind Pierre upon his expulsion from the Eden of Saddle Meadows—finding himself lost "upon actually entering the world." The young man had imagined himself furnished with what he took to be a "true delineation," as "a stranger entering, map in hand, Boston town," yet he finds himself, much as Pierre does in New York City or young Redburn in Liverpool (with his father's long-out of date guidebook), "hopelessly lost" (71).

In the next reflection (chapter 33), Melville takes up the issue of unrealistic portrayals in fiction, once again commenting on a character from the previous chapter in anticipation of the reader's criticism. "How unreal is all this!" he imagines the reader objecting; "Who did ever dress or act like your cosmopolitan? And who, it might be returned, did ever dress or act like a harlequin?" (182). Melville then argues for the freedom of the author to take liberties with "real life", remarking that it is "[s]trange, that in a work of amusement, this severe fidelity to real life should be exacted by anyone, who, by taking up such a work, sufficiently shows that he is not unwilling to drop real life, and turn, for a time, to something different" (182). Such readers, Melville claims, are being inconsistent or illogical: "in books of fiction, they look not only for more entertainment, but, at bottom, even for more reality, than real life itself can show;" "[t]hus," he continues, "though they want novelty, they want nature, too; but nature unfettered, exhilarated, in effect transformed." "In this way of thinking," he concludes, "the people in a fiction, like the people in a play, must dress as nobody exactly dresses, talk as nobody exactly talks, act as nobody exactly acts. It is as with fiction as with religion: it should present another world, and yet one to which we feel the tie" (183).

The most important reflection, however, occurring in chapter 44, itself a profound meditation on the concept of "originality," is as follows:

"QUITE AN ORIGINAL:" A phrase, we fancy, rather oftener used by the young, or the unlearned, or the untraveled, than by the old, or by the well-read, or the man who has made the grand tour. Certainly, the sense of originality exists at its highest in an infant, and probably at its lowest in him who has completed the circle of the sciences. As for original characters in fiction, a grateful reader will, on meeting with one, keep the anniversary of that day. True, we sometimes hear of an author who, at one creation, produces some two or three score such characters; it may be possible. But they can hardly be original in the sense that Hamlet is, or

Don Quixote, or Milton's Satan. That is to say, they are not, in a thorough sense, original at all. They are novel, or singular, or striking, or captivating, or all four at once. More likely, they are what are called odd characters; but for that, are no more original, than what is called an odd genius, in his way, is. (238)

The truly "original" character is, for Melville, a "rarity," a prodigy [...] as in real history is a new law-giver, a revolutionzing philosopher, or the founder of a new religion" (239). What is normally interpreted as a mark of originality in a character is, in fact, "something personal—confined to itself." Melville explains that this type of character "sheds not its characteristic on its surroundings, whereas, the original character, essentially such, is like a revolving Drummond light, raying away from itself all round it—everything is lit by it, everything starts up to it (mark how it is with Hamlet), so that, in certain minds, there follows upon the adequate conception of such a character, an effect, in its way, akin to that which in Genesis attends upon the beginning of things" (Ibid.). As mentioned earlier, Melville is here "ponder[ing] the mystery of human subjectivity in general" (129) and to this topic we now must turn. What, exactly, is Melville saying in these curious, seemingly digressive or aleatory chapters?

One way to explore the notion of individuality, "originality" or subjectivity that is interrogated in these chapters is to look more closely at the concept of "originality," which would imply the related ideas of the "original" and the "copy." Deleuze allows us a way into this problem—that of the "original" versus the "copy," if you will—and in the brief section that follows, I want to look at his formulation of the concept of the simulacrum. This seems especially pertinent in discussing Melville's "masquerade" in *The*

Confidence-Man.[111] Deleuze was, as is well known, a staunch and highly original critic of what he termed the "history of philosophy," or philosophy as traditionally conceived (grounded in a certain reading of Plato and Aristotle, and continuing through Kant and Hegel; a tradition that is in fact grounded in a denial of the simulacrum); in his project, which involved a concerted effort to "overturn Platonism," he attempted to bring together several "minor" or heretical thinkers—Lucretius, for example, Duns Scotus, Spinoza, Nietzsche, Bergson. Provocatively and productively locating elements from within both Plato and Kant's work that threatens to undo their larger projects—and, thereby, displacing them in the so-called "history of philosophy", as avatars of their respective systems ("Platonism", "Kantianism"), which, in fact, form a single tradition (what Deleuze calls "the dogmatic image of thought")— Deleuze's overall project was nothing less than to make thought "dangerous" again, to recover thought as "misosophy" (rather than "philosophy", ruled by the concept of *philein*, friendship or love), to affirm what he called "the powers of the false" and, in the process, to break with the "history of philosophy" as traditionally conceived. Viewed from this perspective, Plato and Kant can indeed be seen as "friends," with Kant extending the Platonic conception of "Dialectics" (as Aristotle, according to Deleuze, interpreted it for all who came after him), based upon a concept of Identity and agreement (or harmony); in fact, Kant's Critical project, taken as a whole, can be seen as nothing but an attempt to produce this agreement, synthesis or harmony, be it among the Faculties or between Nature and Freedom (through the Aesthetic).

For Deleuze, however, and in stark contrast to the above, "Dialectics,"

---

[111]   Significantly, a text that Deleuze explores with his sometime collaborator Félix Guattari in *What is Philosophy?* Trans. Hugh Tomlinson and Graham Burchell (New York: Columbia University Press, 1994): 65–66, and 83.

mistakenly conceived as some sort of "science" with the aim of producing agreement or Identity, via *Aufhebung* or some species of "synthesis" traditionally conceived (I say "traditionally conceived" because Deleuze will speak, in *Difference and Repetition*, of an "asymmetrical synthesis"), from a certain Plato (read through Aristotle), through Hegel, to a certain Kant (one disregarding the Kant of the "Analytic of the Sublime," Deleuze's "Lear-like" Kant), and even Martin Heidegger (who does not, in the end, "escape" this logic or image of thought), and the task of philosophy as a whole, must be built upon encounters between or among enemies, based upon disagreement, Difference, disparity and discord. Plato and Kant, at least in their donnish, "academic" guises (as founders of "Platonism" or "Kantianism"), are no "friends" of Deleuze, and it is imperative that we see exactly why that is. For it is in this Nietzscheo-Deleuzian—and, ultimately, Melvillian—parodic manner that "literature" may, as well, once again become "dangerous." It is certain that critics felt this way about *The Confidence-Man* upon its publication, and the text still possesses an enormous subversive potential.

To that end—in other words, to explore how this text is "dangerous"—in and through what follows, I will first focus upon Deleuze's reading of Plato's aporetic dialogues (*Theaetetus* and the *Sophist*, in particular) over and against more "canonical" or "foundational" dialogues (the *Republic* will serve as my example), assuming the reader's familiarity with Deleuze's reading of the Kantian Critical project refracted (or, indeed, "fractured") through the "Analytic of the Sublime" (found in *the Critique of Judgment*), as well as his dissertation, in particular what has been published as *Difference and Repetition* and *Logic of Sense*, which seems to me to accomplish less an "overturning" of either "Platonism" or "Kantianism" than a subversion of these systems (regimes) of thought (again, as traditionally conceived), from within those very systems. If there are indeed "breaks" within this continuum of thought (again, what Deleuze calls the "dogmatic image of thought"), then Deleuze certainly marks, or at the very least gestures toward, one such break—with the caveat that he never made grandiose claims (a la Heidegger) of "overcoming" or "escaping" metaphysics as a whole. Deleuze's accomplishment was much less, and at the same time, much more than that. And this is precisely why he emphasized "Immanence" over "Transcendence" and characterized his own work as that of "Empiricism," rather than "Metaphysics." For Deleuze, the task of "misosophy" is to subvert the "dogmatic image of thought" and the concept of Identity upon which it relies, as well as the apparatus of representation it engenders (along with a certain Platonism, qua mimesis), by realizing a true "philosophy of Difference" grounded in Nietzsche's Eternal Return and simulacra, or phantasms (not to be confused with "degraded copies," as in mimesis), thereby opening a path for Art, Literary or otherwise, in this subversion. Melville's work, particularly *The Confidence-Man*, follows this path.

For Plato, at least the "canonical" Plato handed down to us via the "history of philosophy," the relationship between *Eidos* and *Mimesis* is absolutely central: Ideas, set apart from the sensible world, are entirely self-productive, the origins of themselves (later they become the *Ding-an-sich*, or the "Noumenal" realm, for Kant); Art, firmly rooted as it is in the sensible world, is understood as mimetic, as mere imitations or copies of Forms or Ideas (again, for Kant, this becomes the "Phenomenal" world). Already, at the very "origin" of the history of philosophy, we have division: *Eidos* (sometimes called *Paradeigma*) versus *Mimesis*; *Episteme* (Knowledge) versus *Doxa* (Opinion); Being versus Becoming; the Intelligible versus the Sensible; the True (or Real) versus the False (or Illusory); even (morally) "good" mimesis versus "bad" mimesis (this is variously described throughout Plato's dialogues, but especially in the *Republic*, Part VII). As Jacques Derrida and others have taught us, in such a "binary opposition" one term is necessarily privileged over the other. In Plato's philosophy, the Ideal (Being) is always given pride of place over the Sensible (Becoming). The task of philosophy and the "true philosopher," therefore, is to love Truth, hate the False, and learn to distinguish between the two. Naturally, this sets the Sophists (itinerant dialecticians-for-hire, so to speak) of Plato's day on the far side of this division: for Plato, speaking through Socrates, the Sophist is a "dangerous" figure, one whose falsehoods must be contained, as in contagion—and "true" philosophers and artists are first and foremost concerned with the health of the *polis*, through strict maintenance of the division between the True and the False.

However, we can already see a crack in the Platonic armature, which Deleuze will fully exploit: when Plato/Socrates attempts to define the Good, for example, he is at a loss, first attempting to define it in contrast to what it is not, in other words, through contradiction and division, but later, when that fails, he has recourse to a tautology (namely, "the Good is Knowledge"—but "what is Knowledge?" Why, "the Good," of course!). He then lapses into simile or analogy, even myth: hence, the various, awkward allegories of the Sun, the Divided Line and the Cave. This is a common move for Plato/Socrates, particularly when pressed for definitions, for descriptions of the essence of the terms they have been dividing throughout the dialogue: in the *Republic* we have the "Myth of Er" when Socrates is pressed to describe the immortality of the soul (and here, we must recall that, years later, Kant takes this for a given, upon which his whole philosophy hinges at one point); in the *Statesman*, when the meaning of the statesman as "shepherd of men" ends in myth; as does the *Phaedrus*, wherein the definition of delirium, particularly the delirium of true love, is sought.

As Deleuze points out in *the Logic of Sense* (as well as in *Difference and Repetiton*), among the three great dialogues dealing with this operation of "division," namely the *Phaedrus*, the *Statesman*, and the *Sophist*, only the last does not end in recourse to myth (and to this, I would add the *Theaetetus*, which is similarly concerned with division, and ends in suspension and irony, as Deleuze says of the *Sophist*). As Deleuze phrases it, in a difficult passage that must be quoted in full:

> How are we to explain [...] that of the three important texts dealing with division—the *Phaedrus*, the *Statesman*, and the *Sophist*—the last one contains no founding myth? The reason is simple. In the *Sophist*, the method of division is employed paradoxically, not in order to evaluate the 'just pretenders' [or 'good copies' as Deleuze has defined Platonic *mimesis*, traditionally conceived], but, on the contrary, in order to track down the 'false pretender' as such, in order to define the being (or rather the nonbeing) of the simulacrum. The Sophist himself is the being of the simulacrum, the satyr or centaur, the Proteus who meddles and insinuates himself everywhere. For this reason, it may be that the end of the Sophist contains the most extraordinary adventure of Platonism: as a consequence of searching in the direction of the simulacrum and of leaning over its abyss, Plato discovers, in the flash of an instant, that *the simulacrum is not a false copy, but that it places in question the very notations of copy and model*. The final definition of the Sophist leads to the point where we can no longer distinguish him from Socrates himself—the ironist working in private by means of brief arguments. Was it not necessary to push irony to that extreme? Was it not Plato himself who pointed out the direction for the 'reversal of Platonism'? (*The Logic of Sense*, Appendix 1, "The Simulacrum and Ancient Philosophy," 256, emphasis added)

Here we have the virtual implosion of "Platonism," or at least the "understand[ing of] Platonic division on the basis of Aristotelian requirements" (*Difference and Repetition* 59), that is, based upon division without *mediation*, "measuring rivals and selecting claimants [...] distinguishing between things and their simulacra within a[n] [Aristotelian] pseudo-genus or a large species" (60). For Deleuze, "[o]verturning Platonism, then, means denying the primacy of original over copy, of model over image; glorifying the reign of simulacra and reflections [or phantasms]" (66)—or, we can add, alongside Melville in *The Confidence-Man*, of "masks." If we return to Foucault's point concerning the simulacrum (versus the copy), discussed earlier (in relation to *Pierre*), we might see what Melville is doing here. Foucault claims that "similitude circulates the simulacrum as an indefinite and reversible relation of the similar to the similar" (44); if this is true, then instead of a hierarchical relation among elements, we have a reversible one—a more equal or democratic one. In essence, any element can take the place of any other. Pierre's discovery of this leads to his dissolution, as a subject, and ultimately to his death; the dizzying masquerade of the confidence-man ends with the mysterious "cosmopolitan" pointing the way toward what Deleuze called "the triumph of the false" over the Model and Copy (which would mean over Platonism, over the order of Representation and Mimesis). If we accept this, then Melville's radical concepts of democracy and freedom, egalitarianism and will (or desire) should come into sharper focus.

What Deleuze accomplished in his subsequent study of Kant (which is beyond the scope of this study)—a "book on an enemy" as he himself described it—was an "un-working" of "Kantianism" from within Kant, much as he illuminated the path toward an "un-working" of "Platonism" from within Plato. He succeeded in showing how Kant can be seen as a "Nietzschean inventor of concepts," an anti-Dialectical Kant (Kant as the anti-Plato or anti-Hegel). As he traced the movement of Kant's thought, characterizing it as a move "from Hamlet to Lear"—from the theme of the "separation which reunites" in the first Critique to the "discord which produces accord" in the third and mightiest Critique—Deleuze shows how the unregulated exercise of all the Faculties would come to define future philosophy (qua "misosophy"), just as Rimbaud's "systematic disorder of all the senses" defined poetry after him.

In short, Deleuze's practice of "misosophy," which must operate by means other than the "dogmatic image of thought" that dominates the "history of philosophy," overturns both "Platonism" (qua philosophy of the Ideal) and "Kantianism" (qua philosophy of the Subject and Reason), or, rather, shows how they implode from within. He accomplishes this by demonstrating how, in order to "reverse Platonism," we must

> make the simulacra rise and to affirm their rights among icons and copies. The problem no longer has to do with the distinction Essence-Appearance or Model-Copy. This distinction operates completely within the world of representation. Rather, it has to do with undertaking the subversion of this world—the 'twilight of the idols'. The simulacrum is not a degraded copy. It harbors a positive power which denies the original and the copy [as the non-distinction between the Sophist and Socrates affirms the power of the *Pseudos*, the False], the model and the reproduction... [It is] a Dionysian machine. It involves the false as power, *Pseudos*, in the sense in which Nietzsche speaks of the highest power of the false. By rising to the surface, the simulacrum makes the Same and the Similar, the model and the copy, fall under the power of the false (phantasm)... It establishes the world of nomadic distribution and crowned anarchies... in order to institute the chaos which creates, making the simulacra function and raising a phantasm... [thereby bringing about] the destruction of Platonism. (*Logic of Sense* 262–263, 266)

And in order to release the subversive, "Lear"-like Kant within "Kantianism," Deleuze points to the aforementioned "tempest in the depths of the chasm opened up in the Subject"; a Subject that has now "dissolved," so to speak. Deleuze, therefore, does not so much represent a "break" with the Platonic-Kantian tradition, but rather a "disjunctive continuation" of that tradition—ultimately, a subversive and ingenious one—which lays out the stakes of a true "philosophy of the future." As Nietzsche once wrote, "there are those who are born posthumously": we could easily see Deleuze as one of these "untimely ones," a precursor (like Zarathustra) who did not come from the Future, but who was the Future. And in that Future, prophet-like, he (or she) awaits us—we "people to come," to use Spinoza's language—as does Herman Melville, to whom we must now return, and who, as an untimely artist, would make (American) literature "dangerous" again, if only we knew how to read him. This is, in fact, nowhere more apparent than in "the masquerade" of interchangeable "identities" or simulacra of his still-misunderstood proto-"(post)modern" novel, *The Confidence-Man*.

How can we contextualize Melville's drama of masks or simulacra, within the larger scope of (American) literature? One possibility is by looking more closely at the work of the late Tony Tanner; specifically, a phenomenon that he argues is on display in Melville's writing, taken as a whole—"reversibility"—and its transformation into what he calls "interchangeability," which may help explain the two-part division, noted earlier, of Melville's late novel. In other words, the infinitely reversible doubles or simulacra (not only avatars of the confidence man, but also his various dupes) that structure the first half of the narrative are transformed, in the second half, into one character, likened to "a Drummond light," and called "an original" ("the cosmopolitan," Frank Goodman), who is the very embodiment of this notion of "interchangeability." To put it another way, following H. Bruce Franklin, who not only reads *The Confidence-Man* as Melville's most structured novel, but also as falling into two distinct halves, described above, we may read the first half of the narrative as a vertiginous play of masks, doubles and reversibility, taken to its absolute limit, before resulting in the "interchangeable" character that dominates the second half of the story, "the cosmopolitan." The question, "who is cheating whom?" becomes unsolvable, impossible to untangle, pushing well beyond the simple reversibility, doubling, and mirroring of the first half of the novel. Also, we must note how the very "identity" of the confidence man—another unsolvable mystery—has, itself, become a "floating signifier," as we saw earlier with the white whale in Moby-Dick and with Isabel's identity, as well as Pierre Sr.'s "true" portrait, Pierre.

These three "floating signifiers," or what Deleuze calls "heterogeneous series," are always (already) deferred, unknowable, beyond our grasp or comprehension—and this is precisely what Melville has discovered in his escape, over the line of the horizon. Before discussing this "discovery," however, we must examine Tanner's work in more detail.

In his Introduction to Tony Tanner's *The American Mystery* (2000), Ian F. A. Bell points out that "Tanner notices [in American literature] a prevailing tendency to fade, [as in] the frequency of words like 'melt' in *The Blithedale Romance*, and asks us to see how 'dematerialization, attenuation, liquidation, vaporization and other words of desubstantiation seem variously to dominate the changing atmosphere'" of American literature and culture (xviii). As Bell puts it, "[w]ords fail here, do not build; deliberately, they create no picture" (Ibid.) in the struggle to deal with the contradictions of American history and society. These contradictions stem from what Tanner describes as the basic idea of America's self-conception: "The new country, the United States of America, depended for its existence both as entity and concept on two things—appropriated, surveyed, legally apportioned land; and a sense of an uncharted, inexhaustibly bounteous west, a plenitude of possibilities: measurement and dream" (xxiii). Tanner conceives of the dematerialization of language in American literature, the move beyond the structure of binary opposites, as a continuous process of self-invention. This move involves literary strategies of transformation: the construction of ontological identity, character, and modes of representation.

As Tanner observers in his chapter on Emerson, if life is in "flux" or constant "metamorphosis," then writing should be as well. Emerson asserts that "Nature hates calculators; her methods are *salutatory and impulsive*. Man lives by *pulses*; our organic movements are such; [...] and the mind goes *antagonizing* on, and never prospers but by fits. We thrive on *casualties* ("Experience"; qtd. in Tanner 6; emphasis in original). Tanner applies these qualities to Emerson's own writing. Emerson believed that the "vast talent and power" of Napoleon's activity comes to no result, while the "vast talent and power" of writers leave definite traces. Power is inseparable from change: "Nothing is secure but life, transition, the energizing spirit ("Circles"; qtd. in Tanner 4). Emerson's style of speech and writing, which seemed to be in permanent transition, oscillated between dissolving and congealing.

Similarly, in *The Blithedale Romance*, Nathaniel Hawthorne's language seems constantly to vaporize or dissolve together with the world being described. In this novel, Miles Coverdale, the narrator, is a writer like Hawthorne and sees his world at Brook Farm dissolve away, as if being inscribed and erased for the reader simultaneously. As Tanner points out, Coverdale undergoes a dissolution of self as he finds his environment becoming completely de-familiarized. Tanner tracks the binaries between fact and fiction, forgery and real money—no doubt looking ahead to Melville's *Confidence-Man*—as a means of determining the "true" copy; whether "forging" the uncreated conscience of one's race or forging money, "both 'forgers' work by putting falsities/fictions into circulation" (16). Ultimately, for Coverdale, America becomes "another spot, and an utter strangeness," as apparently it does for Hawthorne, of whom Henry James said, "He is outside of everything, and an alien everywhere" (37)—or, to put it another way, a "citizen of somewhere else," much like Melville, in fact.

However, our main concern is Tanner's treatment of *White-Jacket*, *Moby-Dick*, and *The Confidence-Man*, in which he further develops the theme of "reversibility" that he sees running through Emerson and Hawthorne, only to reach its culmination in Melville. He defines "reversibility" in terms of repetition or doubling: "All things are potentially double, paradoxically mixed, oddly reversible" (77). Set against Manichean dualism, which Tanner sees embodied in Ahab (echoing Spanos on the "naming" of the whale, as discussed above), the reversibility in Ishmael, for example, reveals a "tolerant inclusiveness." Melville's style, itself, evinces a similar quality, an openness and "careful disorderliness." Tanner finds this quality in America itself as it undergoes an endless metamorphosis in the ongoing process of self-invention. *White-Jacket*, as Tanner puts it, "tears itself free from any hampering orthodoxy and achieves a true Melvillian unsettling power" (59) thus surmounting the problems facing America and finding its unity and stability. *Moby-Dick* for Tanner diagnoses what Nietzsche would later call "the loss of myth, of a mythic home, the mythic womb" (69), and Melville likewise anticipates Nietzsche's insights regarding "perspectivism," which allows for contesting systems of value and different interpretations of the same text. Through Ishmael, who interprets the world with a tolerant inclusiveness, Melville shows how humanity can be brought together into a community by reciprocal dependence. Tanner's reading of *The Confidence-Man* is most pertinent to our present task, however: in this novel, Tanner suggests how "reversibility" can be transformed into what he calls "interchangeability." This term, which Tanner borrows from Thomas Mann, registers "the multiplicity and sheer ontological dubiety of the self" (100) in a world where identity is constantly being transformed, reinvented, revolutionized—precisely what Melville is dramatizing in *The Confidence-Man*. A world of simulacra, of "surface[s] striated upon surface[s]," a masquerade: this was perhaps Melville's final, and harshest, discovery during the period under scrutiny in this study, and by all accounts it left him shattered. But was he in despair, as myriad biographers and critics have assumed? To this question we now turn.

    One question that remains unaddressed, and that is crucial to our purposes, is what we are to make of Melville's "annihilation" comment to Hawthorne. Was he, as the prevailing view would have it, slipping into despair and depression? And did Hawthorne likewise have this impression of his old friend? In other words, how should we read Hawthorne's journal entry (cited earlier)? And is there another possible understanding of this enigmatic comment, which, we should remember, was essentially a private one? At the beginning of this chapter, I quoted Hawthorne's rightly famous journal entry, which recorded Melville's mysterious "annihilation" comment. We are now in a better position to clarify that remark, which Hawthorne undoubtedly took to mean "suicide" or the like (something akin to the extinguishing of the soul, we might assume; in other words, without hope of an afterlife). Naturally, this understanding of Melville's comment horrified Hawthorne; yet, can we not read it in an alternate way? In other words, is there a different way to look at Melville's conception of "annihilation"?

Hershel Parker has convincingly argued for a different reading of this remark, one that supports my emphasis upon the Miltonian echoes that attend the defiant sufferers and their various bachelor-machines throughout Melville's writing of this period. The first thing to notice about Hawthorne's journal entry is that it was written nearly a week after the meeting actually took place, looking back at their afternoon among the sand dunes. Hawthorne places Melville's comment in quotation marks, yet, as Parker notes, it may not be verbatim, given various factors (the time elapsed, the imperfection of memory, and so on). However, as Parker speculates, perhaps "[i]f Melville actually used the [word] 'annihilated,' Hawthorne, like Melville steeped in Milton, [may] have heard an echo of *Paradise Lost*" for, "[a]s both men knew, in book 6 of *Paradise Lost* Milton explains that spirits like Satan cannot be killed piecemeal—'Vital in every part,' they 'Cannot but by annihilating die'" (*Melville*, Vol. II, 301). For proof of this, Parker points to the fact that Melville's older brother, Gansevoort had used this very same passage of Milton in "a fiery [political] speech" and that Melville, in his personal copy of *Paradise Lost*, had underlined "Cannot but by annihilating die" and "put a vertical mark in the margin by the line" (Ibid.). Based upon this reasoning, he concludes that Melville's allusion to Milton, through his use of this resonant word, "annihilation," may have indicated to Hawthorne that "there was still a defiant edge to his [Melville's] resignation: being annihilated at once was better than slow death" (Ibid.). This was most likely the case, though Hawthorne seems to not have understood it in this manner. For support, we need to return to the Miltonian strain in Melville's work—particularly in his "defiant sufferers," such as Ahab and Pierre—and my earlier remarks on the scholarship on this topic.

Miltonian allusion in Melville, particularly the links between Ahab and the Satan of *Paradise Lost*, has long been recognized. During the so-called "Melville Revival" of the 1920s, John Freeman sensed that "man's first disobedience [and the] loss of Eden" constitute one of the whaling adventure's central themes:

> The never-to-be-ended combat typified by Milton's Lucifer and Archangels is typified as boldly by Melville's Moby Dick and Captain Ahab. Vindicating his pride against almightiness, Lucifer is overthrown but unsubdued; by vindicating his perverted spirit against a malignity not less perverse, Ahab is slain by the White Whale.[112]

Most subsequent discussions of Melville's artistic response to *Paradise Lost* have been similarly suggestive and generalized; in Guttmann's view, for example, the equation is simple, involving a broad stroke of the brush: "Milton's fable is used to supplement Melville's own."[113] The drawing of Miltonic connections in the criticism is, furthermore, often associated with the contention that Melville read the epic in a primarily "Romantic" and "Satanic

---

[112] John Freeman, *Herman Melville* (London: Macmillan, 1926): 116–117.

[113] Allen Guttmann, "From *Typee* to *Moby-Dick*: Melville's Allusive Art," *Modern Language Quarterly* 24 (1963): 242.

School" way, attributing to Milton (as did Blake),[114] an unconscious "sympathy for the Devil" (we might say), which is a view that was given support after Melville's personal copy of Milton's poetry was found and its marginalia examined.[115] More than fifty years ago, Henry A. Murray claimed that "Melville's Satan is the spitting image of Milton's hero [...] the stricken, passionate, and often eloquent rebel angel of *Paradise Lost*, whose role [in *Moby-Dick*] is played by Ahab."[116] More recently, Paul Giles similarly noted that Ahab's "desire for revenge on the white whale is as anguished as Satan's quest in Milton's poem for vengeance against God,"[117] while Robin Grey explored the influence of Milton upon Melville's Civil War poetry[118] and John

---

[114] Henry F. Pommer, for example, maintains in *Milton and Melville* (New York: Cooper Square Press, 1970), that "Melville read Milton in a way different from that of many of his contemporaries. He could not accept the Milton praised by piety, but he did accept the Milton who had been accepted and explained by Blake and Shelley" (19–20).

[115] Robin Grey, *The Complicity of Imagination: The American Renaissance, Contests of Authority, and Seventeenth-Century English Culture* (Cambridge: Cambridge University Press, 1997): 213–227.

[116] Henry A. Murray, "*In Nomine Diaboli*," in *Moby-Dick Centennial Essays*, eds. Tyrus Hillway and Luther S. Mansfield (Dallas: Southern Methodist University press, 1953): 11.

[117] Paul Giles, "Bewildering Intertanglement: Melville's Engagement with British Culture" in *The Cambridge Companion to Herman Melville*, ed. Robert S. Levine (Cambridge: Cambridge University press, 1988): 235.

[118] Robin Grey, "Annotations on Civil War: Melville's *Battle-Pieces* and Milton's War in Heaven," *Leviathan* 14:1–2 (March 2002): 51–70.

T. Shawcross and David Urban traced the Miltonian elements in *Clarel*.[119] Regardless of how we measure or read Milton's influence on Melville's writing, it is difficult to deny the continuity between the defiance of these various "heaven assaulters" and the Bulkington figure who Melville apotheosizes. And in his life, Melville remained true to his own "titanic vision," refusing to surrender. His desire to be "annihilated," therefore, must be read in this context—as is the case, as we shall see, with Melville's late work, especially the poetry.

Most importantly, however, Melville's Miltonian defiance brings us back, full-circle as it were, to the point where we began this study: the desire to escape, to flee, to rebel. In other words, to Ahab's bachelor-machine, to Pierre's assault on heaven, now to the confidence man's "masquerade"—and to Melville, himself, and his defiant determination to "write exactly as I please," to risk "sink[ing] in boundless deeps," even if it means that he will fail as a writer, be forgotten, "annihilated" or misunderstood—in other words, wind up "an utter wreck." What did Melville see by the end of this tumultuous period of his life, which indeed ended in shipwreck? What was he trying to express to Hawthorne, to his readers, and to himself? We have seen what he was trying to escape from—but where, we may rightfully ask, was he heading?

For Melville, at this point, writing—indeed, words, language, art— had been transformed, much as he, himself, had been transformed in and through the process of writing. "Now, writing points ahead in time," as

---

[119] John T. Shawcross, "'Too Intellectual a Poet Ever to be Popular': Herman Melville and the Miltonian Dimension of *Clarel*," *Leviathan* 14:1-2 (March 2002): 71–90; and David Urban, "'Rousing Motions' and the Silence of God: Scripture and Immediate Revelation in *Samson Agonistes* and *Clarel*," *Leviathan* 14:1-2 (March 2002): 91–111.

William C. Spengemann writes,[120] "deriving its meaning not once and for all, from unchanging and eternal truths, but endlessly, from its own unforeseeable, inescapable consequences, taking on new meanings with each successive unfolding of events" (xiv)—much as Melville had described the play of masks or simulacra in his last novel, or his own "unfolding," his own growth and development—that it, itself, has set in motion. "Instead of standing for the fixed meanings from which they arose," Spengemann continues, "words now make and continually remake their meanings, accumulating semantic complexity as long as they continue and reverberate, as long as they are read" (Ibid.). In this way, as Melville predicted in the last, resonant line of *The Confidence-Man*, "Something further may follow of this Masquerade" (CM 251).

"When Pierre, for example, sits down to do what Melville is in fact doing—write a novel, 'plagiarized from his own experiences,' as he phrases it (P 302), about a character who is himself a writer—*Pierre* then becomes," as Spengemann teaches us, "at that very instant, autobiographical in the fullest sense of the word: neither a report of the author's life nor an inquiry into that life, but an event in the life itself, one, like getting married or rescuing a secret sister, with unfathomable antecedent causes, unknowable motives, and unpredictable, inescapable consequences" (xv). While virtually every detail in the novel has been put to scrutiny and found to correspond, more or less, to some documented fact in Melville's life before or during the writing of *Pierre*, there is still something that escapes this detail-for-detail mapping onto the text of Melville's "real life." If aspects of Melville's life show up in *Pierre*, they appear there transformed, changed beyond anything but a surface resemblance

---

[120]   See his masterful "Introduction" to *Pierre; or, The Ambiguities* (New York: Penguin, 1996), upon which I draw heavily in this and the following two pages.

to their originals. In *Pierre*, then, "Melville enters a new life, under a new name and new conditions, with a new and unrealized fate awaiting him—awaiting its own unfolding" (Ibid.) in the words that simultaneously record and perform or enact it. Here, Spengemann makes a crucial point: "In autobiography of this profoundly 'modern' or contemporary sort, the author is at once everywhere present and everywhere hidden. Or, as Isabel says of the name inside her guitar, that of Melville lies deep within *Pierre*, 'so secret, wholly hidden, yet constantly carried about in it'" (149; qtd. in Ibid.). The names of our mothers and fathers, in other words, are forever hidden, obscured—and we are foundlings all.

"At that moment when the adventures of Pierre give way to the writing of *Pierre* as the primary subject of the novel," Spengemann continues, "Melville's career arrives at a turning point toward which it can be seen in retrospect to have been heading almost from the very beginning" (Ibid.). His tendency to "unfold," noted above, or to discover in the course of writing unsuspected problems and possibilities that greatly alter if not completely transform his original intentions (and this is why it is so useless to hunt for Melville's "original intentions," as we have seen with Parker) and set the narrative on an altogether different, unanticipated path in turn allows us to trace that very process of "unfolding" with relative ease (relative, say, to more "controlled" authors, such as Hawthorne or James). For, the new direction taken by each of his narratives in mid-passage invariably and unfailingly anticipates a later work in his career; instead of realizing its own "original intentions," Melville's work escapes it, each one unearthing the subject and technique of another work, as yet unwritten (or, perhaps more accurately, "to-be-written"). The experiences that Tommo recounts, for example, in *Typee*, Melville's first novel, as Spengemann demonstrates, turn him into someone quite different from who he was at the narrative's beginning—in fact, into someone we cannot imagine writing the opening chapters, but instead someone closer to the Ishmael who narrates the opening chapters of *Moby-Dick*, himself by the concluding chapters a man who could only write *Pierre*. "As the narrator says of the novel Pierre is writing," each of Melville's works is only one of an interdependent pair, a precursor of a later or repetition of an earlier work: "one 'composed on paper' and another 'writ down in his soul'" (304; qtd. in Ibid.). We must not forget, as well, that these words were composed at precisely the point when Melville and his dream of collaboration had been abandoned by Hawthorne. And once again, Hawthorne precipitated a transformation in Melville's art.

As Spengemann notes, this tendency of writing to change the writer was very much on Melville's mind when he was struggling with *Pierre*: in a letter written to Hawthorne at that time, he warned that an answer addressed to one "Herman Melville" would most likely go astray, "for the very fingers that now guide this pen are not precisely those that took it up and put it on this paper. Lord," Melville continues, "when shall we be done changing?" (qtd. in Spengemann, xvi) He then goes on to make his famous statement concerning his "unfolding:"

> I am like one of those seeds taken out of the Egyptian Pyramids, which, after being planted in English soil, it developed itself, grew to greenness, and then fell to mould. So I. Until I was twenty-five, I had no development at all. From my twenty-fifth year I date my life. Three weeks have scarcely passed, at any time between then and now, that I have not unfolded within myself. But I feel that I am now come to the inmost leaf of the bulb, and that shortly the flower must fall to the mould. (WHM 14: 193)

What Melville became, through this "unfolding" process—in and through writing *Pierre*, for example—is the person, or rather the many, essentially different personae (or masks) whose voices wholly constitute the tales, sketches, poems and fragmented narratives published under the name "Herman Melville" during the next forty years. Of course, it is our ability to contemplate an entire body of work, from *Typee* to *Billy Budd* (unpublished in Melville's lifetime), that enables us to perceive this fundamental change in Melville's career and in his art; to locate its turning point in the struggle that went into producing *Pierre* or the "Agatha" story; to see it approaching in those expository "digressions" that interrupt the narrative stream of *Mardi*, *Moby-Dick*, *Pierre*, and *The Confidence-Man*; and to see its culmination in the enigmatic verse assemblage aptly named "Pebbles," which I will discuss in my conclusion.

With the "annihilation" comment, then, we come full-circle once again, back to Ahab and Pierre, Melville's defiant sufferers, at once mournful and unrepentant, bidding farewell to their lost Edens. This is where we leave Melville, in 1856–57, as well—sorrowful yet unrepentant, defiant to the end, and still standing ahead of us, on the farther shore. What Melville found as he played the confidence man's "masquerade" to its bitter end and crossed over to the other shore was what he would later call "the Inhuman Sea," something that he could only capture in verse, and to which we will turn before concluding this chapter and study; however, before doing so, we must first discuss Melville's farewell to Hawthorne.

Returning once again to Melville's introductory story, "The Piazza," briefly discussed at the end of chapter two, we have now arrived full-circle, with Melville, back at the starting point of this period of intense creativity (as well as this study); in other words, Hawthorne and (Melville's remarkable "review" essay) "His Mosses." The occasion for writing this short, prefatory piece to his collected short stories, *The Piazza Tales* (1856), offered Melville an opportunity to ruminate about his last few years at Pittsfield and about some of the experiences from which the stories had emerged. As an introductory tale, much in the style of Hawthorne's prefaces, it provided Melville with a chance to bring together, in a single work, thoughts he had expressed in several, widely disparate stories. Consequently, he depicts in "The Piazza" a man in the act of looking backwards, reviewing and recapitulating a painful episode in his life and attempting to sum up what he learned from this experience. The story makes several points, as critics have shown, concerning the unreliability of perception,[121] the difference between appearance and reality,[122] and the hollowness of (vulgar) Transcendentalism or Romanticism; however, these are not the main "points," if you will, of the story. "The Piazza" is, as Dillingham has noted, first and foremost "a highly personal account of an emotional crisis";[123] namely, Melville's abandonment by Hawthorne and his dashed dream of collaboration.

The nature of the narrator's emotional crisis is revealed in the reason he gives for undertaking a journey to a mountain cottage that he has admired from afar. He anticipates that he will find "some glad mountain-girl" and that it will do him good to look upon her: it will "cure his weariness" (WHM 9: 6). However, upon reaching his destination, instead of finding a new source of energy and replenishment, the narrator discovers in the mountain cottage weariness personified. Of all the women in Melville's fiction, Marianna seems the most hopelessly alone. Even wretched Hunilla is rescued at last, and even the pathetic maids of the Devil's Dungeon share one another's company in their misery. Marianna lives a life of near-total isolation, weary of her view from her window, weary of the heat in summer and the cold in winter. Her

---

[121] Scott Donaldson, "The Dark Truth of *The Piazza Tales*," *PMLA*, Vol. 85 (1970): 1082.

[122] Richard H. Fogle, *Melville's Shorter Tales* (Norman: University of Oklahoma Press, 1960): 85.

[123] William B. Dillingham, *Melville's Short Fiction: 1853–1856* (Athens: University of Georgia Press, 1977): 320.

brother is gone, as is her favorite companion, a shadow from a birch tree that was felled by lightning.

The emotional crisis depicted in "The Piazza" in both literal and figurative terms is also autobiographical in nature, a thinly disguised treatment of Melville's loss of Hawthorne, who lived in a mountain cottage very near Arrowhead. We do not have to completely agree with Dillingham in seeing "Melville's journeys to Hawthorne's little red cottage at Lenox" as being "like the pilgrimages of some religious enthusiast to the shrine of his idol" (332) to appreciate the parallel between Marianna's abode and that of Hawthorne, who wrote in "The Old Manse" that his "precincts were like the Enchanted Ground, though which the pilgrim travelled on his way to the Celestial City."[124] The many references to enchantment and magic in "The Piazza" suggest that Melville had in mind not only Hawthorne's "The Old Manse," but also his own enthusiastic review of *Mosses from an Old Manse*, where he wrote of the magic spell that Hawthorne's work had cast over him. This may be illustrated by contrasting two resonant passages, one from each text. The first, almost prophetic one, from Hawthorne's "Old Manse" is as follows:

> So far as I am a man of really individual attributes, I veil my face [...] Glancing back over what I have written, it seems but the scattered reminiscences of a single summer. In fairy-land, there is no measurement of time; and, in a spot so sheltered from the turmoil of life's ocean, three years hastened away with a noiseless flight, as the breezy sunshine chases the cloud-shadows across the depths of a still valley. (Mosses from an Old Manse, 33)

---

[124] Nathaniel Hawthorne, *Mosses from an Old Manse*, The Centenary Edition of the Works of Nathaniel Hawthorne, William Charvat, Roy H. Pearce, and C.M. Simpson, eds., Vol. 10 (Columbus: Ohio State University Press, 1974): 28.

The next is from Melville's "Piazza," which seems to be in dialogue with the passage cited above. We should note the repetition of the phrase, "fairy-land," the emphasis on the face, and also the way in which Melville seems to be writing a dark counterpart or sequel to what Hawthorne has written, above—that is, the evening, with its gathering shadows, of that same day which Hawthorne in which time has slipped away as "breezy sunshine chases the cloud-shadows." The following is Melville's passage:

—Enough. Launching my yawl no more for fairy-land, I stick to the piazza. It is my box-royal; and its ampitheatre, my theatre of San Carol. Yes, the scenery is magical—the illusion so complete. And Madam Meadow Lark, my prima donna, plays her grand engagement here; and, drinking in her sunrise note, which, Memnon-like, seems struck from the golden window, how far the weary face behind it. But, every night, when the curtain falls, truth comes in with darkness. No light shows from the mountain. To and fro I walk the piazza deck, haunted by Marianna's face, and many as real a story. (WHM 9: 33)

Here, Melville recounts the loss of Marianna to the narrator and the loss of Hawthorne as a vital force in his own life—as Dillingham points out, this becomes clear once we examine the epigraph to this short story. For this purpose, Melville used a quotation from Shakespeare, the following line from Cymbeline: "With fairest flowers, / Whilst summer lasts, and I live here, Fidele—" These are the words of Arviragus spoken over the "body" of Imogen (pretending to be a boy, Fidele), who is not actually dead but thought to be: as Dillingham notes, this is "a burial speech for a man, Fidele, who is actually a girl and who is not literally dead" (335). It is here that we can better see Melville's reasoning behind the epigram.

In fact, Dillingham takes this a step farther by noting that the line from Arviragus's speech ("Whilst summer lasts") that Melville chose for his epigram is "nearly identical with a line in a similar speech in Pericles," "While summer-days doth last," spoken by a girl called "Marina, a possible source for the mountain girl, Marianna, in "The Piazza" (336). Like Arviragus, Marina is bemoaning the death of a friend, in this case an older woman. The first part of the passage is very similar to Cymbeline, whereas "the rest of the speech," according to Dillingham, seems "pertinent to Melville's own situation and especially to his feelings about the death of a promising friendship" (337):

> Ay me! poor maid,
> Born in a tempest, when my mother died,
> This world to me is a lasting storm,
> Whirring me from my friends.
>   (IV. i. 17–20; quoted in Ibid.)

"In a stormy world that whirred him from his friends, Melville had to find a way," Dillingham argues, of "weathering Cape Horn" (as Melville phrased it in "The Piazza," WHM 9: 3). His solution was building the piazza—in Dillingham's words, "a philosophical stance, a way of surviving for an extraordinary mind" (337). For the piazza, according to the narrator of the story, belongs to two worlds, "combining the coziness of in-doors with the freedom of out-doors" (WHM 9: 1), a dichotomy that for Dillingham reflects Melville's metaphors of "the lee shore" and "the howling infinite," quoted earlier in this study, in the context of Bulkington in *Moby-Dick*. Melville had written, in that section of his masterwork, that it was better, far nobler to perish in the howling infinite than to remain always in the safe confines of the sheltered port, "but his own lifelong attempt," as Dillingham points out, "was to find a way to mediate between the two" (337). His work collectively presents the drama of this struggle, and this is nowhere more powerfully expressed than in the poetry with which Melville occupied himself after *The Confidence-Man*. This poorly understood aspect of his writing career is the focus, however narrow, of the brief conclusion that follows.

The Inhuman Sea: Melville's Poetry

Before concluding, however, we must return to Hawthorne, who, as we have seen, in large part precipitated Melville's remarkable transformation; we must also look closer at Melville's farewell—in writing—to Hawthorne, and to his reaction, years later, to Hawthorne's death. Robert Milder reminds us that Lewis Mumford first asserted that Melville's poem, "Monody" was meant for Hawthorne.[125] The short, poignant lyric runs as follows:

> To have known him, to have loved him
>   After loneless long;
> And then to be estranged in life,
>   And neither in the wrong;
> And now for death to set his seal—
>   Ease me, a little ease, my song!
>
> By wintry hills his hermit-mound
>   The sheeted snow-drifts drape,
> And houseless there the snow-bird flits
>   Beneath the fir-trees' crape;
> Glazed now with ice the cloistral vine
>   That hid the shyest grape. (Clarel 893)

Whether "Monody" is for Hawthorne, however, has been a constant source of scholarly controversy. Walter E. Bezanson extended Mumford's (largely unsupported and anecdotal, as Milder notes) work by "triangulating

---

[125]   Milder is referring to *Herman Melville* (New York: Harcourt, Brace 1929): 264–265.

newfound biographical evidence, the poem *Clarel*, and 'Monody.'"[126] His work, which Milder has shown remains the strongest and most persuasive to date on this issue, came under criticism by Harrison Hayford in an appendix to the Northwestern Newberry *Clarel* entitled, "Melville's 'Monody': For Hawthorne?"[127] Milder himself has assessed the controversy, weighing heavily on the side of Mumford and Bezanson,[128] and critics like Nina Baym and Shirley Dettlaff have built upon or attacked, respectively, the "Monody/Hawthorne" thesis, so to speak, by examining the erotically charged imagery and language of *Clarel* and Melville's later poems.[129] This has also been the focus of Robert K. Martin's study of homosexual desire in Melville, which has perhaps pursued this thesis to its furthest extent.[130]

Poets, as well, have seized upon the image of Hawthorne-as-Monody, and the larger drama of the Hawthorne-Melville friendship or encounter, more generally, in order to draw inspiration. Charles Olson, with whom this study began, recognized the importance of Hawthorne to Melville and his art in *Call Me Ishmael*;[131] while W. H. Auden had earlier written a poem taking this for granted:

---

[126] "Historical and Critical Note," WHM 12: 504–637.
[127] WHM 12: 883–893.
[128] "Editing Melville's Afterlife," *Text: Transactions of the Society for Textual Scholarship* (1997): 389–407.
[129] "The Erotic Motif in Melville's *Clarel*," *Texas Studies in Literature and Language*, XVI (Summer, 1974): 315–328; "Ionian Form and Esau's Waste: Melville's View of Art in *Clarel*," *American Literature*, LIV (May, 1982): 212–228.
[130] *Hero, Captain, and Stranger: Male Friendship, Social Critique, and Literary Form in the Sea Novels of Herman Melville* (Chapel Hill: University of North Carolina Press, 1986): 95–99.
[131] See the chapter entitled, "Man, to man," discussed in chapter one of this study, in particular.

Towards the end he sailed into an extraordinary mildness,
And anchored in his home and reached his wife,
And rode within the harbour of her hand,
And went across each morning to an office
As though his occupation were another island.

Goodness existed: that was the new knowledge
His terror had to blow itself quite out
To let him see it; but it was the gale had blown him
Past the Cape Horn of sensible success
Which cries: 'This rock is Eden. Shipwreck here.'

[...]

He stood upon the narrow balcony and listened:
And all the stars above him sang as in his childhood
'All, all is vanity,' but it was not the same;
For now the words descended like the calm of mountains—
—Nathaniel had been shy because his love was selfish—
But now he cried in exultation and surrender
'The Godhead is broken like bread. We are the pieces.'

And sat down at his desk and wrote a story.[132]

Here, in this final line, Auden is referring to *Billy Budd,* which can perhaps be read as Melville's "testimony to acceptance," if not resignation and surrender, late in life. But perhaps there is another way of reading Melville's post-*Moby-Dick* imagery of decay, isolation, abandonment and shipwreck. If we return to the "Agatha" story, perhaps we can envision an alternative to the by-now

---

[132] From "Herman Melville" (1939) in Auden, *Collected Shorter Poems, 1930–1944* (London: Faber and Faber): 155–156.

well-known, and hopefully discredited, narrative of Melville's defeat, resignation or surrender.

In one of his letters to Hawthorne, noted by R.W.B. Lewis,[133] we can see Melville lingering with mournful affection over a projected account of the slow decay of Agatha's mail-box and the post upn which it stands:

> To this *post* they must come for their letters. And, of course, daily young Agatha goes—for seventeen years she goes thither daily. As her hopes gradually decay in her, so does the post itself and the little box decay. The post rots in the ground at last. Owing to its being little used—hardly used at all—grass grows rankly about it. At last a little bird nests in it. At last the post falls. (WHM 14: 236)

The passage does, of course, reflect Melville's acceptance of mortality and decay, but, at the same time, the lines quoted suggest another significant aspect—namely, the source and nature of Melville's conception of "defeat" or "failure."

"It is easy enough," writes Lewis, "to say that Melville's sensitivity to failure in the mid-1850s was the direct consequence of his own 'failure' as a novelist, after several years of considerable 'success'" (Ibid.). What is important is Melville's view of just what happened, of where the failure lay. In his view, the point was not only that his last two novels had failed to sell widely—though this was a fact of great seriousness to him ("dollars," as he said, always "damned" him). It was not only the fact that American critics were harsh in their judgment of his work, or that they completely neglected it—though, as Lewis points out, "Melville shared with many another

---

[133]   See his "Introduction" to *Herman Melville: A Laurel Reader*, 13, upon which this and the following four pages heavily draw.

American writer a much higher regard for British than for American critics and reviewers" (Ibid.); what had in fact happened, according to Lewis, was something rather different. "What had failed was an effort at communication. A recurring motif during these late years, accordingly, is the motif of the undelivered letter or the misapprehended sign" (Ibid.), noted at the beginning of this study.

Perhaps most famously, in "Benito Cereno," as Lewis notes, both the "wretched Spanish nobleman and members of his crew attempt to convey by sign-language the reality of their desperate situation; and Captain Delano fails consistently to receive their messages." Closer to the "Agatha" passage cited above, and as I hope to have shown, most likely inspired by it, is the picture of an island "post-office" in "The Encantadas":

> And though it may seem very strange to talk of post-offices in this barren region, yet post-offices are occasionally to be found there. They consist of a stake and a bottle. The letters being not only sealed, but corked. They are generally deposited by captains of Nantucketers for the benefit of passing fishermen, and contain statements as to what luck they had in whaling or tortoise-hunting. Frequently, however, long months and months, whole years glide by and no applicant appears. The stake rots and falls, presenting no very exhilarating subject. (WHM 9: 172; qtd. in Lewis, 14)

"A still less exhilarating subject," as Lewis phrases it, "and the most memorable example of this theme occur at the end of 'Bartleby, the Scrivener,' when the narrator reports the rumor that Bartleby had at one time worked as a subordinate clerk in the Dead Letter Office in Washington." "What could be more terrible for a man prone to helplessness like Bartleby," Lewis asks (echoing the narrator of the tale), "than the business of 'continually handling these dead letters, and assorting them for the flame... On errands of life,' he adds, appalled, 'these letters speed to death'" (Ibid.).

As Lewis so eloquently puts it: "So," in this way, "Melville's letters of life—his novels—had in his view of the matter sped to death, undelivered, unread by the addressee, the public; destined only to be destroyed" (Ibid.). Melville felt, according to Lewis, that he had "somehow failed to deliver the messages that shaped themselves so urgently in his imagination; and for a writer as profoundly personal and expressive as Melville, a failure of this kind was apt to be devastating. What Melville did was to convert his sense of the failure of communication into a central fictional theme; and to make expert short fiction out of the failure of his longer fiction" (15). In many ways, it was, as Lewis contends, a "courageous undertaking; and it has been properly celebrated by Hart Crane, in his poem, 'At Melville's Tomb,'" as the artistic effort by which Melville is perhaps best to be remembered:

> Often beneath the waves, wide from this ledge
> The dice of dead men's bones he saw bequeath
> An Embassy. Their numbers as he watched
> Beat on the dusky shore and were obscured (qtd. in 15).

In what has become a rather notorious episode, described by Lewis, "Crane had to explain to his editor that his intention had been to relate the bones of dead mariners, men who failed to reach the shore alive, with 'certain messages undelivered,' certain experiences not finally communicated; both the bones and the messages beat on the dusky shore and get obscured. The passage is complex; but it testifies in its oblique way to an essential aspect of Melville," and it also shows us that, as Lewis notes, Crane most certainly understood this. The poem in full, following the first stanza, cited above, is as follows:

> And wrecks passed, without sound of bells,

> The calyx of death's bounty giving back
> A scattered chapter, livid hieroglyph,
> The portent wound in corridors of shells.
>
> Then in the circuit calm of one vast coil,
> Its lashings charmed and malice reconciled,
> Frosted eyes there were that lifted altars;
> And silent answers crept across the stars.
>
> Compass, quadrant, and sextant contrive
> No farther tides... High in the azure steeps
> Monody shall not wake the mariner.
> This fabulous shadow only the sea keeps.[134]

Here, in concluding this chapter, we must also note that we, once again, see Hawthorne make an appearance, now in the guise of "Monody." But returning to my final point, we must recognize that "to formulate success and failure in terms of communication is also to find the focus of human experience in the question of community—that is, of the relation between the individual and community," as Lewis has claimed; and Melville's work of the mid-1850s "contains some of the most extreme and disturbing images of isolation that modern literature, American or otherwise, has recorded" (Ibid.). This has, in turn, led scholars to focus upon such figures, characters Melville himself (in Moby-Dick, describing the crew of the *Pequod*) called "isolatoes." Though one aspect of their isolation is surely grounded in their spiritual or religious condition—witness Ahab's, Pierre's or, years later, Clarel's lonely quests, for

---

[134] "At Melville's Tomb" (1926) in *The Voice That Is Great Within Us: American Poetry of the Twentieth Century*, Hayden Carruth, ed. (New York: Bantam Books, 1970): 214–215.

example—it seems more to the point to focus upon their relation to the larger community, to their attempts to negotiate their identity between the self and other, be it a crew of sailors, a family, or even a nation. Consequently, this is where Melville's overtly "political" orientation is made manifest, where his undelivered message still awaits us, unread, and where I will end my study. In my conclusion, I will briefly address some of Melville's late poems, a topic that I hope to examine in greater detail elsewhere.

Conclusion

In hollows of the liquid hills / Where the long Blue Ridges run, / The flattery of no echo thrills, / For echo the seas have none; / Nor aught that gives man back man's strain— / The hope of his heart, the dream in his brain. (Melville, "Pebbles," iii)

Gilles Deleuze, following the work of D.H. Lawrence, claimed that the highest purpose of Herman Melville's writing—indeed, the highest purpose of the greatest of American writing—is to "escape." Deleuze argued that Melville was attempting to escape from the English "paternal function," while Lawrence famously asserted that it was from "Home" and "Mother." Other scholars and critics have followed suit, echoing this thesis in various ways while altering the object from which Melville was attempting to escape—the lingering shadow of his dead father, for example, or the "torture box" of his wife and family (as Lawrence phrased it), various aspects of contemporary American society and culture, or even the unreceptive and uncomprehending reading public and literary establishment of his day. Clearly, we can also easily point to various episodes drawn from Melville's biography, when he literally "escaped"—for example, before he turned to writing, during his years at sea, a period in which he had temporarily escaped from his duties and responsibilities on shore, in what was once a large, proud family, but was now—after the untimely death of his father—impoverished and deeply in debt. In fact, Melville's biographical details have fueled a great deal of scholarship and speculation about his writing (and vice-versa). However, as useful and provocative as the Lawrence-Deleuze thesis may be, it has not yielded a general consensus among Melville scholars, and the question as to what exactly Melville was attempting to escape from—a question whose answer has important ramifications for how we read or understand Melville, and as such is absolutely crucial—remains an open one. This study attempted to address this question, by bringing it together with another, equally mysterious and long-standing problem: Melville's brief but intense friendship with Nathaniel Hawthorne, and the impact of this relationship upon Melville's work.

It is the wager of this study that the Melville-Hawthorne encounter, and the work it helped inspire, can in some way contribute to illuminating these and other mysteries of Melville scholarship. It is not by accident that Melville's most feverish period of writing followed his initial encounter with Hawthorne, nor is it by chance that these texts are in dialogue with Hawthorne's work. This dialogue, in turn, helped transform Melville's art, forcing him to revisit earlier work and retrieve and rework certain figures, motifs and themes. That Melville's literary career—its "major phase," roughly 1850 to 1857, a period which saw the publication of *Moby-Dick*, *Pierre*, *Israel Potter* and *The Confidence-Man*, as well as all of his short stories, several of them masterpieces of the form—also ended with the demise of this enigmatic friendship is likewise no coincidence. By putting a sharper edge on the point of Melville's critique—in other words, clearly identifying that from which he was attempting one way or another to "escape"—this book attempted to fill a gap in current scholarship and contribute to discussion and debate concerning those tumultuous and still-poorly understood years of Melville's "major phase." I argued three main points: that Melville was desperately trying to escape from the confines of, first, the nation-state, second, the family, and third, subjectivity. His encounter with Hawthorne— its initial shock of recognition and joyful passion, its deepening affection and maturity, as well as its eventual dissolution and subsequent disappointment and pain—provided Melville with the impetus to construct various "bachelor machines," a term taken from Deleuze and Guattari (who adapted it from Marcel Duchamp via Michel Carrouges) that I employ in order to articulate the manner in which Melville attempts to "escape." Ahab's transnational, interracial, and even interspecies ship, Pierre's community of outcasts and lover-siblings, and the confidence man's dizzying masquerade aboard a riverboat that is a veritable microcosm of Antebellum America all profit from being read in light of this concept, which Deleuze and Guattari describe in the following terms: "With no family, no conjugality, the bachelor is all the more social, social-dangerous, social-traitor, a collective in himself" (71). For these three figures—Ahab, Pierre and the confidence man—are undeniably dangerous, traitors, figures who subvert the order of things while turning away or fleeing society. In this manner, Melville was conducting a kind of thought-experiment and expressing his innermost desires. My study, as incomplete or unsatisfactory as it may be, attempts to map this process.

Returning to Melville at the end of the period under scrutiny here, and the intriguing question of whether or not "Monody" was truly meant for Hawthorne, we may rightfully ask the question why Melville turned to poetry, in the first place, after his farewell to prose in *The Confidence-Man*. Though he had been asked to contribute to *The Atlantic Monthly*, as Spengemann points out, he never submitted any stories. Melville briefly tried his hand at lecturing, but that endeavor seemed halfhearted and ended rather unsatisfactorily. We might assume, based upon this and other circumstantial evidence (gathered by Spengemann, Milder and Miller, among myriad others), that Melville had simply exhausted all other possible outlets for his writing; however, this would seem to discount the overwhelming evidence that Melville had for a long time admired poetry, to which he makes constant reference throughout his work, and that he was for many years a dedicated student and practitioner of verse. Parker makes exactly this point, which he elaborated at length in his recent monograph. Unfortunately, however, Melville's first collection of poems, drawn from his Mediterranean travels in the winter of 1856–1857—which he began shortly after his walk with Hawthorne amidst the sand dunes of Southport—failed to find a publisher; ten years later, *Battle-Pieces* (1866), his first published collection (and final commercially funded publication in any genre, as Miller notes) received a "decidedly cool reception from reviewers, who mainly lamented what they saw as the once popular novelist's mistaken turn to verse." After another decade, *Clarel* (1876) appeared, thanks to the largess of Melville's uncle Peter Gansevoort, to whom he dedicated the book, but as Milder tells us, it went unread for the most part and was eventually recalled by the author. Twelve years later still, Melville himself paid for the private printing of *John Marr and Other Sailors* (1888), which contains "Pebbles," an extraordinary poem that I will briefly discuss, below, and then of *Timoleon* (1891), in which the aforementioned "Monody" appears; both were printed in very limited, private editions, meant, as Bryant and others have stressed, to be given away to friends. Apparently, the idea for what would become *Billy Budd, Sailor* (published posthumously, in 1924, after it was discovered in a bread tin) had also begun as verse (ostensibly a sea-shanty, which Melville transformed into a poem): "Billy in the Darbies," which remains as a kind of appendix to Melville's late, exquisite though still poorly understood novella.

At the end of chapter three, we discussed "Monody," but there is a lesser-known poem that seems to bear an unmistakable relation to Hawthorne. This is the uncollected "Madame Mirror," which was almost certainly written in response to Hawthorne's "Monsieur du Miroir," a short story on which Melville commented in his "Mosses" review—and a passage of which, "He will pass to the dark realm of Nothingness, but will not find me there," he marked in the margin of his copy. We should note the fact that Melville changed the gender of the mirror in the title, from male to female, and the language from French to English; we may even speculate as to why he chose to respond to this story of Hawthorne's—perhaps the answer lies in the last paragraph, where Hawthorne bids "Farewell, Monsieur du Miroir!" In any case, we must look more closely at the original story and then examine Melville's response in greater detail. First, a short passage that must have appealed to Melville in which the narrator of Hawthorne's tale addresses the mirror: "Oh, friend, canst thou not hear and answer me? Break down the barrier between us! Grasp my hand! Speak! Listen!" (*Mosses from an Old Manse* 171). Next, we have Melville:

> With wrecks in a garret I'm stranded,
> Where, no longer returning a face,
> I take to reflections the deeper
> On memories far to retrace.
>
> In me have all people confided,
> The maiden her charms has displayed,
> And truths unrevealed and unuttered
> To me have been freely betrayed.
>
> [...]
>
> What pangs after parties of pleasure,
> What smiles but disclosures of pain!
> O, the tears of the hopeless unloved,
> O, the start at old age drawing near,
> O, what shadows of thoughts unexpressed
> Like clouds on a lake have been here!⁽¹³⁵⁾

We see, yet again, images of shipwreck, clouds and water, as well as the face of the beloved, now lost, and the theme of confidence betrayed. There is also a sense of weariness, much as we have seen in "The Piazza," when the narrator

---

[135] *Tales, Poems and Other Writings*, ed. John Bryant (New York: Modern Library, 2001): 319–320.

goes abroad to remedy his own weariness and finds weariness personified in the person of Marianna.

But there is a vastly more powerful poem, more of a verse assemblage, called "Pebbles," to which I now wish to turn. It concludes the collection *John Marr and Other Sailors*, and contains seven stanzas of irregular verse fragments, of which I will focus upon two that I find particularly moving. The first, "Pebble v," is one in which the sea speaks for itself. As William C. Spengemann notes, this stanza "completes the movement from the land [a reference to the first stanza] to utter landlessness ('myriad wrecks in me') by way of land's end and the beach's nautical envoys ('embattled fleets')."[136] It is as follows:

> Implacable I, the old implacable Sea:
> Implacable most when most I smile serene—
> Pleased, no appeased, by myriad wrecks in me.[137]

Here, we can see Melville repeating the shipwreck imagery, now changing the point of view, from that of a sailor to that of the sea itself. We can also clearly see, looking at the entire sweep of the poem with Spengemann, that the sea is "[a]t first ambiguous, then inscrutable, then silently indifferent, then potentially destructive, [but] now openly hostile" (595). In this way, we can chart Melville's stages on the way to "what should have been a blessing but has turned out to be annihilation;" [d]ry land, sea beach, sea surface, sea bottom; dissatisfaction, desire, hope, disappointment, daring, drowning; irony, reverence, doubt, realization, extinction;" or, in other words, Melville seems to discover, through this poem, "a watery grave" (Ibid.). Though Spengemann

---

[136] "Melville the Poet," *American Literary History*, Vol. 11, No. 4 (1999): 595.
[137] Quoted in Spengemann, 591.

reads the next stanza, "Pebble vi," in a Miltonian vein (595–597), linking it to "God-defying Ahab at the moment of his apotheosis" (595), which lends support to my argument in this study, in the interests of space, I must limit my discussion to "Pebble vii," the final stanza, which reads as follows:

> Healed of my hurt, I laud the inhuman Sea—
> Yea, bless the Angels Four that there convene;
> For healed I am even by their pitiless breath
> Distilled in wholesome dew named rosmarine. (501)

Here, I wish to focus solely upon the first line of that stanza, "Healed of my hurt, I laud the inhuman Sea—," which seems to speak directly to the "infinite series of the waves" cited earlier, from "The Mast-Head" chapter of *Moby-Dick*, but also, and perhaps more crucially, to Melville's disappointment in life, particularly with regard to Hawthorne and their dream of collaboration. Yet Melville rises from the depths. The speaker is like one reborn, having been baptized not in holy water but in the "inhuman sea" itself; and, as Spengemann points out, the "angels four" should recall not only Revelation (7:1)—"And I saw four angels standing on the four corners of the earth, holding the four winds of the earth, that the wind should not blow on the earth, nor the sea"— but also *Pierre*, in which the defiant heaven-assaulter who would "gospelize the world anew" finds himself staring, "transfixed at sea-born Isabel" (597), as he hears a strange music: "Every downward undulating wave and billow of [her] tossed tresses gleamed here and there like a tract of phosphorescent midnight sea; and, simultaneously, all the four winds of the world of melody broke loose" (WHM 7: 150; qtd. in Spengemann 597).

With this ethereal melody, we leave Melville, whose messages still go undelivered, unread or un-deciphered, and who still awaits us on the far, dusky shore. Why did he turn to verse? That is a topic deserving of a study in its own right, but, to bring the current study to a close, perhaps we may wish to agree with Spengemann in thinking that poetry, for Melville, "has done, poetically, what neither faith nor philosophy could do: make some sense of a nonsensically fragmented world without pretending that the world itself makes sense" (599).

Bibliography

Argersinger, Jana L. and Leland S. Person. "Hawthorne and Melville: Writing, Relationship, and Missing Letters." In *Hawthorne and Melville: Writing a Relationship*, Ed. Argersinger and Person. Athens: Univ. of Georgia Press, 2008. 1–24.

Arvin, Newton. *Melville*. New York: William Sloane Associates, 1950.

Auden, W.H. "Herman Melville" (1939). In *Collected Shorter Poems, 1930–1944*. London: Faber and Faber. 155–156.

Baym, Nina. "The Erotic Motif in Melville's *Clarel*." *Texas Studies in Literature and Language*, XVI (Summer 1974): 315–328.

Bercovitch, Sacvan. *The American Jeremiad*. Madison: University of Wisconsin Press, 1978.

Blau, Richard. *The Body Impolitic: A Reading of Four Novels by Herman Melville*. Amsterdam: Rodopi, 1979.

Branch, Watson G. "The Genesis, Composition, and Structure of *The Confidence-Man*." *Nineteenth-Century Fiction*, Vol. 27, No. 4 (March 1973): 424–428.

Browne, Ray B. *Melville's Drive to Humanism*. Lafayette: Purdue University Studies, 1971.

Bryant, John. *Melville and Repose: The Rhetoric of Humor in the American Renaissance*. New York: Oxford University Press, 1993.

Casarino, Cesare. *Modernity at Sea: Melville, Marx, Conrad in Crisis*. Minneapolis: University of Minnesota Press, 2002.

Cohen, Hennig. "Herman Melville (1819–1891)." In *Dictionary of Literary Biography, Volume 3: Antebellum Writers in New York and the South*. Ed. Joel Myerson. Detroit: Gale Research, 1979.

Cook, Jonathan A. "Christian Typology and Social Critique in Melville's 'The Two Temples.'" *Christianity and Literature* Vol. 56, No. 1 (Fall 2006): 5–33.

Clymer, Jeffory A. "Property and Selfhood in Herman Melville's *Pierre*." *Nineteenth-Century Literature*, Vol. 61, No. 2 (September 2006): 171–199.

Crane, Hart. "At Melville's Tomb" (1926). In *The Voice That Is Great Within Us: American Poetry of the Twentieth Century*. Ed. Hayden Carruth. New York: Bantam Books, 1970. 214–215.

Delbanco, Andrew. *Herman Melville: His World and Work*. New York: Random House, 2005.

Deleuze, Gilles. "On the Superiority of Anglo-American Literature." In *Dialogues II*, Trans. Hugh Tomlinson and Barbara Habberjam. New York: Columbia University Press, 1987. 36–76.

——. *The Logic of Sense.* Trans. Mark Lester. New York: Columbia University Press, 1990.

——. "Bartleby; or, the Formula." In *Essays Critical and Clinical.* Trans. Daniel W. Smith and Michael A. Greco. Minneapolis: University of Minnesota Press, 1997. 68–90.

——, and Félix Guattari. *Kafka: Toward a Minor Literature.* Trans. Dana Polan, trans. Minneapolis: University of Minnesota Press, 1986.

——, and Félix Guattari. *What is Philosophy?* Trans. Hugh Tomlinson and Graham Burchell. New York: Columbia University Press, 1994.

Dettlaff, Shirley. "Ionian Form and Esau's Waste: Melville's View of Art in *Clarel.*" *American Literature*, LIV (May 1982): 212–228.

Dillingham, William B. *Melville's Short Fiction: 1853–1856.* Athens: University of Georgia Press, 1977.

Donaldson, Scott. "The Dark Truth of The Piazza Tales." *PMLA*, Vol. 85 (1970): 1082–86.

Donoghue, Denis. "Melville Beyond Culture." *The Sewanee Review*, Vol. 118, No. 3 (Summer 2010): 351–366.

Dryden, Edgar A. "From the Piazza to the Enchanted Isles: Melville's Textual Rovings." In *After Strange Texts: the Role of Theory in the Study of Literature*, Ed. Gregory S. Jay and David L. Miller. Tuscaloosa: The University of Alabama Press, 1985. 46–68.

——. *Monumental Melville: The Formation of a Literary Career.* Stanford: Stanford University Press, 2004.

Duban, James L. "Transatlantic Counterparts: The Diptych and Social Inquiry in Melville's 'Poor Man's Pudding and Rich Man's Crumbs.'" *The New England Quarterly*, Vol. 66, No. 2 (June 1993): 274–286.

Durand, Régis. "'The Captive King': The Absent Father in Melville's Text." In *The Fictional Father: Lacanian Readings of the Text.* Ed. Robert Con Davis. Amherst: University of Massachusetts Press, 1981. 48–72.

Fisher, Marvin. *Going Under: Melville's Short Fiction and the American 1850s.* Baton Rouge: Louisiana State University Press, 1977.

Fogle, Richard H. *Melville's Shorter Tales.* Norman: University of Oklahoma Press, 1960.

Foucault, Michel. "Nietzsche, Genealogy, History." In *Language, Counter-Memory, Practice: Selected Essays and Interviews.* Ed. and trans. Donald F. Bouchard. Ithaca: Cornell University Press, 1977. 139–164

——. *This Is Not a Pipe.* Illustrated by René Magritte. Translated by James Harkness. Berkeley: University of California Press, 1983.

——. "Of Other Spaces." Trans. Jay Miskowiec. *Diacritics*, 16 (Spring 1986): 22–27.

Franklin, H. Bruce. *The Wake of the Gods: Melville's Mythology.* Stanford: Stanford University Press, 1963.

Freeman; John. *Herman Melville.* London: Macmillan, 1926.

Fruscione, Joseph. "'What is Called Savagery': Race, Visual Perception, and Bodily Contact in *Moby-Dick.*" *Leviathan,* Vol. 10, No. 1 (March 2008): 3–24.

Giles, Paul. "Bewildering Intertanglement: Melville's Engagement with British Culture." In *The Cambridge Companion to Herman Melville.* Ed. Robert S. Levine. Cambridge: Cambridge University Press, 1988. 224–249.

———. *Virtual Americas: Transnational Fictions and the Transatlantic Imaginary.* Durham: Duke University Press, 2002.

Giovannini, G. "Melville's *Pierre* and Dante's *Inferno.*" *PMLA,* Vol. 64, No. 1 (March 1949): 70–78.

Gollin, Rita. "*Pierre*'s Metamorphosis of Dante's *Inferno.*" *American Literature,* Vol. 39, No. 4 (January 1968): 542–545.

Grey, Robin. *The Complicity of Imagination: The American Renaissance, Contests of Authority, and Seventeenth-Century English Culture.* Cambridge: Cambridge University Press, 1997.

———. "Annotations on Civil War: Melville's *Battle-Pieces* and Milton's War in Heaven." *Leviathan,* Vol. 14, No. 1–2 (March 2002): 51–70.

Guttmann, Allen. "From *Typee* to *Moby-Dick*: Melville's Allusive Art." *Modern Language Quarterly* 24 (1963): 237–244.

Hawthorne, Nathaniel. *Mosses from an Old Manse.* The Centenary Edition of the Works of Nathaniel Hawthorne. Ed. William Charvat, Roy H. Pearce, and C.M. Simpson. Vol. 10. Columbus: Ohio State University Press, 1974.

———. *The English Notebooks, 1856–1860.* The Centenary Edition of The Works of Nathaniel Hawthorne. Ed., Thomas Woodson and Bill Ellis. Vol. 12. Columbus: Ohio State University Press, 1997.

———. *The Scarlet Letter: A Romance.* New York: Penguin Books, 2003.

Hayford, Harrison. "The Significance of Melville's 'Agatha' Letters." *ELH: A Journal of English Literary History,* XIII (December 1946): 299–310.

———. "Melville and Hawthorne: A Biographical and Critical Study." Ph.D. diss., Yale University (1945).

Hecht, Roger. "Rents in the Landscape: the Anti-Rent War in Melville's *Pierre.*" *ATQ,* Vol. 19, No. 1 (March 2005): 37–51.

Higgins, Brian and Hershel Parker. "The Flawed Grandeur of Melville's *Pierre.*" In *New*

Perspectives on Melville. Ed. Faith Pullin. Edinburgh: Edinburgh University Press, 1978. 162–96.

Hiltner, Judith R. "From Pisgah to Egypt: Narrative Continuities in Melville's *Israel Potter* and 'The Two Temples.'" *Journal of Narrative Technique* Vol. 19, No. 3 (1989): 300–311.

Howard, Leon. *Herman Melville: A Biography.* Berkeley: University of California Press, 1951.

Karcher, Carolyn. *Shadow Over the Promised Land.* Baton Rouge: Louisiana State University Press, 1980.

Kearns, Michael S. "Interpreting Intentional Incoherence: Towards a Disambiguation of Melville's 'Pierre; Or, The Ambiguities.'" *The Bulletin of the Midwestern Language Association*, Vol. 16, No. 1 (Spring, 1983): 34–54.

Kelley, Wyn. "Hawthorne and Melville in the Shoals: 'Agatha,' the Trials of Authorship, and the Dream of Collaboration." In *Hawthorne and Melville: Writing a Relationship*, Ed. Argersinger and Person. Athens: Univ. of Georgia Press, 2008. 173–195.

Lawrence, D. H. *Studies in Classic American Literature.* New York: Thomas Seltzer, 1923.

Lee, Maurice. "Melville's 'Mistakes': Correcting the Politics of 'Poor Man's Pudding and Rich Man's Crumbs.'" *ESQ*, Vol. 41, No. 2 (1995): 153–175.

Leyda, Jay, ed. *The Complete Short Stories of Herman Melville.* New York: Random House, 1949.

Madsen, Deborah L. *American Exceptionalism.* Edinburgh: Edinburgh University Press, 1998.

Mansfeld, Luther S. "Glimpses of Herman Melville's Life in Pittsfield, 1850–1851; Some Unpublished Letters of Evert A. Duyckinck." *American Literature* 9 (1937).

Martin, Robert K. *Hero, Captain, and Stranger: Male Friendship, Social Critique, and Literary Form in the Sea Novels of Herman Melville.* Chapel Hill: University of North Carolina Press, 1986.

——, and Leland S. Person. "Missing Letters: Hawthorne, Melville, and Scholarly Desire." *ESQ: A Journal of the American Renaissance*, Vol. 46, Nos. 1&2 (2000): 99–122.

Marx, Leo. *The Machine in the Garden: Technology and the Pastoral Ideal in America.* Oxford: Oxford University Press, 1964.

Matthiessen, F.O. *American Renaissance: Art and Expression in the Age of Emerson and Whitman.* New York: Oxford University Press, 1941.

Mayoux, Jean-Jacques. *Melville.* Trans. John Ashberry. New York: Grove Press, 1960.

McCarthy, Paul. *The Twisted Mind: Madness in Herman Melville's Fiction.* Iowa City:

University of Iowa Press, 1990.

Melville, Herman. *Typee: A Peep at Polynesian Life.* Ed. Hayford, Harrison, Hershel Parker, and G. Thomas Tanselle. Vol. 1 of The Writings of Herman Melville. Evanston, Ill., and Chicago: Northwestern University Press and The Newberry Library, 1968.

———. *Mardi; and a Voyage Thither.* Ed. Hayford, Harrison, Hershel Parker, and G. Thomas Tanselle. Vol. 3 of The Writings of Herman Melville. Evanston, Ill., and Chicago: Northwestern University Press and The Newberry Library, 1988.

———. *Redburn: His First Voyage.* Ed. Hayford, Harrison, Hershel Parker, and G. Thomas Tanselle. Vol. 4 of The Writings of Herman Melville. Evanston, Ill., and Chicago: Northwestern University Press and The Newberry Library, 1969.

———. *White-Jacket; or, The World in a Man-of-War.* Ed. Hayford, Harrison, Hershel Parker, and G. Thomas Tanselle. Vol. 5 of The Writings of Herman Melville. Evanston, Ill., and Chicago: Northwestern University Press and The Newberry Library, 1970.

———. *Moby-Dick; or, The Whale.* Ed. Hayford, Harrison, Hershel Parker, and G. Thomas Tanselle. Vol. 6 of The Writings of Herman Melville. Evanston, Ill., and Chicago: Northwestern University Press and The Newberry Library, 1988.

———. *Pierre; or, The Ambiguities.* Ed. Hayford, Harrison, Hershel Parker, and G. Thomas Tanselle. Vol. 7 of The Writings of Herman Melville. Evanston, Ill., and Chicago: Northwestern University Press and The Newberry Library, 1971.

———. *Israel Potter: His Fifty Years of Exile.* Ed. Hayford, Harrison, Hershel Parker, and G. Thomas Tanselle. Vol. 8 of The Writings of Herman Melville. Evanston, Ill., and Chicago: Northwestern University Press and The Newberry Library, 1982.

———. *The Piazza Tales, and Other Prose Pieces, 1839–1860.* Ed. Hayford, Harrison, Hershel Parker, and G. Thomas Tanselle. Vol. 9 of The Writings of Herman Melville. Evanston, Ill., and Chicago: Northwestern University Press and The Newberry Library, 1987.

———. *The Confidence-Man: His Masquerade.* Ed. Hayford, Harrison, Hershel Parker, and G. Thomas Tanselle. Vol. 10 of The Writings of Herman Melville. Evanston, Ill., and Chicago: Northwestern University Press and The Newberry Library, 1984.

———. *Clarel: A Poem and Pilgrimage in the Holy Land.* Ed. Hayford, Harrison, Hershel Parker, and G. Thomas Tanselle. Vol. 12 of The Writings of Herman Melville. Evanston, Ill., and Chicago: Northwestern University Press and The Newberry Library, 1991.

———. *Correspondence.* Ed. Hayford, Harrison, Hershel Parker, and G. Thomas Tanselle. Vol. 14 of The Writings of Herman Melville. Evanston, Ill., and Chicago:

Northwestern University Press and The Newberry Library, 1993.

———. *Journals*. Ed. Hayford, Harrison, Hershel Parker, and G. Thomas Tanselle. Vol. 15 of The Writings of Herman Melville. Evanston, Ill., and Chicago: Northwestern University Press and The Newberry Library, 1989.

———. *Herman Melville: Tales, Poems, and Other Writings*. Ed. John Bryant. New York: Modern Library, 2001.

Milder, Robert. "Editing Melville's Afterlife." *Text: Transactions of the Society for Textual Scholarship* (1997): 389–407.

———. "Brief Biography." In *A Historical Guide to Herman Melville*. Ed. Giles Gunn Oxford: Oxford University Press, 2005: 29–47.

———. *Exiled Royalties: Melville and the Life We Imagine*. New York: Oxford University Press, 2006.

Miller, Edwin Haviland. *Melville*. New York: Persea Books, 1975.

Miller, James E. Jr. *A Reader's Guide to Herman Melville*. New York: Noonday Press, 1962.

Mumford, Lewis. *Herman Melville*. New York: Harcourt, Brace, 1929.

Murray, Henry A. "In Nomine Diaboli." In *Moby-Dick Centennial Essays*. Ed. Tyrus Hillway and Luther S. Mansfield. Dallas: Southern Methodist University Press, 1953.

Nixon, Nicola. "Compromising Politics and Herman Melville's *Pierre*." *American Literature*, Vol. 69, No. 4 (December 1997): 719–741.

O'Brien, Fitz-James. "Our Young Authors—Melville." In Higgins and Parker, *Critical Essays on "Pierre."* 75–76.

Olson, Charles. *Call Me Ishmael*. San Francisco: City Lights Books, 1947.

Otter, Samuel. "The Eden of Saddle Meadows: Landscape and Ideology in *Pierre*." *American Literature*, Vol. 66, No. 1 (March 1994): 55–81.

———. *Melville's Anatomies*. Berkeley: University of California Press, 1999.

Owens, W.R. "Introduction" to *The Pilgrim's Progress* by John Bunyan. Oxford: Oxford University Press, 2003.

Parini, Jay. *The Passages of H.M.* New York: Doubleday, 2010.

Parker, Hershel. *Herman Melville: A Biography, Volume I, 1819–1851*. Baltimore: The Johns Hopkins University Press, 1996.

———, ed.. *Pierre; Or, The Ambiguities* (Kraken Edition). New York: HarperCollins, 1997.

———. *Herman Melville: A Biography, Volume 2, 1851–1891*. Baltimore: The Johns Hopkins University Press, 2002.

———. *Melville: The Making of the Poet*. Evanston: Northwestern University Press, 2008.

Pommer, Henry F. *Milton and Melville*. New York: Cooper Square Press, 1970.

Renker, Elizabeth. *Strike Through the Mask: Melville and the Scene of Writing.* Baltimore: The Johns Hopkins University Press, 1996.

Rogin, Michael Paul. *Subversive Genealogy: The Politics and Art of Herman Melville.* Berkeley: University of California Press, 1985.

Rowland, Beryl. "Sitting Up with a Corpse: Malthus according to Melville in 'Poor Man's Pudding and Rich Man's Crumbs.'" *Journal of American Studies*, Vol. 6, No. 1 (April 1972): 69–83.

Sanborn, Geoffrey. *The Sign of the Cannibal: Melville and the Making of a Postcolonial Reader.* Durham: Duke University Press, 1998.

Sealts, Merton M. Jr. "Melville and the Platonic Tradition." In *Pursuing Melville: 1940–1980.* Madison: University of Wisconsin Press, 1982. 326–327.

Sedgwick, Eve Kosofsky. *Epistemology of the Closet.* Berkeley: University of California Press, 1990.

Shawcross, John T. "'Too Intellectual a Poet Ever to be Popular': Herman Melville and the Miltonian Dimension of *Clarel.*" *Leviathan* 14:1–2 (March 2002): 71–90.

Smith, Hubert F. "Melville's Master in Chancery and His Recalcitrant Clerk." *American Quarterly*, XVII (Winter 1965): 734–741.

Spanos, William V. *The Errant Art of Moby-Dick: The Canon, the Cold War, and the Struggle for American Studies.* Durham: Duke University Press, 1995.

———. *America's Shadow: An Anatomy of Empire.* Minneapolis: University of Minnesota Press, 2000.

———. *American Exceptionalism in the Age of Globalization: The Specter of Vietnam.* Albany: SUNY Press, 2008.

———. *Herman Melville and the American Calling: The Fiction after* Moby-Dick, *1851–1857.* Albany: SUNY Press, 2008.

Spengemann, William C. "Melville the Poet." *American Literary History*, Vol. 11, No. 4 (1999): 571–609.

Tanner, Tony. *The American Mystery: American Literature from Emerson to DeLillo.* Cambridge: Cambridge University Press, 2000.

Thomas, Brook. "The Writer's Procreative Urge in *Pierre*: Fictional Freedom or Convoluted Incest?" *Studies in the Novel*, Vol. 11, No. 4 (Winter 1979): 16–30.

Thompson, C. E. "Melville's 'Cock-a-Doodle-Doo!' A Case Study in Bipolar Disorder." *ATQ* Vol. 17, No. 1 (March 2003): 43–58.

Urban, David. "'Rousing Motions' and the Silence of God: Scripture and Immediate Revelation in *Samson Agonistes* and *Clarel.*" *Leviathan* 14:1–2 (March 2002): 91–111.

Watson, Charles N. Jr. "The Estrangement of Hawthorne and Melville." *The New England Quarterly*, Vol. 46, No. 3 (September 1973): 380–402.

Watson, E.L. Grant. "Melville's *Pierre*." In *Critical Essays on Herman Melville's "Pierre; or, The Ambiguities.*" Ed. Brian Higgins and Hershel Parker. Boston: Hall, 1983.

Weaver, Raymond. *Herman Melville: Mariner and Mystic*. New York: George H. Doran, 1921.

Winter, Aaron. "Seeds of Discontent: The Expanding Satiric Range of Melville's Transatlantic Diptychs." *Leviathan*, Vol. 8, No. 2 (June 2006): 17–35.

Wright, Nathalia. "*Pierre*: Melville's *Inferno*." *American Literature*, Vol. 32, No. 2 (May 1960): 167–181.

Zeigler, James. "Charles Olson's American Studies: *Call Me Ishmael* and the Cold War." *Arizona Quarterly*, Vol. 63, No. 2 (Summer 2007): 51–80.

Index

A

Agatha (character) 18, 80, 81, 82, 83, 84, 85, 86, 89, 137, 138, 139, 140, 141, 185, 192, 193, 194
Albany, NY 59, 103, 158
American Exceptionalism 59, 65, 67
American Jeremiad 57, 67
Arrowhead (Melville homestead) 17, 29, 32, 63, 81, 137, 187
Auden, W. H. (Wystan Hugh) 191, 192

B

Bulkington (character) 36, 37, 38, 116, 117, 127, 181, 189

C

Carrouge, Michel 15, 200
Chaucer, Geoffrey 147, 148
Christianity 44, 65
Crane, Hart 195

D

Deleuze, Gilles 11, 15, 17, 18, 19, 21, 23, 39, 41, 54, 61, 76, 77, 90, 97, 100, 109, 115, 119, 120, 121, 129, 133, 137, 143, 166, 167, 168, 169, 170, 171, 172, 173, 175, 199, 200, 201
"Bachelor Machines" in 15, 200
Difference and Repetition 168, 171
"Difference" in 168, 169, 170, 171
"Dogmatic Image of Thought" in 168, 169, 172
Essays Critical and Clinical 61
Kafka: Toward a Minor Literature 15, 54, 100, 119, 133
"Kantianism" in 167, 168, 172, 173
"Misosophy" in 167, 169, 172
"Oedipal Incest" in 120
"On the Superiority of Anglo-American Literature" 11, 21, 39, 77, 91, 143
"Originality" in 158, 166
"Overturning Platonism" in 167, 168, 171, 173
"Reoedipalization" in 54, 109, 133, 157
"Repetition" in 16, 17, 19, 65, 101, 102, 105, 108, 132, 142, 168, 171, 176, 184, 188
"Schizo-Incest" in 17, 100, 109, 120
The Logic of Sense 171
"The Powers of the False" in 167
What is Philosophy? 167
With Felix Guattari 167
Dialectics 167
Difference (see Deleuze)
Diptych 64, 65
"Dogmatic Image of Thought" (see Deleuze)
Donoghue, Denis 14
Duyckinck, Evert A. (Augustus) 31, 32, 33, 34, 87

E

Emerson, Ralph Waldo 24, 30, 151, 175, 176
Enceladus 115, 122, 126, 127, 128, 130
Errand in the Wilderness 57, 67

F

Foucault, Michel 13, 96, 98, 103, 110, 131, 172
  "Nietzsche, Genealogy, History" 96
  "Of Other Spaces" 13
  This is Not a Pipe 130, 131, 172
Franklin, H. (Howard) Bruce 61, 83, 84, 86, 153, 159, 160, 161, 174
Freud, Sigmund 35

G

Ganesvoort (family) 95
Genealogy 95, 96, 136

H

Hawthorne, Nathaniel 11, 12, 13, 15, 16, 18, 19, 20, 24, 25, 26, 27, 28, 29, 32, 33, 34, 35, 36, 37, 38, 40, 62, 75, 79, 81, 82, 83, 84, 85, 86, 87, 89, 90, 91, 93, 94, 114, 123, 132, 134, 135, 137, 138, 139, 140, 141, 142, 144, 147, 151, 152, 153, 154, 157, 158, 176, 177, 178, 179, 181, 183, 184, 185, 186, 187, 188, 190, 191, 193, 196, 200, 201, 202, 203, 205
  "Monsieur Du Miroir" 202
  Mosses from an Old Manse 16, 32, 187, 203
  The Blithedale Romance 83, 94, 175, 176
  "The Old Manse" 16, 141, 187
  The Scarlet Letter 11, 12, 36
Hunilla (character) 18, 133, 135, 137, 139, 140, 141, 186

I

Ishmael (character) 14, 21, 25, 32, 36, 40, 42, 45, 50, 53, 75, 107, 109, 112, 118, 122, 123, 148, 149, 152, 176, 177, 184, 191

J

Jonah (Biblical figure) 117

K

Kafka, Franz 15, 54, 100, 110, 119, 120, 121, 133, 137
  "The Judgment" 110
Kant, Immanuel 167, 168, 169, 170, 172, 173
  "Analytic of the Sublime" 168

L

Lawrence, D. H. (David Herbert) 11, 13, 14, 115, 129, 199
  Studies in Classic American Literature 13
Leyda, Jay 17, 63, 64, 122
Liverpool 30, 59, 60, 61, 83, 86, 87, 138, 144, 145, 164

M

Mann, Thomas 177
Magritte, René 131
Marianna (character) 18, 140, 141, 186, 187, 188, 189, 204
Marx, Leo 13, 40, 41, 72
Matthiessen, F. O. (Francis Otto) 24, 30
Melvill, Alan 11, 12, 13, 14, 15, 16, 17, 18, 19, 20, 21, 22, 23, 24, 25, 26, 27, 28, 29, 30, 31, 32, 33, 34, 35, 36, 37, 38, 40, 43, 44, 45, 46, 47, 48, 49, 50, 52, 53, 56, 57, 58, 59, 60, 61, 62, 63, 64, 65, 66, 67, 68, 69, 71, 72, 73, 74, 75, 77, 78, 79, 80, 81, 82, 83, 84, 85, 86, 87, 88, 89, 90, 91, 92, 93, 94, 95, 96, 97, 98, 99, 101, 102, 103, 105, 110, 111, 113, 114, 115, 116, 117, 120, 121, 122, 123, 124, 126, 127, 128, 129, 131, 132, 133, 134, 135, 136, 137, 138, 139, 140, 141, 142, 143, 144, 145, 146,

147, 148, 149, 150, 151, 152, 153, 154, 155, 156, 157, 158, 159, 160, 161, 163, 164, 165, 166, 168, 169, 172, 174, 175, 176, 177, 178, 179, 180, 181, 182, 183, 184, 185, 186, 187, 188, 189, 190, 191, 192, 193, 195, 196, 197, 199, 200, 201, 202, 203, 204, 205, 206

Melville, Herman 11, 12, 13, 14, 15, 16, 17, 18, 19, 20, 21, 22, 23, 24, 25, 26, 27, 28, 29, 30, 31, 32, 33, 34, 35, 36, 37, 38, 40, 43, 44, 45, 46, 47, 48, 49, 50, 52, 53, 56, 57, 58, 59, 60, 61, 62, 63, 64, 65, 66, 67, 68, 69, 71, 72, 73, 74, 75, 77, 78, 79, 80, 81, 82, 83, 84, 85, 86, 87, 88, 89, 90, 91, 92, 93, 94, 95, 96, 97, 98, 99, 101, 102, 103, 105, 110, 111, 113, 114, 115, 116, 117, 120, 121, 122, 123, 124, 126, 127, 128, 129, 131, 132, 133, 134, 135, 136, 137, 138, 139, 140, 141, 142, 143, 144, 145, 146, 147, 148, 149, 150, 151, 152, 153, 154, 155, 156, 157, 158, 159, 160, 161, 163, 164, 165, 166, 168, 169, 172, 174, 175, 176, 177, 178, 179, 180, 181, 182, 183, 184, 185, 186, 187, 188, 189, 190, 191, 192, 193, 195, 196, 197, 199, 200, 201, 202, 203, 204, 205, 206
 "Agatha" story in 82
 Clarel 68, 83, 145, 154, 181, 190, 191, 196, 202
 Escape in 11, 12, 13, 14, 16, 18, 20, 22, 23, 27, 35, 38, 44, 46, 57, 65, 71, 76, 98, 105, 116, 120, 124, 129, 142, 168, 175, 181, 182, 183, 199, 200, 201
 Failure in 38, 134, 135, 137, 146, 153, 193, 195, 196
 "Hawthorne and His Mosses" 16, 36, 62, 85, 134
 Homosocial/Homosexual desire in 15, 90, 191
 Israel Potter 17, 56, 57, 58, 59, 60, 61, 62, 64, 65, 81, 86, 123, 134, 135, 139, 153,

200
Machines in 15, 178, 200
"Madame Mirror" 202
Mardi 22, 23, 28, 29, 38, 62, 86, 152, 185
Moby-Dick 13, 14, 16, 22, 24, 25, 27, 28, 30, 31, 32, 33, 34, 35, 36, 37, 39, 41, 44, 45, 46, 56, 57, 63, 67, 70, 75, 77, 84, 85, 87, 91, 92, 93, 94, 95, 103, 105, 107, 108, 111, 112, 113, 114, 116, 117, 118, 120, 122, 124, 127, 130, 131, 134, 135, 147, 148, 152, 153, 161, 174, 176, 177, 179, 180, 184, 185, 189, 192, 196, 200, 205
"Monody" 83, 190, 201, 202
Omoo 28, 44, 152
"Originality" in 158, 166
"Pebbles" 185, 199, 202, 204, 205
Pierre 13, 14, 16, 17, 18, 19, 20, 36, 56, 57, 60, 62, 63, 64, 76, 77, 78, 79, 80, 81, 83, 86, 87, 88, 89, 91, 92, 93, 94, 95, 96, 97, 98, 99, 100, 101, 102, 103, 104, 105, 106, 107, 108, 109, 110, 111, 112, 113, 114, 115, 116, 117, 118, 119, 120, 121, 122, 123, 124, 125, 126, 127, 128, 129, 130, 131, 132, 133, 134, 135, 136, 142, 145, 148, 149, 152, 155, 161, 163, 164, 172, 174, 179, 181, 182, 183, 184, 185, 196, 200, 201, 205
"Poor Man's Pudding and Rich Man's Crumbs" 68
Portraits in 60, 103, 104, 106, 113, 119, 133, 134, 147
Redburn 17, 23, 30, 31, 38, 56, 57, 59, 60, 61, 62, 63, 64, 65, 149, 152, 158, 164
The Confidence-Man 13, 14, 19, 22, 38, 46, 62, 64, 81, 87, 109, 123, 124, 126, 129, 131, 135, 142, 143, 145, 146, 147, 149, 152, 153, 154, 155, 157, 158, 159, 160, 161, 163, 166, 168, 169, 172, 174, 176, 177, 182, 185, 189, 200, 201
"The Encantadas" 64, 132, 133, 135, 194

Index 217

The Isle of the Cross 18, 80, 82, 87
"The Paradise of Bachelors and the Tartarus of Maids" 17, 63, 70, 80
The Piazza Tales 16, 18, 64, 81, 86, 135, 139, 185, 186
"The Two Temples" 17, 73, 81
"The Vanquished" in 23, 99, 135
Typee 23, 33, 44, 79, 152, 157, 179, 183, 185
White-Jacket 30, 31, 86, 149, 152, 155, 158, 176, 177
Melville Revival, The 179
Milton, John 20, 36, 38, 40, 52, 55, 56, 108, 117, 121, 122, 123, 127, 158, 166, 178, 179, 180, 181, 205
Paradise Lost 52, 121, 123, 178, 179, 180
Mimesis 131, 169, 172
Monumentalism 98, 99, 123

N

New York City 13, 29, 62, 69, 98, 121, 133, 145, 158, 164
Nietzsche, Friedrich W. (Wilhelm) 96, 98, 110, 167, 168, 169, 172, 173, 177

O

Olson, Charles 21, 25, 26, 32, 36, 37, 40, 42, 123, 191
Call Me Ishmael 21, 25, 32, 36, 40, 42, 123, 191

P

Paintings (portraits) 60, 103, 104, 106, 113, 119, 133, 134, 147
Parker, Hershel 22, 33, 79, 80, 82, 87, 90, 91, 92, 93, 94, 99, 120, 122, 156, 157, 159, 161, 163, 178, 183, 201
Plato 150, 167, 168, 169, 170, 171, 172, 173

Phaedrus 170, 171
Republic 168, 169, 170
Sophist 168, 170, 171, 173
Statesman 170, 171
Theaetetus 168, 170
Platonism 167, 168, 169, 171, 172, 173
Pynchon, Thomas 135
"The Preterite" in 135

R

Romantic Satanism 56

S

Shakespeare, William 25, 26, 29, 32, 40, 78, 85, 86, 115, 188
Shaw, Lemuel 30, 32, 88, 137, 144, 145, 181
Simulacrum 171
Spanos, William V. (Vaios) 17, 40, 41, 56, 57, 59, 92, 96, 98, 103, 107, 110, 111, 112, 122, 135, 148, 176
St. Elmo's Fire 52, 107, 111, 114

T

Tanner, Tony 19, 66, 146, 155, 174, 175, 176, 177
"Interchangeability" in 19, 146, 155, 174, 177
"Reversibility" in 19, 146, 155, 174, 176, 177
The Bible 58, 67, 149, 154
The Inferno (Dante) 71, 115, 136, 137, 153
Thoreau, Henry David 151
Timonism 26, 123
Transcendentalism 186
Typology 58, 60, 65, 67

V

Van Rensselaer (family) 95, 98

Taras Alexander Sak earned a Ph.D. in Comparative Literature from the State University of New York at Binghamton, focusing upon 19th and 20th century American Literature, the work of Herman Melville, and Critical Theory. He has published widely on Melville, Poe, Don DeLillo, Thomas Pynchon, Saul Bellow, and Cormac McCarthy, as well as on music (Lou Reed, Bob Dylan) and film. He is currently an Associate Professor at Yasuda Women's University in Hiroshima, Japan.

The Art of Escape: On Melville's Bachelor Machines

2025年3月3日　　初版発行

著者	Taras Alexander Sak（サック・タラス）	
発行者	三浦衛	
発行所	春風社 Shumpusha Publishing	

横浜市西区紅葉ヶ丘53　横浜市教育会館3階
〈電話〉045・261・3168　〈FAX〉045・261・3169
〈振替〉00200・1・37524
http://www.shumpu.com　　info@shumpu.com

印刷・製本　シナノ書籍印刷株式会社

装丁　　　長田年伸
本文設計　長田年伸

乱丁・落丁本は送料小社負担でお取り替えいたします。
© Taras Alexander Sak. All Rights Reserved. Printed in Japan.
ISBN 978-4-86110-995-9 C0098 ¥6000E

ISBN978-4-86110-995-9
C0098 ¥6000E

定価 |本体**6000**円| ＋税

|**6600**円|（10%税込）